Paradoxes and Dragons
Volume 2
A Science Fiction and Fantasy Anthology

Joseph R. Lallo

ISBN: 978-1951240073

Table Contents

Foreword

I must say, when I started my Patreon with what I was calling "The Shorts of Dubious Canonicity Project," I really didn't expect it to last very long. I've had a blast using the Patreon as a testbed for strange ideas and fun concepts that I couldn't find places for in full books or existing series. Strangely often these stories include either time travel or dragons. You'd think I was a fan of those topics or something…

These stories mostly come from 2020, a year which… occurred.

Uncle Easy

Joseph R. Lallo

Uncle Easy

Among the first batch of Patreon stories was something called *Wasteland*. I really enjoyed writing the story, and it turned out you folks liked it a bunch as well. I got enough positive feedback from it to make it the first Patreon story to have an official sequel. Originally I called this Uncle Robot, and like another recent story it was ideated when I was having a conversation with one of my illustrators, Fable. There are actually a handful of other "Wasteland Series" stories I was thinking of writing, but this was the first to be fully fleshed out. If you like it, let me know and we'll continue adding to this weird little setting.

Light filtered through a hand-woven curtain. Lana grumbled and buried her head under the pillow. She hadn't gotten a wink of sleep that night. She was too excited. But that didn't change the fact that she wasn't a morning person. Right around sunrise, her giddy anticipation of what the day held turned to irritation at the entire concept of wakefulness.

She wasn't sure what time it was, only that it was too early. Sure, she could look at the clock, but that wouldn't really improve her situation at all. She'd *made* the clock, and she'd had the bright idea to make it solar-powered like just about everything else in the camp. It was thus less of a clock and more of a daylight timer. Not her finest creation.

An unwelcome rolling clatter jolted her brain. There was no hiding from it any longer. It was time to wake up.

Again the clatter rang out, precisely the same as last time. She pulled herself out of bed and straightened out her pajama top, then shoved her curtain aside.

"I'm *up!* I'm up already," Lana said, rubbing her eyes.

A squat, beetle-like robot clung to the windowsill from the outside. Assorted highly visible signs of damage and repair left little of the once-mirror-polished shell in its original form. Rather than appearing rundown, the overall effect was one of sturdy care and personality, culminating with the word "Easy" etched onto the shell with the skill and care of a jeweler. A sensor-strewn apparatus pivoted at the end of an actuator, giving it the semblance of a many-eyed head with smoldering blue lights.

"Good morning, kiddo," squawked the robot.

Technically the thing spoke in a pre-recorded, chopped up version of her father's voice. The specific intonations and the subtle distortion were distinctively Easy's, such that she'd never thought of it as anything but his own voice.

"Today's the day, Uncle Easy!" she said, the simmering excitement already starting to shove her weariness aside.

"Today is the day, kiddo," Easy replied.

Lana shielded her eyes from the sun and peered over the family compound. Long, exquisitely orderly rows of crops waved gently in the breeze. Little sparkling points of silver revealed the scurrying forms of other robots like Easy as they tended to this and that, basked in the sun, or generally amused themselves. Patches of jewel-blue solar panels drank in the sunlight, and beyond it all, a horseshoe-shaped lake sparkled with the morning sun. It was a perfect little nugget of paradise in the middle of an endless, dusty nothing.

Just beyond the edge of the lake, a peculiar vehicle was angled toward the rising sun. She could see her mother and father loading it up already.

"Hey! They're doing it without me!" Lana objected.

She pulled open the window and hefted Easy inside, then threw on her slippers and her tool belt. She rushed down the stairs.

"Go slow. Be careful, kiddo," Easy squawked behind her.

Lana hopped onto the banister and slid down.

"I've done it a million times, Uncle Easy," she said.

"You have done it one thousand four hundred sixty-one times," he corrected. "You have hurt yourself one hundred thirty-four times, kiddo."

"That's only nine point… one percent, Uncle Easy."

"Nine point one seven one eight percent, kiddo."

"Same difference."

She hustled across the ceramic tiles meticulously arranged into a patterned walkway. Every dozen or so rows of tiles she passed one with a hand imprint and a date. They were just a few weeks away from adding one to celebrate her tenth birthday, but that wasn't what she was so excited about. Not at the moment, anyway.

"Hi, Tango! Hi, Rosemary! Hi, Whiskey." she shouted as she dashed by various robots.

Each of them stopped and turned to waggle a spidery leg in her direction.

"Hi, Cardamom! Hi, Zulu! Hi, Fiddlehead! Today's the day!"

"Today's the day!" the robots echoed back.

Just like Easy, they all had their own specific take on their borrowed voice. Some borrowed their words from her father, some from her mother. Her aunt voiced a few, her older sister voiced one. So far *she* hadn't become the voice template for one, but that would probably change in the next few weeks.

She trotted across the pier on the moat. Easy skittered up to the head of the skiff. A panel flopped open on his underbelly and a wire harness dropped down to interface with a matching socket. The motor of the skiff spun up and it glided across the surface of the moat.

"Mom! Dad! Why didn't you wait?" Lana called.

A lean and ruggedly equipped couple turned from the cargo hatch of a well-engineered, albeit clearly piecemeal, vehicle. Her father had perpetually neglected hair, both on his head and his chin. They were black and threaded with gray. Combined with the amount of time he'd spent in the sun, it left him looking a good two decades older than he really was. Her mother had longer brown hair with a dash less gray. Lana's infant brother Benny was strapped to her chest in a papoose.

Her father turned and crouched to hug her.

"Lana, what's the daily yield of the buggy's solar panels?" he asked.

"Six kilowatt-hours," she said with the singsong tone of someone who knew this was the beginning of a tired routine.

"And what's the average power consumption of the buggy?"

"One hundred-forty watt-hours per mile."

"So what's the daily range without running a deficit?"

"Forty-two point eight miles."

"Forty-two point eight five seven miles, kiddo," Easy clarified.

"Same difference," said Lana and her mother at once.

"What your father is getting at is that we needed the cargo loaded up before sunrise so that we didn't waste any range. And *someone* is a sleepyhead," her Mom said.

"I didn't sleep barely at all! I could have helped," Lana said.

"Well, there's two more cases of tinned beans if you want to pitch in," her Dad said.

Lana crouched and hefted at the crate. It was a bit too heavy for her to haul it off the floor on her own, but Easy pitched in. She heaved it up onto the tailgate. Her mom shoved it forward and she loaded the process for the second case.

"You know, it's not too late for her to come along," her dad said.

Her mom turned to him.

"David, what's the average calorie consumption per day to maintain the weight of two adults and a child."

He rolled his eyes. "Five thousand three hundred."

"And how many calories in a pound of beans?"

"Fifteen hundred."

"So how many pounds, per day, are we going to need?"

"Three point five three three," he said.

"Between that and the water, how many days short would we come if she came along?"

"We could scavenge along the way!" he said. "I did it for years before I met Easy."

"And you were what, ninety pounds when you met him? We've been through this."

"But she's only *nine,* Elizabeth," he hissed under his breath.

"Julia was twelve when she started going out on her own."

"Which is more than nine," he said.

"I'll be fine, Dad," Lana said.

"She's great at maintaining the robots, she's a good gardener, and you and I both know the whole crew adores her and wouldn't let anything bad happen to her. We'll only be gone for a month."

"Lana will be fine, David," Easy said.

"See!" Lana said.

Her dad sighed and tousled her hair. "You're right, kiddo. Your old dad is just a little overprotective thanks to traveling the continent for years without any evidence of any other surviving human beings, I guess. Silly me. Tell you what. Before we head out, I still need to balance the battery charges and your mom still needs to prep some bean sprouts. Which do you want to help with?"

"Uh… bean sprouts."

"Then get to picking! Easy, you're with me for this one."

Easy clattered after him as he pulled a dolly from the side of the buggy and dropped it to roll underneath. Lana trotted after her mother.

"Now I know we've been over it—" her mother began.

"Like a million times," Lana said.

"But let's make it a million and one. We'll be gone for a month. Fifteen days out, three days there, fifteen days back. That's the *best* case. The radio will only be good for the first day or so. After that, you and the bots are on your own. Keep the receiver on. You never know. I feel *terrible* missing your tenth birthday, but your father, Easy, and Tango ran the numbers and we won't get a better shot at contacting the satellite, and if we can get some semblance of global communication up, who knows how many more little enclaves like ours will show up? It's the difference between surviving and being part of a society."

"I know. It's okay. Uncle Easy said he'd make a cake!"

"Oh, he did, did he?" Her mom cast a glare at the little robot, who scuttled a little farther under the buggy.

"And we can celebrate when you get back," Lana said.

"Remember, you need to double check the irrigation system every morning. The bots can get bogged down in the mud and that's dangerous."

"I know, Mom."

"You *need* to check the machine shop every six hours for newcomers. We're really hurting for U-joints and some of the other jelly-bean parts. Hopefully some of the wanderers will bring some, but if you have any spare time between the hydroponics upkeep and the compost turnover, maybe fabricate some. For the *life* of me, I can't get the feeds and speeds right on that mill…"

"That's okay, Mom. Dad can't fix the pH in the soil to save his life, so it evens out."

"Right… oh! And keep the beacon up. Check it every night."

"It's not going to break, Mom," Lana said.

"It's broken six times since you were born. You just don't know because your dad caught it twice, I caught it once, and Easy caught it three times. So make sure it's up."

She took a breath and crouched down to the bed of bean sprouts. The pair started selecting sprouts that looked healthy enough to thrive even while in a planter being toted along in a buggy.

"Two more things and then we should get going. The sun's nearly strong enough. First, at the risk of sounding like your dad, stay safe. You are the most precious thing in the world right now."

"Mo-o-o-m."

"And second, don't eat all the sugar snap peas. If I come back and you ate all the sugar snaps, you're on phosphorus duty for a month, you got that?"

"Cross my heart," she said.

"And crossed fingers behind her back," Easy said, trotting up to them.

She shot the little robot an angry look. "You snitch!"

"Okay! We're up to charge, the voltage looks good, let's get rolling!" her dad said. "Lana, if everything goes right, your birthday present is going to be a way to talk to the rest of the world. Come here!"

He scooped her up into a hug.

"I'm going to miss you so much."

"I'll miss you too, Dad. Love you."

#

After a lingering hug, Lana watched her parents climb into the solar buggy and head off to the east. She watched them until they were nothing more than a rising cloud of dust in the endless, dry expanse around their little island of green. Easy stood beside her, sensors focused on the same point on the horizon. Lana felt uneasy, like a safety harness that had been strapped to her since birth had just been cut free.

But, for better or worse, that unease quickly vanished behind the same giddy excitement that had kept her up all night.

Lana was well aware that she was living in a world that was very different than it had once been. She knew that, for much of her parents' lives before finding each other, every day was spent living in fear that they might be alone in the world. But that was not the world Lana had grown up in. In the nine years she'd walked this arid earth, she'd not been alone for a single moment. Between Easy, the other robots, and her parents, she'd always been a part of something larger than herself. It was nice—as far as she knew. She'd never had a taste of being in charge of herself. On her own. Unsupervised. At least, not until now.

"Okay, Uncle Easy," she said. "I'm officially the only human in the camp."

"Yes, kiddo," he said.

"That means everything that is just for humans is just for me, at least until Mom and Dad come back."

"Sort of, kiddo."

"Sort of is good enough for me! Let's go see what I've been missing."

She crouched down. Easy clattered around behind her, then sprang from the ground. Two little legs hooked over her shoulders, two more swung under her arms to form loops like the straps of a backpack, and the remaining ones lightly clamped her sides. Once he was properly piggybacked, his head swung aside to watch over her shoulder as she hurried back through their strange little community.

First stop, Daddy's secret stash.

#

"Come on, Zulu! It's got to be here somewhere," Lana said.

She'd recruited the usual suspects when it came to mischief. All of the robots had their own personalities, but Zulu was definitely her partner in crime. They were the one robot who absolutely refused to start using recordings to communicate. It was all pantomime and posture with them. Nodding and shaking their head was as complex as they got with social interactions, but when it came to doing something naughty, they never hesitated. This had contributed to a considerably larger proportion of replacement parts on the little critter. They had a terrible habit of getting banged up.

Right now Zulu was perched on a precarious spire of wind-scoured rock, their head rigidly sweeping back and forth as some manner of ground penetrating radar did its thing. Their search had brought them a half-mile south of the main camp. It was right at the edge of where their constant upkeep gave way to the general decay of the surrounding wasteland. Dust heaped in dunes. The air had the zero-percent humidity sting of endless desert. No good soil. No water. No reason for anyone to be here. And that's why she was checking it out.

"Every time Dad gets any free time, he's always wandering around back here. He's *got* to have something hidden," Lana said.

"Your dad doesn't hide things, kiddo," Easy said.

"Maybe it only *seems* that way because he's so *good* at it," she said. "How come you're not helping Zulu scan?"

"Someone has to be the responsible one, kiddo."

"You're my uncle. And Dad says uncles are there for letting you taste your first beer and stuff."

"We don't have beer, kiddo."

Zulu clacked each of their legs in a rolling sequence, like someone drumming their fingers, then scampered toward a specific point in the distance.

"We'll just see about that," Lana said, dashing after him.

Zulu scrabbled at a particularly gravelly dune. Lana pulled a folding shovel from her belt and pitched in. Three minutes of digging unearthed a beat-up old metal crate. It was one of the older ones, from back before they started making their own. Faded green paint still colored it what few sections hadn't been scraped clean by years of being buried and dug up. She cleared the top and fiddled with the latch. It was locked, but like most things her father had dug up in his travels, it would have needed a lot of tender loving care to actually work as intended. The robots had obviously been worth the effort. This thing, not so much. She rattled the latch a bit. While it wouldn't open with simple jiggling, it clearly wouldn't take much.

"I didn't bring my tools," she said. "Zulu, can you open it?"

Zulu's head retracted. The center of their shell split and a heat-scorched metal tube rose up and took aim.

"*No lasers!*" Lana urged. "We've got to do it careful, so Dad won't know."

The shell snapped shut and Zulu's head re-emerged. They rattled it in a clear negative, then scampered off toward the camp.

"Oh, come on!" she called after them. "I'll polish your panels extra good!"

Zulu ignored the attempted bribe.

"Zulu lacks finesse, kiddo," Easy said.

She glanced at her uncle. "Well *you* don't. What do you say? Can't you get it open?"

"Yes. But that would make David angry, kiddo."

"Only if he finds out about it. If he *doesn't* find out about it, he won't be angry. So if it is your goal to make sure Dad doesn't get angry, you *have* to do this for me," she reasoned.

Easy held perfectly still. Fans inside him flared as he did some processing.

"Your logic is sound, kiddo," he said.

He retracted all of his legs at once, plummeting from her back. Before he reached the ground his legs snapped back out and flipped him to the proper orientation. He clattered fluidly up to the crate and swept his sensors back and forth over the lock. One leg, raised to deliver a calculated tap to the side of the luck, caused it to fall open.

"Oh, boy, oh boy!" Lana squealed, heaving the lid open.

The inside was a veritable treasure trove. Stacks of books she'd never seen before. Little trinkets and gadgets she didn't recognize. She plucked the thickest book from the pile like she had unearthed a holy relic.

"One thousand and one rude jokes..." she said in awe.

The desert air had preserved the book incredibly well. She flipped through to a random page.

"Hey, Easy!" she said. "Did you hear about the constipated mathematician?"

"No, kiddo."

"He worked it out with a pencil!" she squealed.

Easy's fans flared again.

"Constipated," he said, in Lana's voice, as the word had evidently never come up in conversation with David. "... Worked it out with a pencil... Are you talking about poop, kiddo?"

"*You said poop!*" she said, consumed with helpless laughter. "This is gold..."

#

She spent most of the first week memorizing as many of the jokes as she could and stuffing herself with dates. Her mom hadn't said anything about eating too many dates, after all, and the trees were just about to start growing a fresh harvest of them anyway.

10

But being the only human in the camp wasn't all fun and games. As noon crept forward on the eighth day, it was time once again to do her rounds. She marched along the tiles and surveyed her home like a general reviewing her troops. Right now there were close to seventy robots as a part of the camp, with probably another three hundred or so that came and went. The locals all had names, and ever since she figured out she had more of an aptitude for machinery than agriculture, she'd probably had a hand in fixing most of them. They were her extended family, and it wasn't lost on her that there were some tasks they simply couldn't do for themselves. They needed her as much as she needed them.

Lana grabbed a bag from inside the door of a shed and paced to a courtyard between the main solar array and the first of many fields of crops. It was a popular hangout for robots with nothing better to do. They sprawled out like fat cats, deep-blue solar panels soaking up the sun.

"Okay!" She clapped. "I need the busy bees. Who wants to be the busy bees today?"

A few of the robots glanced in her direction, then lazily retracted their heads like turtles. Four of them eagerly hopped up and scuttled over.

"How did I know you'd be one of the volunteers, Cardamom? But, Tango, I'm surprised. You don't usually like the costume."

"Uniform," Tango corrected.

"Right, right, *uniform*," she said in an overly placating way.

She pulled open the bag as the volunteer robots lined up. One by one she affixed what looked like feather dusters to the "elbows" of their legs. The wind did a reasonable job of pollinating their crops, but without any insects, there was still a lot of manual pollination going on. A few robots with the proper equipment could do it well enough. In this case the proper equipment included the aforementioned dusters and a pair of entirely unnecessary googly eyes and springy pompoms. She still remembered the day a handful of the roving robots had come in for repairs and had dropped off the big box of craft supplies as barter. Many a robot earned a glittery makeover that day.

"Okay, Cardamom? You go to field one. Tango, field two, Fiddlehead, field three. And…" She squinted. "Who's squeaking?"

She stood up straight.

"Hey! Everyone! I heard a squeak. Who's squeaking?" she bellowed.

One by one, each of the robots did a quirky little shimmy that tested each joint in sequence. When a rather jagged and heat-blued robot twitched its fourth leg, a cricket-like chirp squealed out.

"Ah-*ha!* Front and center, Lilac. What does Dad always say?" Lana said to the offending robot.

"Today's squeaks are tomorrow's grinds," Lilac said, in her mother's voice with some devastating reverb.

"And no one likes grinds." Lana pulled an oiler from her tool belt and applied some. "There, how's that?"

"No squeak," Lilac said.

"Next time come and see me. Now does everyone know where they're going?"

"Yes!" the robots replied.

"Great, have fun!"

The robots skittered away. One of the others bounced up from its basking and tapped up to her, almost sheepishly.

"Need something, Eta?" Lana asked.

"Hide and seek?" Eta asked.

Every robot in earshot, or at least sensor-shot, perked its head up. They sprang to their feet and scuttled over until Lana was surrounded by two dozen robots looking eagerly in her direction and urging her.

"Hide and seek!"

"Hide and seek?"

"Hide and seek *please*."

Lana crossed her arms. "First of all, hide and seek is a baby game, and I'm the adult here now. Second, *you're too good at it*. You're seek and destroy robots. It's no fun for you and it's no fun for me if you all find me at once as soon as you start looking."

"Incorrect," said Eta. "It is very fun for us."

The other robots nodded in agreement.

"Please," the robots said in unison.

They tapped in place, all sensors turned to her. Her resolve started to weaken. Then a thought came to mind and a grin lit up her face.

"Okay!"

"Hooray," they proclaimed.

Limited to whatever degree of enthusiasm the person providing their voice could muster up on the day they recorded the word, it led to a strangely lackluster celebration for some of the robots.

"But there are special rules," she said. "Only audio and video sensors. No radar."

One of the robots raised a claw.

"Yes, Honeysuckle?" she said.

"What about infrared?" the curious robot asked in her mother's voice.

Others nodded.

"Yes, infrared is visual," said Eta.

"Not for me it isn't. We're trying to make this fair, and maybe to make it last it more than a couple minutes. And that's the other thing. I get to use Dad's scooter to find a hiding spot."

"David didn't give you permission to use the scooter, kiddo," Easy said quickly.

"He didn't *forbid* me from using it, did he? And if there was an emergency, he'd let me use it then, right?"

"Yes, he would, kiddo."

"So, this is enrichment for you guys. Super important. And I'm supposed to take care of you all, so this is basically an emergency."

"It is not an emergency, kiddo," he said.

"Anyone who's playing the game, turn off all sensors and count to three hundred at one hertz. When you're done, audio and video sensors on and come find me. If you can't find me in an hour, I win."

The robots nodded and tucked themselves into their shells. Muffled voice clips started counting out slowly.

"*Now* it's an emergency, because if I don't do a good job hiding, they'll all be disappointed."

Easy stared impassively at Lana.

"Please! You're supposed to be my cool uncle. If we don't have beer for me to taste you can at least do this."

"Fine. But I'll drive, kiddo."

"Good enough for me!"

She sprinted to the same shack where the bee equipment had been and hauled the scooter out into the light. The vehicle was one of only a handful of devices that were effectively built from scratch by her father. It used salvaged parts for the important stuff, like the batteries, solar panels, motor, and wheels, but the structure was all his doing, and it showed. The wheels were oversized for a vehicle barely larger than a go-kart, the better for getting traction in the dusty wastes. It had a downright ingenious suspension that made it profoundly stable. And— most importantly, as far as Lana was concerned—it was *fast*. She'd ridden on it with her dad dozens of times. The pair of them were about the maximum the thing could handle, and even *then* she could feel the wind whip through her hair as they went. With just Easy and Lana on the thing, it would be *flying*.

She popped on her helmet and strapped into the seat. Easy clattered up to the steering wheel and dropped down his cable to click into the receptacle.

"Don't spare the throttle. We've got to make this a good game for the others!"

"Okay, kiddo."

The motor whirred, the wheels slung gravel, and the pair streaked off into the dusty world beyond the camp.

"Where do you want to go, kiddo?" Easy asked, amplifying his voice over the whistling wind.

"Let's go to the old base," she called back.

"That is the first place they're gonna look, kiddo."

"Sure, but it's so big, and there's so many places to hide. I'll be perfect!"

#

Right around when the robots back in the camp would have been waking picking up their heads and starting their search, Easy and Lana arrived in the abandoned military base a mile west of the camp. The base was a big part of the reason they'd set up camp where they did. Her parents said it was probably some sort of bunker that, for one reason or another, was empty. The place was dug deep into the ground and had held up remarkably well. Half of the higher quality bits of equipment that made the camp run in the early days had been scavenged from the base, and several thousand gallons of water had been waiting in its tanks to help them start the irrigation moat that they now depended upon. Best of all, the place had been a "strategic seed vault," providing them with a tremendous amount of nutritional variety beyond the random assortment of vegetables that her parents had been able to scrounge up seeds for.

Easy parked outside the main gate, which had long ago been lasered off and carted back to be made into pipes or whatever else the camp had needed that day. It seemed like the sort of place that she would have been kept away from, but such couldn't have been further from the truth. This place had practically been her private electronics lab in the old days. Truth be told, she was sort of tired of it. They hadn't needed any parts that were available in this place for a while. This was her first time coming out here in over a year.

Lana pulled an LED flashlight from her belt and hurried inside.

"Let's go downstairs. Sub-Level 3. There are all of those desks. I'll hide under one of those."

She and her robotic uncle scurried down a few flights of stairs, past the stripped-clean levels until she passed the sign for SL-3.

This had been the first level they'd cleared out, long before she was born. It had their stores of non-perishable food, which kept the camp afloat while they were getting the first few harvests of crops ready. She paced through the cool hallway, looking for the room she remembered from their last trip. Her father had said it was probably a classroom. The desk in her room had come from here.

"You better not snitch on me, Easy," she said as she pushed the door open. "Remember, you're on my team, not theirs. A mile and three floors still isn't much of a hiding place for a whole bunch of you guys."

She hurried to the larger desk at the head of the room and huddled underneath it.

"Just gotta make it an hour," she whispered, clicking off her flashlight. "You make sure you tell me when an hour's up, okay? Uncle Easy?"

He wasn't beside her. When she peered up, he wasn't even in the room with her. She crept out from behind the desk.

"Psst! Come on. You'll spoil things, come on!"

She poked her head into the hall. The blue light of Easy's "eye" was stationary.

"Easy! Come on!" she hissed.

He didn't respond. She paced over to him and knocked on his shell. He still didn't respond.

"Your batteries can't be dead. We swapped them out last month and you're definitely charged. Your light would be off otherwise."

She gave him another knock.

"Come on, this isn't funny," she said.

She clicked the flashlight on and shined it on his solar panels. Still nothing. Finally she turned to match the gaze of his sensors. There should have only been a set of blast doors that had signaled the end of the line for their old trash-picking trips. The thing had been scorched by several hundred attempts by the robots to burn holes through it to no avail. But when she shined the flashlight on it, something had changed.

A puddle of oil had formed on the floor. The blast door had slumped aside. One corner had lifted up, like one of the rails that held it had fallen away and allowed it to become crooked. A hydraulic seal must have finally given way on the other side of the door. The corner of the door that had lifted revealed a flickering light within.

"Easy… Easy, is that thing in there messing with you?"

Her uncle remained stone still. She hefted him from the floor and hurried him out into the stairwell. Even when he was well clear of the mysterious device, he remained completely immobile.

"No, no, no…" she fretted. "I've got to fix this. The rest of them are coming here and if whatever that is effects them, too…"

She didn't want to think about it. These robots were her family and they were her responsibility. Any danger that might be facing her in that room was nothing compared to what would happen to the camp if something like this existed to pose a threat to all of the robots.

Lana dashed down the stairs and slid across the oily floor. She crouched low and shined her flashlight into the room, mindful of any threats. The air was heavy with the scent of hydraulic fluid and… something else. Something musty and unsettling. She swept the light slowly. It revealed assorted control panels, some still flickering. Maybe this place still had a solar array somewhere? That seemed unlikely. Solar panels were among the most useful items in the wasteland. Surely they'd picked the whole countryside clean of them, and it wasn't as though you could just *hide* one. They needed the sun. It must have been some other power source.

She shook her head. That didn't matter right now. All that mattered was finding out what had locked Easy up and stopping it. She continued to scan the room. The pool of light settled on a chilling sight. On the far end of the blast door was a desiccated, long-deceased figure. The faded remnants of a laboratory uniform still clung to the corpse. Tools were clutched in its hands, and parts had been scattered around the body.

They had been trying to escape, trying to dismantle the blast door. That's why the formidable thing had failed at all. Decades ago this person had been working at it, and it had taken this long for their efforts to pay off.

Lana shuddered and turned away. That skeleton wasn't going anywhere, and she had a job to do.

The lights were too dim for her to see much of what the panels read with the flashlight on, so she gathered her courage and clicked the flashlight off. In the darkness, the glimmers of failing technology led her to a small control panel. As she drew closer, she could hear the odd, edge of her hearing hiss of high-voltage electronics. The indicator lights were a distinctive color, the very glow Easy's sensors had been locked onto. She turned on the flashlight.

"Drone countermeasures," Lana read.

A grid of toggle switches beneath the label each had its own indicator. The labels on the switches used confusing, military terminology. *Strategic, Tactical, Operational.* Beneath each of those toggles were smaller buttons labeled with quadrants. None of it made any sense. But she knew that drone was just another name for robot, and countermeasures meant things that were supposed to stop other things. So if something was hurting Uncle Easy, it was probably this.

She reached out with a shaking hand and flipped the switches one at a time. Strategic. Regional, Tactical. One quadrant after another. The lights in the room flickered a bit as she did. Each switch she deactivated seemed to cause the lights to brighten. When the last of toggles had been switched off, the place was almost fully lit.

A clattering of metal legs drew her eyes to the door. Easy slid into the room and desperately scanned the room.

"What happened? Where are you, kiddo?" Easy asked.

He lacked the inflection to sound frightened or concerned, but his posture made it more than clear he was vexed.

"You're okay!" she squealed, plucking him up and hugging him. "What happened to you just now?"

"I stopped. Interrupt requested. Countermeasure engaged, kiddo." His head turned to the panel. "Did you flip these switches, kiddo?"

"Yeah! I had to do something to snap you out of it."

He looked over the panels again.

"This might not have been good, kiddo."

"What do you mean? You woke up. That's what I wanted."

Easy wriggled free of her grip and clattered up along the control panel. One by one he tapped the labels of switches.

"Operational. Quadrant-002. That switch is for us. The seek and destroy drones. Switch on others, now, kiddo."

"What? Why?"

"Things will change. Maybe not good changes if you don't, kiddo."

"Okay, okay. Better to leave things the way you find them, anyway. That's what Mom says."

She switched on all of the other quadrant switches, then reached up to switch on the three main ones. When she flipped the toggle for "Strategic", there was a worrisome pop and sputter behind the control panel and everything went dark. No lights, no indicators, no hiss of voltage. Nothing.

"Uh-oh…" Lana said.

#

Needless to say, Lana lost that particular game of hide and seek. She probably would have anyway. Even without their advanced sensors, a coordinated grid search conducted by hexapod robot drones is a stunningly efficient way to track someone down. For the next few days Lana and Easy were particularly vigilant of anything that might be even the slightest bit wrong. But the days rolled by and nothing seemed wrong. The robots happily did their jobs and played their games. Lana did her job and played with the robots. All was well.

Easy clacked along over the counters in their kitchen. He was dusted with flour, his sensors trained on the handwritten recipe on a poorly bleached bit of home-made paper.

"450 grams. Powdered sugar," he said.

He tapped over to a canister and, quite delicately, pinched a measuring spoon with his front legs. When he'd dosed them into a canister with an oddly specific clay lid, he returned the sugar to the cabinet and inserted his center two legs through holes in the top. Horrifying slicing and dicing sounds rang out from inside the sealed bowl as he viciously vibrated his legs. When he was through, he popped the top of the container open and a plume of fine sugar dust rose out of it. He tipped the sugar into a bowl of wet ingredients, placed the same lid on top, and stuck his legs through to mix it until it was a smooth frosting.

A timer sounded. He raised his head.

"The cake is ready, Zulu," he stated.

The robots had their own, far more information-dense method for communicating, but in the years that they'd been working with the humans, they'd found that using voice commands for human tasks worked remarkably well. It also helped humans who were nearby to know what was being done.

Zulu tapped into the kitchen and plunked into the sink to wash off, then crawled out and opened the oven. They waked directly into the oven, its heating elements still glowing, and carried out first one pan, then the other to cool.

"Are there fresh strawberries, Zulu?"

The silent robot rattled their head in the affirmative.

"Three fancy ones, Zulu."

Zulu nodded once and sprang to the floor to fetch them. Vibration sensors in Easy's legs picked up motion upstairs. Lana was awake. He finished blending the frosting and quickly rinsed his legs, then placed covers over both cake and frosting.

"What *day* is it?" Lana trilled from the top of the stairs.

"Happy birthday, kiddo," Easy said at amplified volume.

He climbed up into a cabinet and returned with a bowl awkwardly pinched between his center legs. As Lana pranced into the kitchen, he hopped to the table and placed the bowl down, then bounced to the stovetop to load dip a custom designed scoop into a simmering pot. He bounced to the table again and dumped some of the porridge-like concoction into the bowl.

Proximity sensors sent up an alert and his head pivoted upside down to spy Lana reaching for the bowl of frosting.

"Hey. Cake for dessert. Breakfast time, kiddo."

"But it's my birthday!"

"You get cake for dessert. Breakfast time, kiddo."

She paused for a moment.

"*Cake* is for dessert, but I just want to steal some frosting."

"Frosting is for dessert, kiddo."

"But frosting is just sugary topping, and *jelly* is sugary topping. And jelly is for breakfast. Therefore, frosting is for breakfast."

Easy's fans flared.

"Your logic is sound, kiddo," he said.

She took a big scoop of frosting out of the bowl with her finger and sucked on it while Easy got her a spoon.

"So what are we doing today?"

"Cake, kiddo."

"Is it *only* cake?" Lana said slyly. "Or are there *surprises?*"

"You will see, kiddo."

She giggled in excitement.

#

Lana finished her breakfast and watched as Easy deemed the cake ready for frosting. The robot slipped two of his legs into rigged up holsters on the outside of spatulas and began to ice the cake. What he lacked in creativity and artistry, he more than made up for in precision, as when he was finished the cake was a perfect, flawless cylinder of white-iced glory. When he was finished, Zulu trotted in with an adorable little basket hanging around their neck.

They climbed up and positioned the strawberries precisely at the twelve, four, and eight o' clock positions. They then flipped out their laser and did a complicated little dance around the cake, pulsing the laser along the way. When they were through, they reached out and pivoted the strawberries, which unscrewed along a perfect helical cut to make a beautiful corkscrew sculpture of each berry.

They turned, took a bow, and sprung off to go about their day.

Lana clapped.

"This is going to be a great day!"

"Are you done with breakfast, kiddo?" Easy asked.

"Yep!"

He hopped down to the floor. "Follow me, kiddo."

"I knew there was more!"

She practically bounced along as Uncle Easy clattered along the floor and out into the sun. She pulled a shammy from her tool belt and crouched to give his solar panels a quick buff, lest the residue of the cake prep slow his charge. Along the way, she wondered what her surprise might be. The robots meant well, but most of them had a very basic understanding of the things humans might enjoy. Most of this crew were around when things were a lot harder, so the bar for a great gift was much lower. Last year they'd gotten her a gallon jug of spring water and a coil of salvaged copper wire. The year before, they'd gotten her a single work boot.

Her dad had drilled it into her that it was the thought that counted, particularly since it was borderline miraculous that they'd figured *this* much out, but hope sprung eternal that they'd get her something good each year.

Outside, all of the robots skittered out from among the crops and buildings as she followed Easy. She was being led toward a small metal box in the middle of the pathway leading to the moat. When she reached it, she crouched down to grab it.

"Not yet, kiddo," Easy said.

He stretched is legs for a few extra inches of height. In a wave of motion, the other robots did the same.

"Ready. Go," Easy said.

A tiny chorus rang out.

"Happy birthday to you…"

She smiled as the song echoed across the courtyard. Every year, for every birthday, they sang this song. The robots had a different song, a frankly much catchier tune her mom wrote that was called "Arrival Day." Every year, when the family sang, the robots would record it. When they sang, they played back their favorite rendition. She could hear her own voice from last year, and the year before. She could hear her parents from up close and far away. It was nice. And for a moment it reminded her, despite how exciting it was to be "on her own," she really missed her parents.

"Happy birthday, dear Lana. Happy birthday to you."

She clapped.

"Go ahead, kiddo."

She grabbed the box and pulled off the lid.

"Oh… Hahaha… they're… great!" she said, unconvincingly.

The box contained a pacifier that had been bleached white by the sun and a metal tin of sardines.

"David said we would do the handprint when he gets back, kiddo."

"Oh! Okay, sure. It sort of means more to them than it means to me anyway."

"David said since he was going to make you wait, he had a surprise for you, too, kiddo."

She turned around and shrieked in excitement. A handful of the bots were hauling out a two-wheeled contraption. It had the distinctive look of her father's engineering, but was slick and new. It looked *fast*. She had a two-wheeled scooter already, but it was the sort you pushed with your feet and overall it just wasn't very good for the dusty ground of their home. This looked like the next logical evolution of it, powered, with larger wheels. It halfway between a scooter and a dirt bike.

"This is for me? This is really for me?"

"Only if you wear the helmet and pads, kiddo."

Two more robots sifted out from among the crops with pads and a helmet. They were both a little big for her, and looked like something that a fighter pilot would wear, but she didn't care. With an incomprehensible squeal she snatched them up and started to put them on.

"Best birthday ever!"

The robots clattered and tapped their legs, doing the fidgety little dance they did when they were excited. She fumbled with the straps for her kneepads, already wondering if she would be able to get any height ramping off dunes with this thing like her dad's scooter did. She was so lost in her own thoughts, she didn't notice that the clattering and clacking was slowing to a stop. Then came the murmurings.

"Look."

"Wow."

"I remember that."

She cocked and eyebrow and glanced at her friends. All of the robots had their heads turned to a point in the sky, far to the south. She squinted, and soon was able to make out a small point of darkness.

A cold anxiety fluttered through her. The exciting thing about being alone was that it was new, and there was very little new in her life from day to day. But it had been something new that she'd expected. This was something new that was unexpected. It was a *bad* sort of new.

"What is it? What is that?"

All at once, the robots answered.

"Strategic."

"Strategic what?" she said. "What's strategic?"

"We are seek and destroy drones. Operational. We find humans. If we are near humans for long enough. Tactical comes. After that, Strategic comes, kiddo."

"Comes for what? Are they here to help?"

"Help us. Not you, kiddo."

"What do you mean?"

"David told you. Elizabeth told you. We had orders, before the people who gave the orders were gone, kiddo."

"But… but you're not following orders anymore. We're working together now."

"We are. Maybe not them. Maybe they still follow old orders, kiddo."

"S-so what do I do?"

Easy looked to the approaching point in the sky, then looked to the other robots. They all looked back to her. In unison, they answered:

"Hide and seek."

It wasn't the eager, pleading request for a game, though the precise same audio files were used. This was a deadly serious piece of advice from a collection of beings who were most certainly in a position to know. She nodded and pulled the helmet a little tighter, then stepped onto the two-wheeled scooter. Easy hopped on and clamped into his piggy-back position. It took two twists of the throttle for her muscle memory to kick in. In minutes she was streaking along the dry ground, hurdling toward the old base. Even if it was a lousy hiding place, it was worlds better than the camp, and at least it put some earth and stone between her and whatever the mysterious flying speck might have in store for her.

"Do you know what that thing will do? If it's still following orders?" she said anxiously.

"No. Probably destroy, kiddo."

"Th-they can't do that! I'm in charge! Mom and Dad will blame me!" she objected.

"Sorry, kiddo."

"Can you do that listening and talking thing? Where the bunch of you sort of whisper with the radio waves? So I can communicate with the rest of them? What are they going to do without me?"

"No. Bad for hide and seek. The Strategic Drone will find us, kiddo."

"Can you just listen, then? At least so I know what's going on? And let *me* know?"

"Yes, kiddo."

The little voice of excitement in her head grumbled about how she had to weave between dust-mounds rather than vaulting over them like she wanted, but it was more important to be safe than have fun right now. Her present wasn't quite as fast as her dad's scooter, but it was close. Close enough that if she'd wasted the time to dig his scooter out it would have been too late.

The thing in the sky had been moving fast, but it was slowing down as it got closer and lower. She was approaching the entrance to the base. Just a few minutes had gone by. In that time the thing had resolved from an indistinct black point on the horizon to what was clearly a massive, flying wing. It was easier to compare its size to the camp itself than anything smaller. A wide swoop of a shape cutting through the air. A flying wing. She could see the shadow it cast racing along the ground. Its entire surface had the deep blue iridescence of a solar panel.

It was close enough for her to hear the fearsome whine of electric turbines when she reached the shade of the base entrance. She was beginning to get a genuine sense of its scale. Thin silver lines traced out the familiar grid of a standard solar panel layout. Engineering instincts trained into her since birth by her father started to roll through her head. Rather than letting the aching concern consume her, she found herself muttering through the calculations aloud.

"How many panels do you count, side to side?" she asked.

"One hundred-two, kiddo."

"It looks like eight or nine long?"

"Nine, kiddo."

"Nine times one oh two. Uh, uh. Nine eighteen. Four hundred watts each. That's… uh… Thirty-six… And… seventy-two. Plus two zeroes. So, three thousand… thirty thousand… Three hundred sixty-seven thousand two hundred watts."

"Good math, kiddo."

"How many watts is Zulu's laser?"

"Six thousand, kiddo."

"So… does that thing have… Take off three zeroes. Six… No…" She shook her head. "Does it have a bunch of those lasers?"

"No. Two big ones, kiddo."

"How big?"

The shadow of the massive drone slid over them. It was moving incredibly slow now, its massive wingspan and relatively low mass meaning the gentlest breeze was enough to keep it aloft. Lana looked up to its belly and saw a host of sensor nodes, similar to those found in Easy's head but much larger and likely far more sensitive. The whining of turbines died away and blades flipped up from the four corners of the curved rectangle of its chasse. They pivoted forward and back, giving it a more efficient low-speed propulsion as it shifted to a circling trajectory. It was patrolling and analyzing.

"Hide, kiddo."

She didn't need to be told twice. The scooter was small enough to drive right through the doors of the base and into its bowels.

"Is it… uh… Is it saying anything?" she asked.

Easy pointed his head upward. A small parabolic dish deployed like a flower in his bonnet. He pointed his head.

"Yes, it is talking, kiddo," Easy said.

Lana angled the scooter and rattled it down a flight of stairs.

"Well what's it saying? Is it friendly?"

"It wants to know our nation or corporation of allegiance, kiddo."

"What the heck is a corporation? Or a nation?"

"Things that used to exist when there were more people, Kiddo."

"Tell it we don't have those!"

"Honeysuckle is telling it that, kiddo."

"And?"

Easy twitched his dish a few times.

"The drone wants a representative of the corporation or nation, kiddo."

"*But we don't have one!*"

"If the drone doesn't get a representative, it will destroy the camp, kiddo. … Honeysuckle is saying that she is the representative, kiddo."

"Smart! Remind me to give Honey some of that good grease Dad found."

"It says a representative is a human. Needs credentials, Kiddo."

"What are credentials?"

"Papers that say someone is in charge. From when there were nations and corporations, kiddo."

"But Mom and Dad just *told* me I was in charge. They didn't write it down. Why is this thing asking for so many things from the old world? Doesn't it know that's all over?"

"No, kiddo."

"It should be obvious! It wouldn't be hard to *find* someone if things weren't different now. Why can't it figure it out?"

"That's not how robots work. We don't figure things out, kiddo."

"You all did!"

"We were out of orders and out of choices. And we met your dad, who was nice, kiddo."

"So if I'm nice to that one it'll come to its senses?"

"It thinks it has orders, kiddo."

"So I need credentials."

Easy nodded.

"What do they look like?"

"I don't know. We didn't need them. We just found people, kiddo."

"Okay… Okay… Important people would have them, right?"

"Yes, kiddo."

"I guess… Eugh… This is going to be gross…"

#

A few very unpleasant minutes later, Lana and Echo were on their way back to the camp. With no time to come up with a real plan, and no way to know what exactly the Strategic Drone was after, she made the only choice she could. Layered atop her outfit was the musty lab coat from the desiccated remains from the control room. It was a small mercy that the dry environment had reduced the unfortunate person to something akin to a scarecrow, so there wasn't any… *juice* to deal with.

Lana glanced up to the flying wing. It was circling like a vulture, with one of its many nodes focused precisely on her.

"Why isn't it doing anything?" Lana asked.

"I don't know. Nothing is better than bad thing, kiddo."

"I guess so. But I wish it wouldn't just stare. It's making me nervous." She swallowed hard. "*More* nervous."

She swept and swerved around mounds of dust. The thing in the sky watched her. Slowly, sparkling little carapaces scuttled toward Lana. Each one shouted as she came near.

"Lana! Hide!"

"I'm in charge! I can't hide!" she shouted back.

Her trusty new scooter skidded into the courtyard, but there was still no response from the circling aircraft.

"Hey! Hey!" she shouted, waving. "You wanted a representative? That's me! You wanted credentials? I've got them."

Easy trained his dish on the drone.

"It is asking for your credentials, kiddo"

"I have the credentials. See? Look! Credentials!" Lana said, gesticulating wildly at the entirety of her ensemble.

Easy's dish twitched.

"It wants your ID number, kiddo."

"ID… ID! I have one of those!" She felt the front of the lab coat and pulled the ID card off. She squinted at it.

"Registration Number 6F9289AC-EF," she said.

A hatch flipped open on the belly of the wing.

"Laser charging, kiddo," Easy stated.

Before he'd gotten the second syllable out, he had spun around and clicked himself into place on her chest. The other robots surged toward her like a wave, clattering over her and interlinking their legs until she was entirely cocooned in their resilient bodies.

"It's not even me! It's not even me I stole the coat!" she squealed, teetering under the weight of her impromptu suit of armor.

Clacking legs snagged the ID and passed it to the outside to present to the circling sensors.

"It says ID image does not match ID holder, kiddo."

"Yeah! See! I'm not the person you want to shoot, so don't shoot!"

"It wants to know our nation or corporation of allegiance, kiddo."

"There aren't any of those! It's done! It's over! Whatever you were supposed to do, you did it!" she shouted.

She trembled, certain the next thing she'd feel would be the bite of a laser. None came. Heartened by the possibility that the thing was actually listening, she continued.

"Don't you think you'd *notice* if there was a world left? If whoever told you to do what you think you're supposed to do was still around? Did you see anyone on the way here? Do you have any readings or anything from anyone but us? You're done! Congratulations! You did it! You killed everybody! Now you can rest!"

There was another long silence.

"It is announcing his other orders, kiddo."

"Are they good orders?"

"Mutually assured destruction. The elimination of its corporation of allegiance requires the destruction of any unallied societies. Laser charging, kiddo."

The robots forming her armor rolled backward and began clattering across the ground as quickly as they could.

"We can't! There's nowhere else to go!" she shouted. "Listen, you stupid sky wing. Look at this down here! This is what society is now! It's humans and robots, together. No sides. We take care of them. They take care of us! All humans. All robots. All together. And that includes you! You can't finish destroying society without destroying *you*."

The robots hauling her away like a colony of ants did not slow, and she couldn't see past the shell they'd formed over her to tell what was happening, but there was no sound of sizzling chaos. The robots slowed, then stopped. They heaved her to her feet and scattered off her. The wing was still circling, but the laser was notably tucked away again.

"It says it has reached an internal contradiction. It must destroy society. That requires it to destroy itself. But it is mandated to defend itself, except at the expense of its nation of allegiance, but it is a part of its own nation of allegiance. It is seeking conflict resolution, kiddo."

"Easy," she said. "Just ignore the old rules. They don't fit anymore. If you're willing to follow the new rules, we'll be happy to have you aboard."

"It wants to know the rules, kiddo."

"They're easy. Don't hurt anybody. No humans, no robots. If you need fixing, we'll fix you if we can. First one's free, but after that you've got to help bring back stuff to keep our little society afloat. And if you see any signs of anyone, you let us know. That's it."

The flying wing circled twice. It was the longest few minutes of Lana's life. The propellers flipped up and the turbines flipped down. Dust scoured away from the dry stone outside the camp. The flying wing slowly lowered to the ground and powered down.

"It says it needs new bearings in turbine three, kiddo."

Lana blinked and scanned across the massive drone. "Okay… Okay, that might have to wait until Dad gets back. But until then, you're going to need a name, and you're going to need a voice. And before *any* of that, I'm going to need some cake."

#

Several weeks later…

"I'm getting some blips and pings," David said, doing his best to feed the baby while monitoring a cobbled together communicator.

"It can wait, Dave. We're almost home." She leaned on the accelerator to drag the sluggish buggy up a slope. "And not a minute too soon. We're almost out of charge."

"I'm just still amazed we got the satellite network to wake up. And how many of them are still active. Eventually people are going to *have* to notice. Maybe some automated—"

"Dave, something's wrong," she said suddenly.

"What? Where?" he said, looking up from his dual tasks.

He looked up and instantly spotted what she had. The massive expanse of solar panels just beyond the east edge of the camp. He pulled out a pair of binoculars.

"There's no damage. Everything seems intact. Are we in range? We must be in range. I'm checking the radio."

He set down the satellite communicator and picked up the old-fashioned radio.

"Hello? Kiddo! Are you there? Answer fast, young lady!"

After a punishing few minutes, there was a reply.

"Mom! Dad! You're home!"

"Yeah, we'll be back in an hour. I can see the camp now. Maybe you could explain exactly what I'm looking at?"

"Oh, right. That's our newest resident. Say hello, Madras!"

A much louder, booming version of Lana's own voice burst over the radio.

"Hi, Mom. Hi, Dad. I need new bearings on turbine three, please."

"Lana, what the heck is that and where did it come from?" she said.

"It's a long story, but it's fine. She's super nice."

"Where did you get a name like Madras?" Elizabeth said.

"It was in this funny poem I read," Lana said gleefully.

"Oh, no…" David said.

"What poem?" Elizabeth asked.

"I don't think you really need to—" David began.

"There once was a girl from Madras, who had the most magnificent—"

"Okay, yes, that's fine," David said quickly. "We'll talk about it when we get home. I'm just glad you're safe."

"Okay! See you soon!"

David turned off the radio.

"Did our daughter name a flying fortress after a dirty limerick, Dave?"

"It would appear so."

"Why do I get the feeling you're somehow to blame?"

"Because you are a very astute woman."

Elizabeth sighed. "We're never leaving her alone again."

Comfortable Dragon
Joseph R. Lallo

Comfortable Dragon

Ever since I decided to name the first collection of Patreon stories *Paradoxes and Dragons*, it became necessary to include at least one dragon-based story in each cluster of Patreon shorts. There was very little fear of this not happening naturally, as I've got dragons on the brain to the point that I find ways to include them in settings where they don't even make sense. In the instance of *Comfortable Dragon*, the setting makes sense, but the fact that the entire premise came from a single adjective is a little weird.

I actually have been wanting to write this story for quite a while. Way back when I went to LA for a conference and I was getting super stressed out, I sat on my friend Fable's couch and said, "I want to write a story where there's a dragon just being comfortable, loving life." Eventually, that became this. I hope you enjoy it!

A haggard-looking man riding a rather *more* haggard horse approached the edge of a small mountain village. He'd begun this little journey in the depths of summer, and had dressed accordingly. At the time, his wide-brimmed hat had been the most important piece of protection he had, as the biggest threat had been being baked to a crisp by the sun. He'd believed at the time that it would be simple enough to find a new place to line his pockets and put down some roots.

His travels had not gone as he had planned. Now the harsh mountain winds were blowing right through his lightweight ensemble and he scarcely had two coins to rub together to equip himself with something more suitable. This place, however, was looking rather promising as a means to correct that financial shortcoming.

The homes here were pointlessly large and sprawling for so cold a place. It must cost a fortune to heat them. And yet every chimney in every home was billowing. He knew, without a doubt, that were he to knock on the door of any of these monuments to avarice, he would find it to be stuffed with rare and exotic trinkets whose worth was more important than their appearance. The head of the household would fit one of perhaps five descriptions, each worthless beyond the contents of his or her coffers. He grinned and stroked his long, curled mustache. Exactly the sort of person he needed.

"Too much money and the unquenchable desire to show it off," he murmured. "Smashing. It won't take much of a search to find a man in need of a good blade and a daring hand."

He spurred his horse forward. Unlike the last half-dozen towns he'd passed through, there was little in the way of commerce here. No blacksmith. No market. None of the things that typically kept a village functioning. Another good sign. It meant that all of the work done here was done by those in service of the nobles. Each of the manors may as well have been a city-state in and of itself. A large staff could always use another member.

There were but two buildings that did not amount to lavish private residences. One was a social club that he was quite certain would turn him away at the door. The other was a public house. Unless he missed his guess, it was owned by one of the people in town, and served as a means to ensure the wages to those who actually received them would eventually come right back where they came from.

He tied his horse in the adjoining stable and stepped through the door. Interior was warm and close, the air heavy with a combination of tobacco smoke and burning green wood.

"Hello, sir. Can I help you?" said a weary-looking woman on a stool beside the door.

"I rather think you can, Miss. You see, my name is—"

"You're selling something," she interrupted.

"I beg pardon?"

"You're selling something and we're not buying," she said.

"My dear lady, I assure you, while I offer services, and of course I expect a fair fee, I wouldn't think to attempt to separate you or any of the purveyors of this establishment from your hard-earned money."

"Looking to bilk one of the nobles, then."

"Err… Not in so many words."

"Job board is on the back wall. And if you want an ale or something to eat, money up front."

"You don't trust me, madam?"

"No, sir."

"Well." He dusted himself off. "At least you have my title correct. Sir Ronin, to be specific."

"Welcome to town, Sir Ronin. Job board is in on the back wall, and if you want ale or something to eat—"

"Money up front. You've been clear on that point."

He marched to the back of the room and gazed over the board. Small slips of paper, written out in the same clear but rough hand. Most of them were quite beneath him. Quests to fetch this or that. The sorts of things that wouldn't be necessary at all if the place had had a market or trader. The payment was a pittance, set by someone who didn't understand what time and labor were truly worth. But one of them was *precisely* the sort of task that he prided himself upon.

"Ah!" he said, tugging the page away from the tack. "Wanted immediately. A tracker, bounty hunter, or other mercenary to return an abducted individual. Great peril. Only the bravest need apply."

He marched up to the woman beside the door.

"This may as well have been addressed to me personally. This is requested by a Lord Milhaus. Where might I find them man?" he asked.

"Top of the hill. Milhaus Manor. You can't miss it." She rolled her eyes. "No matter how hard you try."

\#

To call Milhaus Manor ostentatious would be an understatement. In a part of the kingdom where most homes were the color of sun-bleached wood, layers of brightly colored paints, slathered on with little regard to taste or artistic expression, proclaimed this place to be the home of a Very Significant Individual. This, at least, was the aim of the place. The staff was similarly festooned with ornaments. The young woman who answered the door may as well have been a circus performer for how brilliant her uniform was.

And then there was Lord Milhaus himself. He was a tall man, though very slight of build. This fact must have been a sore one for him, as the baffles and ruffles of his multi-color outfit bulked him out considerably. Not unlike the plumage of a bird from far-off lands… he wondered if a pail of water over the head would leave this man a scrawny and miserable husk of his former self.

"So," he said, his voice thin and reedy. "I am told you are interested in returning that which was taken from me?"

Ronin stroked his mustache and flashed a smile. "I am, sir. I am *quite* interested."

"You *are* aware that this is a treacherous journey. You are the fifth adventurer who has offered me his services and I've yet to have one return. What makes you think you are equal to the task?"

"Have you ever paid a visit to the southern lands?"

"My business keeps me here."

"Ah, a pity. It is a land of beauty and grandeur. And more relevant to the matter at hand, it is where I made my reputation. I have served under no fewer than seven lords."

"Difficulty maintaining employment?"

"I prefer to interpret myself as a man whose services are so highly in demand that I could not be expected to serve a single lord."

Milhaus narrowed his eyes. "You are selling something, aren't you?"

"I do wish I knew why people kept saying such a thing. The fact is, I am a master tracker, and quite the demon with a sword. I will find the scoundrel who took your… May I ask, who was abducted? Your daughter, perhaps?"

"Hardly."

"Your wife?"

"My tailor."

Sir Ronin held his tongue and kept his expression neutral, just in case the man was joking. No laughter came.

"A crime! A travesty! To have deprived the household of the man no doubt responsible for the work of art you are wearing now is an act of the purest violence."

"My feelings exactly."

"If I could be so bold as to ask, you say that I am the fifth adventurer to undertake this mission."

"You are."

"And are we to suppose that my predecessors met their end?"

"I can only suppose such is the case. I've heard nothing from them, and my tailor has not been returned."

"May I ask, why not procure a new tailor?"

"I scoured the world for him. He is, bar none, the finest textile artisan of our generation. He has no equal. And I shall have him returned to me."

"If it is your will, then it is my quest. Er… Provided my compensation is sufficient."

"You shall be given supplies for your quest and what little we know about his potential whereabouts and, when you return with him, you shall be showered in riches."

He twisted his mustache.

"Evocative though it is, might I have more solid a figure than 'a shower'?"

"Thirty gold pieces," he said flatly.

"A princely sum." He stood and clicked his heels. "You will have your precious seamster before the month is out!"

#

Two weeks later…

"Thirty gold pieces was not enough…" he muttered.

This wasn't his first bounty. Ronin's talk of being an expert tracker wasn't bluster. And unlike many such missions, the information regarding the missing person was in ready supply. All knew where he'd gone, and retracing the path lead him in a single direction. The tailor had been traveling through a part of the trade route where precious fabrics from the west were bought and sold—spoke of a single culprit.

A dragon.

In his experience, most such claims could be chalked up to some combination of hysteria and intoxication, but some very sound, very sober people had been matter-of-fact on the subject. They hadn't even said "a dragon." They'd said, "*the* dragon." And all had pointed to the same mountain.

Every moment since then had been worse than the last. The only moderately accessible method to reach the mountain was a windy, howling pass and a sheer cliff. His horse had barely made it through the pass, and nearly six hours had passed since he'd started scaling the cliff and he'd yet to reach a walkable slope. He wasn't foolish enough to try climbing the cliff while wearing his plate armor for the climb, and the leather underpadding was taking a terrible beating on the jagged stone. Some fairly fresh breaks along the way told the tale of less careful climbers than he who had met their end at the bottom of the rocky slope. The thought had crossed his mind that he should turn back. The more sensible of his predecessors probably had, taking the equipment they'd been given by Milhaus as payment for their trouble and abandoning the full reward. Chances were good that those who hadn't done so were the aforementioned fallen climbers and who had abandoned far more than just the reward for their lack of discretion.

Two things were keeping him from turning back now. The first was his sense of pride. He was Sir Ronin, after all. Who was he if not the man who would succeed where others had failed? The larger reason however, was that climbing down was a great deal more difficult than climbing up, and the only thing worse than dying was dying in retreat.

Numb fingers dragged him farther. A crust of ice from his breath had frosted his mustache. Still he pressed on. Another hour passed. It felt like an eternity. Just as the last of his grip was threatening to give out on him, he pulled himself onto a ledge that could only be his destination.

It wasn't just that this ledge was large enough for a dragon to perch upon. It wasn't that it was perfectly level in a way that suggested the work of a mason rather than wind and snow. It was that it didn't even deserve to be *called* a ledge. This was a porch. Lines had been etched into the ledge to mimic the gaps of cobblestones. The face of the mountain had been smoothed and similarly etched. His past clashes with dragons had each been at the mouths of yawning, forbidding caves. The sort of place that was hung with fang-like rock formations. A portal that may as well lead to the depths of darkness. This was a door. A massive one, perhaps five times his height, but a genuine door. Wood slabs, metal hinges. Even a knocker, albeit one that probably weighed more than he did. It was shaped like an ox's head, with the ring hinged to strike the door. A chain connected to the bottom of the ring dangled down to eye level for him, where it connected to a fist-sized lump of brass that was itself connected to the door by a slack bit of chain.

The list of things one most likely to encounter when hoping to slay a dragon was longer than his arm. He had to watch for fire. He had to be mindful of the wind, for fear of their acute sense of smell. He had to watch the skies to avoid swooping attacks from above. But fortifications were not among them. It would take a battering ram to get through this door. All he had was a sword.

He huddled close to the door and pressed his ear to it. It was warm to the touch. Not just sheltered from the cold wind, which it mercifully was, but physically warm. This wasn't some unexplained relic of a forgotten age. Something lived here. For now, anyway.

Sir Ronin dropped down to his belly and began to feel his way across the bottom of the door. It was astoundingly well made. He could scarcely fit a finger beneath it. The thing probably didn't let a breath of breeze through. There was no window, not that there would be. It didn't even make sense that there was a door. Any further searching would require him to leave this porch, and until his fingers regained their sensation, that was unwise. But perhaps it would not be necessary.

He pulled his blade from its sheath. Its edge gleamed with an unnatural brilliance. A single slice was all it should take. It was all it had taken before. He preferred to have the element of surprise. Particularly in situations such as this where his target could end him with a single breath. But surviving the trip here was tricky enough. Making his way back to the mountainside to search for another entrance that might not exist? That might well be more dangerous than the alternative.

This would take razor-sharp reflexes. He might only have moments to do what needed to be done. With sword held ready, he stalked to the low-hanging lump of the door knocker. It would take three men such as himself to knock with the actual ring, but the lump would make plenty of noise for a dyed in the wool hunter like a dragon.

He pulled it back and thumped three times. The air was still echoing with its impact. A few sprinting strides took him clear of the door. He trained his eyes at the approximate height he would expect a dragon's head to be. The whole battle played out in his mind. It would turn. A diving roll. Jaws open. Flame. Another roll forward. Upward thrust. And it would be done.

"May I help you?"

He nearly jumped out of his skin. The door was still shut, but when he looked back to where he had been, there was a short bald man in a neat jacket and tidy trousers. Sir Ronin blinked.

"Did you need something, sir?" the man said.

Ronin had not expected conversation. It took him a moment to gather his wits.

"Would you… Er… Would you be the man of the house?"

"No. That would be Mister Comfortable."

"Mister Comfortable?"

"Yes. Did you have an appointment?"

"Is Mister Comfortable what I think he is?"

"Do you think he is a dragon?"

"I do."

"Then he is precisely what you think he is."

"I take it that he is not about."

"Oh, he is, but if you do not have an appointment I am afraid he won't be pleased to see you. He doesn't like to be disturbed."

"In my experience, dragons generally don't. Tell me, sir, have you made the acquaintance of a Mr. Webb?"

"I am he."

"Mr. Janus Webb."

"The same."

"I've been sent by Lord Milhaus."

The man's expression became considerably less neutral, though he remained polite.

"Ah. Please send Lord Milhaus my regrets that I will not be joining you."

"If you are frightened that the dragon—"

"Mr. Comfortable."

"Yes, that Mr. Comfortable will kill you, I assure you, I can protect you."

"I am utterly unconcerned, sir. Now do you require anything else, or shall I bid you good day?"

Ronin looked down the cliffside, then back to the curious little man.

"I've come an awfully long way and I'm really not interested in climbing back down the mountain quite so soon. Could I warm my bones for just a moment or two?"

"Of course! Of course, come in!" He said. "But the sword will have to wait outside. And any other weapons you might be carrying. A basic precaution, you understand."

"If those are the rules of the house," he said.

He sheathed the weapon and removed it from his belt. As he approached, he discovered the curious fellow had exited the dragon's lair through a hinged portion of the main door that Ronin had mistaken for simply another plank during his investigation.

This was not going as he had anticipated. Normally that would trouble him, but considering he'd anticipated a battle with a dragon, this was in no uncertain terms an improvement. At least for the moment. And he wouldn't be alive today if he'd not developed a knack for adapting to changing circumstances.

Passing through the door was a glorious relief from the elements he'd braved to reach this place.

"I'll ask you to keep your voice down. Mr. Comfortable is resting," Webb said quietly.

"Resting."

"Yes."

"A creature of the night, is he?"

"Oh, heavens no. He sleeps through the night. That is why we must be so quiet, you see. He sleeps so well during the night that the slightest sound wakes him during the day."

The tailor, who at the moment seemed to have instead taken the role of a butler, led him through the home. Ronin was inclined to call it a cave, but having seen the inside, the term really didn't suit the place. The chambers had seen the same care as the outside. Walls were smooth and artful. Doorways between the alcoves were graceful arches large enough for a creature of considerable stature to pass through. Beyond the etched faux brick of the floor and walls, it was only lightly decorated. What little decoration he could spot was quite contrary to the typical dragon's den. It wasn't scattered with gold and jewels. This dragon favored rugs and tapestries. And even within that narrow lens, they defied expectation. The tapestries were intricate and exquisite, but the rugs were simply fluffy. Downy soft threads stood almost ankle-high as he walked across it, like he was walking through a field with cotton grass.

Flickering oil lamps served to both light and warm the place, nestled nicely within wall sconces. Most of the place was at least dimly lit. The exceptions were a far more brightly lit chamber branched off to the right, and a very dark chamber tucked away to the left. He didn't need to ask what could be found within that darkness. A soft, deep, rumbling breath came and went every few seconds.

Ronin eyed the darkness as he walked.

"You seem awfully casual about your unique circumstances, Mr. Webb," he said.

"Not terribly unique, Mister…"

"Sir, if you would. Sir Ronin."

"Sir Ronin. I am one of seven people here, as you'll soon find."

"Not to contradict you, my good sir, but that would only serve to make your circumstance more remarkable, not less. In my experience, it is the nature of a dragon's prisoner to seek rescue."

"You are a knight, Sir Ronin. Are you a noble?"

"Not by birth, but occasionally by deed."

"You are, at least, a free man."

"I am. And I am here to restore your freedom as well."

"No, sir. You are here to return me to Lord Milhaus, the holder of considerable debts. Now that I'm not within earshot of him, I feel comfortable in adding to that a man of horrid and garish tastes. My present circumstance is one of relative isolation, perhaps, but my lodgings are more spacious, my work more fulfilling, and the food is of royal quality."

"What work do you do while in the clutches of a beast?"

"I am a tailor, Sir Ronin. And it is in that capacity that I am called to serve."

Sir Ronin looked upon the man curiously. "What sort of jobs could a tailor do for a dragon?"

"Very, very large ones, sir."

The pair finally stepped fully into the well-lit chamber. Sir Ronin abandoned all further speculation about the sort of things he might find here, as he clearly was not having any success with his predictions thus far. The chamber was a veritable industry in and of itself. Thread shuttled back and forth on great looms, steadily weaving long bolts of fine cloth. Two more men and four women worked at assorted bits of textile equipment. Spinning wheels, embroidery hoops. Great shears slicking through fabric. A pillowcase large enough to upholster the outside of a cottage hung along one wall. Large storage closets had been carved along the back wall of the chamber, each overflowing with wool, feathers, flock, and other assorted stuffing.

"Ladies, gentlemen, this is Sir Ronin. He has been hired by Lord Milhaus to liberate me," Webb said.

The others stopped their work and glared at the newcomer.

"I informed him his services would not be required," he added.

A look of relief replaced the distrust and they all went back to work.

"Would you have some tea, sir? I'm afraid we only have chamomile, but we have it in abundance. And something to eat?" Webb said.

"If it wouldn't put you out?"

"Dragons are fine hunters, sir. Even a rare trip keeps the larder well stocked."

Just to the left of the entrance was a small nook outfitted quite nicely with a table, some chairs, a cupboard, and a hearth. Sir Ronin took a seat. A bit of refreshment was quickly assembled.

"Cream, sir? Or lemon," Webb asked.

Ronin raised an eyebrow. "Mr. Comfortable must be a *very* capable hunter to be bringing back cream and lemon."

"He is kind enough to take one of the ladies along to a market up north."

"They let dragons come and go?"

"He doesn't take her *all the way* mind you."

"And she does the shopping and comes back, does she?"

"Naturally."

"Back into the clutches of a dragon."

"Yes."

Sir Ronin sipped his tea. "I think I may have to meet this Mr. Comfortable. He seems like a very interesting fellow."

The walls rumbled with a half-hearted wail. It was deep and resonant, and powerful enough to jostle Ronin's nerves.

"Ah! Then you are in luck. If you act fast, you may have your chance. Our benefactor is rolling over. Do hurry, though. He's a terrible grump if you bother him when he's started to doze again."

The knight set down his cup and stood, trotting swiftly back through the lair. He approached the darkened chamber with a good deal less trepidation than he'd approached the door not a half hour ago. In both cases he was expecting to come face to face with a dragon, but after the overall attitude among the tailors and weavers, he very much doubted he had anything to fear from whatever beast was lurking ahead.

As he stepped into the doorway, two things struck him. The room, even without the benefit of crackling flames, was much warmer than the rest of the lair. It was a heavy, pervasive warmth that made his eyes heavy. And then there was the smell. It was potent, earthy, but not wholly unpleasant. It put him in mind of when his father's hunting dogs would come in from the rain and bake themselves in front of the fire.

He stepped as far into the darkness as he dared, then softly cleared his throat.

"Er… Hello?"

"Mmm?" a low voice murmured thickly. "Need something?"

The voice was low and powerful enough to rumble in his chest.

"I wondered if I could have a word with you."

"Mmm… Very well."

"Lovely. You see, I was sent here with the intent—"

A flash of light and a rush of heat startled him to silence. A breath of flame curled to the ceiling. It splashed against a previously unseen chandelier, igniting it.

The glow of the light gradually revealed the dragon's inner sanctum. The room itself was something of a bowl. It dipped down a few paced beyond where Sir Ronin was standing and was utterly heaped with cushions, pillows, and blankets. Some had the dull gleam of satin or silk. Others were quilted, still others knitted, and everything with any stuffing at all was overstuffed. Fabric that had been the bed of any sort of animal tended toward rattiness, but this bedding looked pristine and perfect. And then, there was the dragon himself.

Like his decadent furnishings, he was pristine, soft, and overstuffed. He was sprawled on his back, wings spread out to either side and curled up against the curve of the bowl that he'd filled with his cushions. His head was hidden behind his great belly, so it took a grunt of effort and a curled neck to heft his head into view to look upon his visitor. He was short-necked, as dragons went, with a long narrow snout that bore what seemed to be a permanent expression of ease and relaxation. Half-lidded, sleepy eyes blinked.

"You're new," he said. "Friend or foe?"

"My name is Sir Ronin."

"A sir. A knight sort of sir or just the formal sort."

"A knight, but an unarmed one."

"Mmm. So a smart friend or a stupid foe. In either case, the sort

I prefer to deal with. What brings you to my home?"

"I was charged with returning Mr. Webb to his former employer."

"Mmm. No. Have a safe journey back, Sir Ronin."

He flopped his head back again and released a long, luxurious sigh. It truly seemed as though this creature breathed exclusively in blissful sighs.

"May I ask why you require a battalion of tailors?"

He grumbled and hefted his head up again.

"You are a pain in the neck, Sir Ronin."

"I'd say I'm a good deal more polite than most knights would be in this situation."

"No. I mean literally. You are giving me a pain in my neck."

The pudgy tail tufted with silky hair whipped up from the bowl and wrapped around him, ensnaring him with startling speed for something that seemed perfectly sedentary a heartbeat earlier. He was hauled out over the monster's belly, and dumped unceremoniously onto it.

He bounced a bit, then sunk down into its pudgy plushness. The hide was pale green, smooth, and yielding. Sir Ronin rose and fell, wobbling slightly at the top and bottom of each breath. From this vantage, the dragon was able to gaze up at him with his head nicely nestled in a few strategically propped pillows.

It was clear Comfortable was the source of the warmth in the room. Having his hands dimple down into his supple hide was like dipping them into a hot bath.

"Now, you were saying?"

"Why do you need seven tailors and seamstresses?"

"Look around you. Who do you suppose made my bed?"

"But you've got the bed now. Why do you still need them?"

"Because it can *always* be better. And even a proper cushion wears out. So I have a new set made every month."

"Every *month!?*"

The beast huffed, softly smoky breath ruffling his mustache.

"Do you know why dragons sleep on a mound of gold?"

"I'd always chalked it up to avarice."

"That's why we *hoard* the gold… more or less. But my kin sleep on their gold because, as metals go, it is rather soft. A properly broken-in mound of gold can last hundreds of years without needing to be churned or fluffed up. But a pillow? But there are better ways."

He wriggled back and forth, almost dislodging Sir Ronin from his perch. The motion burrowed him into the mound of pillows until only his belly, his snout, and his tail stuck out.

"So much better," he breathed.

"What happens to the older pillows?"

"I haul them out and leave them with the staff. Then I haul in the new ones and arrange them nicely. By the time I'm back from a hunt they've done whatever they do. None of my concern."

"It seems like grunt work to simply manufacture pillows. Surely you don't need someone as skilled as Mr. Webb."

Comfortable poked his head up again, smaller pillows tumbling aside. He gave Ronin a pitying look.

"You've never experienced a proper pillow."

He leaned up a bit more.

"I scarcely see how one pillow can differ so greatly from anoth—"

His skepticism was interrupted by a burst of breath as Comfortable blew him from his belly to flop onto one of the pillows perched on the dragon's thigh. The soft, smooth cushion practically enfolded him, gloriously supporting every bit of his body.

"Oh…" he breathed. "Oh, my…"

"Night and day," Comfortable said. "I'll be keeping my tailors, thank you."

"I understand. Entirely."

"Then run along."

The pudgy tail emerged from beneath the pillows and ensnared him once again, hefting him from the mound of pillows and plopping him on the edge of the dished-out pillow pit.

"Er… There are still some problems."

"Not for me there aren't," he said.

"I've come here at great risk to my life, and I was anticipating a rather substantial payment for returning Mr. Webb."

"Must I squish you? Is that how this must end? Because I do find that distasteful."

"No! I will leave quietly, but I would much prefer not to risk my life on the return only to have nothing to show for it when all is said and done. And to speak to your interests, Lord Milhaus clearly has no issues hurling fortune seekers in your direction, so I'll merely be the first of many."

"So must I squish *him?* That seems like the beginning of a tiresome sequence of squishings."

"I can head back and tell him Webb was killed. He doesn't seem to be the sort who would demand revenge for the death of an employee. But there is still the matter of my payment and my safe return."

"If you can bear spending a few days, I can drop you off somewhere when next I hunt. I'm not making a special trip. As for money, I have none to give you, and you haven't exactly earned it from me."

"What do you mean you don't have money? Where do you get the materials for the pillows? And the little creature comforts for the tailors?"

"Ask them," he said simply.

A curl of his tail pressed his chandelier to the ceiling such that it was snuffed out, then rolled over, burrowing himself into his pillows to drift off to sleep again.

#

"Ah, so you'll be staying with us," Webb said, walking with Ronin back to the work area. "I'm sure we can find a way to make you useful."

"Yes, yes. I was rather hoping to discuss it. Mr. Comfortable doesn't seem to know how all of this is paid for."

"Ah. It's nothing sinister. Even after being used for a month or two by a dragon, the fine fabrics still have quite a bit of life in them. One can make a tremendous amount of fine clothing from the remains of a single cushion. Whoever makes the trip to the market sells what we've crafted and it is more than enough to fulfill our needs, his needs, and a considerable amount besides. Even with the unavoidable discount we must apply."

"Discount?"

"The scent of a dragon is a rather enduring one. We can't very well charge full price for an odd-smelling garment."

Sir Ronin gave him an incredulous look.

"My dear Mr. Webb. You have a dearth of imagination. If you'll provide me with an assortment of your wares, I can assure you, a return trip to this place will be *well* worth both my time and yours. As a matter of fact… If you feel comfortable you still recall Lord Milhaus's measurements, I believe I can wrap all of this up nicely."

#

Two weeks later…

Sir Ronin, now dressed in a rather fetching outfit, marched into Lord Milhaus' chambers.

"Greetings, m'lord!" Ronin said. "I bring sad tidings."

"And you are?" the Lord said.

"Sir Ronin, m'lord."

Lord Milhaus eyed him dispassionately, awaiting further clarification.

"You sent me to seek Mr. Webb, your tailor. A task that claimed the lives of four other men."

"Ah. I'd assumed you were the fifth. Have you retrieved him then?"

"No, m'lord. As I said. I bring sad tidings. Mr. Webb has been killed. The world has lost a fine tailor. "

"I see. Unfortunate indeed. I shall have to seek a replacement." He crossed his arms. "In the meantime, I do home you don't expect me to pay you. If I recall correctly the payment was conditioned upon his return."

"Mmm. I rather suspected that would be your attitude. However, all is not lost, both for me and for you."

Lord Milhaus looked askance at him.

"You're selling something…"

"Yes, m'lord! I am indeed selling something. In my travels, I came upon a very secretive vendor with the most marvelous of wares."

He opened his pack and revealed a frilled blouse.

"I think you will find this piece to be the match for anything your poor, departed Mr. Webb could produce."

Milhaus took the garment and gave it a measuring glance.

"Excellent threadwork. Fine fabric… Yes… Yes this is expertly made. The colors are a bit drab for my taste, but certainly a serviceable piece for a less formal occasion."

He sniffed and wrinkled his nose.

"What is that odor?"

Sir Ronin leaned back and gasped rather more theatrically than was necessary.

"M'lord, surely you understand that the 'odor' you've identified is the greatest treasure of all. This fabric is perfumed with the rarest of exotic scents. I assure you, no nobleman in a generation has worn something with so precious and exclusive a fragrance. Its source is the most closely defended secret in a dozen kingdoms. That a source has been found is nothing short of miraculous. And you, sir, have the tremendous fortune of being the first to have a chance at purchasing it."

With each superlative, the fashion-hungry lord's eyes sparkled more.

"Yes, yes… I shall purchase it. What is the fee?"

"As it so happens, I can part with this masterpiece for a piddling price. Just thirty gold pieces…"

#

A few minutes later, Sir Ronin left Milhaus's estate with a pack full of gold. He wasn't certain what delighted him more: that he would very shortly be an extremely wealthy man, or that he would earn that fortune ensuring that the very wealthiest nobles would be paying through the nose to smell like a dragon's laundry.

But it was going to be an awful lot of fun finding out.

Joseph R. Lallo

Time Loop

Time Loop

What follows is part of the "Shorts of Dubious Canonicity" project I started in 2018. In an attempt to keep my mind sharp and fresh, I started taking votes on short stories to write each weekend. Some of them stayed short. Some of them grew into full novellas. But almost all of them were the result of my fans and followers casting their votes to give them support.

There are two topics that seem to be perennial favorites among my readers. One of them is dragons, the other is time travel. Specifically time loops. This is one of those rare stories where I just got a flat out (and vague) request for "A Time Loop Story." The idea for this one was kicking around in my head for a while, but boy oh boy was it more complicated to write than I expected. I actually made a flow chart to keep track of it. I didn't stick to it perfectly but it kept me from contradicting myself (I hope).

52

Damon Robbins set down his recently emptied cup of morning joe. It had been lackluster, thanks to the local convenience store having run out of non-dairy creamer. He didn't exactly expect top-quality stuff from a place that displayed most of its food on greasy rolling bars, but generally the quantity made up for it. If the universe were a fair and equitable place, he'd be nursing thirty-two glorious ounces of wake-up juice from a comically large thermal mug, but the mug was conspicuously missing from where he'd left it in the cabinet of his dorm. The largest size offered by the store barely lasted to the lobby of the research building.

If he was going to get through this day, he was going to need a lot more caffeine. Fortunately, the university knew that academia was fueled by coffee. The k-cup machine in the lounge was perpetually well-stocked, and he fully intended to hit it up when he got the chance. But first, there was work to do.

He flipped through his handwritten notes. In theory, it would be more efficient to keep his notes in a spreadsheet or memo document so he could copy and paste. Then again, in theory he would be working on a computer that had been manufactured *after* he was born. As it was, all he had was an old, practically bulletproof IBM mechanical keyboard that clicked obnoxiously as he loaded up the boot sequence. According to the department heads, this was the newest piece of PC hardware that could still run the code and the interface for the transceiver array in the basement.

Information on the project was kept vague. Damon wasn't entirely certain if the vagueness was thanks to some sort of NDA, classified status, or if even the people running the project didn't know what it was about. He didn't mind that he didn't know what it was. He didn't want to know what it was. The only thing that mattered right now was the whole project was still funded by some long-forgotten bit of political pork, and that meant he could work off his student loans without having to enter the gig economy.

The test system, which made the sort of charming whirring and clicking sounds you just didn't get out of modern PCs, began to execute the commands. He squinted at the green glow of the monitor and waited for the blinking cursor to populate the message that was still burned into the screen from the several thousand prior tests.

"Come on, come on. Fail already so I can go hit the lounge before Jerry finishes the French roast," he grumbled.

The computer produced a sickly beep.

Processing readings.

Damon grimaced and slumped in his chair. He flipped to a clean page and clicked his pen. Technically, these readings were what he was hoping for. When he'd been given this job, the previous guy pointed him to a sagging bookshelf filled with three-ring binders. They held "the procedures." Painstakingly detailed flow charts described what he was to do in the event of success. The layer of dust across the entire collection suggested just how often they'd had to be consulted in the last few decades. In the three months he'd been doing this job, he'd never had to venture past the coffee-stained index card taped to the side of the monitor.

Fail = Wait for Cooldown, Enter the most recent set of readings

Processing Readings = Write Down A New Set of Readings (Fewer = Better)

Failures were great. He had a mandatory ten-minute break while the rat's nest of a system caught its breath, then had to enter in the most recent of the numerical strings he'd jotted down from prior tests. Now that it was processing readings, he would have to sit and wait for it to start spitting out numbers for him to write down and use in future tests.

"How many will it be this time?" he grumbled, jotting numbers in the margins of the cleanest page of notebook. "If it's under five, I'm treating myself to a cruller."

He snickered. The numbers were hexadecimal, thirty-two digits long. For as long as he'd been working here, he'd never seen this thing produce less than fifteen of them. The current record for the most entries was sixty-five, mercifully set by his predecessor. It must have taken half an hour for him to write all of them down. He conservatively prepared ten lines for the alphanumeric strings, then looked up to see if the set had finished populating on the screen.

There was one.

"One set of readings? Wow. That's… if fewer is better, that's pretty darn good, I guess."

He jotted the sequence of digits down and tapped enter. More grinding, more clicking. The data entry prompt appeared in its burned-in spot on the screen and he quickly typed in the numbers. When he was sure he'd entered them correctly, he tapped enter.

"Come on, baby. Fail. I can just *feel* Jerry eying up that last French roast pod…"

The clicking went on longer than usual. On his home computer, and even on his phone, he was well accustomed to things randomly taking their time. Spinning beachballs and rotating circles were a fact of life. Heck, there were even some systems in this university that would still treat you to a flipping hourglass. But this hunk of hardware was well before the years of pings and multitasking. It had one job to do. It didn't do it well, but it at least did it consistently. A half-second longer than usual would have been noticeable. This thing was chewing on the command for a good fifteen seconds and counting. Finally, it made its decision.

Equilibrium Established. Execute Program 11-A.

He frowned. This was new. He didn't like new. Not in this context, anyway. New meant potentially talking to his superiors. He'd long ago come to terms with the potentially nefarious nature of this little project. The official policies around the position already required he maintain scrupulous security. No discussing the findings. All doors locked at all times. Anything out of the ordinary to be reported to security. Things that were unexplained and exuded a "don't ask questions" kind of vibe tended to have origins with agencies that called their employees "operatives" and did their interviewing in locked rooms with plain white walls. He really didn't want to have to tell someone that their project was acting up, even if that meant it had finally succeeded.

"Maybe it's not bad," he muttered. "Maybe it's just a procedure that didn't fit on the card."

He swiveled in his wobbly office chair and clicked on the lamp on the table in front of the procedure manuals.

"What the… Oh, no…"

The manuals were mostly covered with a layer of dust that was approaching "prop in a haunted house" levels of thickness. The security measures meant this room never saw the janitor's touch, and they certainly weren't paying him enough to do janitorial duties. He was presently the only one certified for this position. Technically, everything that was done in this place *should* have been his doing. But one of the manuals had clearly been accessed recently. There were clear-as-day fingerprints in the dust, and big section of the table was clear in front of it.

"This *would* happen on a day when I was low on caffeine…" he grumbled, already fishing out his phone.

He looked up the building security number and dialed.

"Hey… Yeah, this is Damon Robbins, over in the monitor room on the research level? Yeah. There's some evidence that someone's been in this room recently. I… Yeah, I know you're busy, but it's the Litmus Project. There's rules I've got to… Oh, okay. Thanks for—"

The call dropped. Damon tucked the phone back into his pocket. The tone at the beginning of the call had been gruff. He'd only crossed paths with the head of security a few times, but the man had quickly established himself to be the kind of guy who was perpetually on the verge of an angry rant. The audacity of the suggestion that he might have to actively secure the place was enough to push him over into "do you know who you're talking to!?" territory. At the mention of the Litmus Project, his tone changed, assuring that he'd do "a sweep" before hanging up.

"Okay… Okay, so this is probably nothing. Nothing's missing. If someone came in here, they'll be on camera. If they got in here, it either means they jimmied the lock or I left it unlocked. I *know* I didn't leave it unlocked. So… I guess I'll just keep doing my job."

He glanced back at the screen.

"Execute program 11-A," he repeated. "Let's see."

He swept his gaze across the row of binders. On the opposite side from the incriminatingly dust-free binder was one marked "Programs." He slipped it free from the row and carried it over to the computer desk to avoid further contaminating what might be a crime scene. This was literally the first time he'd opened a binder since he'd arrived. Aside from the plume of dislodged dust that rushed out when he opened it, he really didn't know what to expect. What he got was a series of folders loaded with punch cards of all things.

"Seriously? *Seriously?* What *century* is this?" he growled.

A few flipped pages brought him to a stack of six cards in a folder labeled 11-A. The folder had a handwritten note.

"All programs in series 11 of the specification need to be fed into the card reader on the main processing rack of the apparatus. Once in place, press the LOAD and EXECUTE programs in order," he read. "I have to… I have to go *into the basement for this one?*"

He shuddered. The less Damon thought about the stuff in the basement the better. He didn't know the details, but the whole mess looked like an exquisite corpse of a science experiment. Wave after wave of researchers and interns must have cobbled together equipment ranging from the 1940s to the early 1990s. They'd built a veritable time capsule of the Cold War out of gear they'd coaxed into what could charitably be called a working state. Stolen Russian components with vacuum tubes, experimental bleeding edge computer systems that he now knew needed punch cards to start up. Big antennae with faded warning labels featuring worrisome terms like "Maximum Permissible Exposure." The whole room smelled like burning copper, overheated plastic, and whatever weird chemical they flushed it with every morning. It was usually best to keep his visits to the equipment room brief. So far he'd been able to keep them *so* brief that he'd not been back since his orientation a few months ago.

Damon turned to the doorway and flipped up a laminated card.

"Don't be ready, don't be ready, don't be ready," he muttered to himself as he looked over the automated maintenance schedule.

The only other thing he'd remembered from orientation was that the room was off limits for two hours a day, one in the morning and one in the evening. During those times the room was flushed with aforementioned chemical. If he recalled correctly, the chemical was "a perfectly safe, non-toxic gas, which nevertheless will displace the oxygen in the room." This fell quite short of his own definition of "perfectly safe" but since the door auto-locked during the flush, he mostly just had to be mindful of when it was happening so that he would know not to be in there at the time.

Just his luck, the flush had happened thirty minutes prior. Plenty of time for the room to be rendered safe, at least by whatever standards governed government research.

Somewhere, a piercing whine echoed through the halls. It didn't take him long to determine it was the door to the stairwell. He knew it all to well, as did any other newcomer to the building. The fire escape doors were alarmed, a fact that most people found out the hard way after attempting to use them instead of the otherwise identical non-alarmed stairs at the opposite end of the hallway. Normally he'd disregard the sound, but in light of the current situation, it was better to be safe than sorry.

"Alarms are going off, people are screwing with the manuals, new procedures are happening. That's it. I'm calling the boss."

He pulled out his phone and tapped the contact for the professor who was overseeing the project.

"Dr. Wells. How can I help you?" his supervisor answered in her the sharp, studious voice.

"Hi. Damon here."

"As the caller ID indicated, yes."

"Did security call you or anything?"

"Why would security call me?"

"There was… I don't want to call it signs of a break-in, but someone definitely screwed with the manuals since I left yesterday."

"I see. Has the security footage been reviewed?"

"I reported it, but that was just a few minutes ago."

"I'm sure it is being handled then."

"Should I take a couple hours off until he gives the all-clear?"

"Not unless he contacts you suggesting there is reason to be concerned."

"Of course…" Damon griped under his breath. "Okay, Dr. Wells. Um, since I've got you on the phone. There's been a development with the project."

"What sort of development?"

"It wants me to execute a program. Is that normal?"

"A program… Which program, Mr. Robbins?"

"11-A."

"I will be there in twenty minutes."

"Why?"

"Because that's the program we've been waiting for."

"Should I wait until you get here to do anything?"

"What are the last four digits in the number that produced that prompt. You wrote it down, didn't you?"

"Yeah, of course. Procedure, you know? It's… 5da7."

He heard some tapping of keys.

"Excellent. Excellent. Enter it as soon as the machine is ready. There might be an over-temperature prompt, but that'll go off in a minute or two. These numbers are time-sensitive. Get down there now and execute the program. And take notes on what happens. This is a very big day, Mr. Robbins. A very big day."

She hung up. He stared at the phone for a moment.

"You don't suppose you could have told me what to expect, do you?"

He grabbed the program packet. There was time enough to flick through his phone notifications during his brisk walk toward the floor lobby and past the coffee machine. There wasn't time to stop and partake of it, but that didn't mean he couldn't give it a longing glance as he swept by. Three or four disposable coffee lids were scattered on the floor, but his muscle-memory locked his eyes onto the French roast row of the k-cup rack. It was, of course, empty.

"Frickin' Jerry…" he muttered to himself. "Taking the last coffee and leaving a mess."

Damon pressed the elevator button. Sure, he could take the stairs and it would probably be faster, but he wasn't really in a hurry to get down to the basement and expose himself to whatever emissions that machine was belching into the world.

A minute or two later, the light tapping of footsteps approaching down the hallway ended in an abrupt squeak-stop. He glanced up just in time to see someone ducking out of view of the elevator bank. Damon took a whiff and detected the incriminating scent of French roast.

"Jerry? I know that's you. You're the only other one who drinks that coffee."

The footsteps quickly departed.

"You're supposed to refill the row when you finish it, Jerry!" Damon called.

The elevator doors opened and he stepped inside.

"Social contract, Jerry!" he shouted before the doors closed.

His ride down was as slow and irritating as he'd expected. Three floors listening to the rhythmic rattle and squeak of an elevator older than his father. He'd long ago given up trying to figure out why they'd placed the monitoring room three floors above the equipment it was monitoring. The whole thing felt like they knew it wasn't great to spend a lot of time close to the equipment, which made him wonder if the residents of floors one through three had been informed of just what was lurking below while they went about their business.

The doors shuddered open in the basement level, and he was treated, once again, to the scent of French roast. It permeated the floor, though it seemed a bit stale, like an old spill.

"The universe is taunting me," Damon muttered. "No one else even uses this floor but the Litmus Project. Unless one of the department heads was down here inspecting it, someone's been trespassing and wasting coffee."

The dim corridor with the door to the equipment room was, sure enough, thick with the smell of spilled coffee. He tested the door. Still locked. At least the room hadn't been tampered with. He tugged the keyring he'd been entrusted with from his pocket and unlocked to door. The faint scent of "perfectly safe" chemicals rolled out along with the terribly thick stench of coffee to form a particularly unpleasant bouquet. He groped for the light switch and flicked it. There wasn't any coffee on the floor, but there was a telltale clean spot where it had been mopped up.

"Who would have done this? Who could have done this? Great. I'll probably have to report that, too. This is going to be a day with a *lot* of paperwork."

He set the concern aside to look upon the beast he'd been monitoring for all this time. Rack after rack of equipment filled the room. Some had been clearly designed to fit in the rack. Others had cobbled together adapters composed of twine, plywood, and cardboard keeping them in place. Patch wires in tangled bundles ran from rack to rack. Most of the room was shrouded in shadow, the old-fashioned tungsten light bulbs having long since burned out. There was no unifying aesthetic to the room, with beige, discolored boxes mounted beside weird olive drab cases with chipping paint. The thing didn't even have a monitor. He might not have known the thing was classified as a computer if not for the ominous whirr of fans and click of assorted memory devices. The business end of the monster was a brushed metal control panel with some slots, some buttons, a tray, and indicator lights labeled with grease pencil.

"Just make it quick," he instructed himself, hurrying to the control panel.

He opened the packet of punch cards and positioned them in the receptacle as the faded diagram instructed. Just above the input slot were two plastic buttons the same approximate shade of a smoker's teeth. He pressed the one marked LOAD.

The machine sprung to life, slurping up the stack of cards with frightening speed and efficiency. A sound not unlike an electric typewriter—something he'd *also* only experienced because of this antiquated job—clacked away inside the machine and it rocketed the pile back out, to settle into the output receptacle. Two flickering lights illuminated on the control panel. One was labeled "POGRAM LOADED" and the other read "EXECUTION READY."

"A typo on a control panel. Always a great sign."

He stowed the program back in the packet and reached for the button.

"No, wait!" yelped a voice behind him.

The sudden outburst startled him. He flinched, jamming the button a bit harder than he intended. When he did, a few things happened at once. A crackling clap assaulted his ears, and a terrible electronic scent of burnt wire filled his nostrils. Something like the opposite of a flash filled his vision, with all of the light in the room fading to pure black before popping again. He would have assumed it was some sort of a power dip caused by the machine overtaxing the circuit feeding it, but it felt different. It was too sharp, too sudden. It recovered too quickly.

He put his hand over his hammering heart and took a breath. He quickly wished he hadn't. The smell in the room was far worse than before. Both the weird chemical smell and the coffee stink were a good deal stronger.

There was no sign of the person who'd shouted. He hurried out the door, hoping to catch them, but the hallway was empty. He clenched his fist and reached for his phone.

"Way to do your job, security guy," he growled, angrily jabbing the redial option on his recent call.

He held the phone to his ear, waiting for the ring, but it never came. When he took it away, he found it displaying as strange error code he didn't recognize. Two more attempts produced the same result, and he realized that both the Wi-Fi and cell indicators on the notification tray were marked with Xs.

"This behemoth better not have busted my phone."

Damon marched angrily into the hallway and hammered the button for the elevator. It was there waiting for him. He rode it to his floor and stepped off. It was his intention to return directly to the monitoring room, where he could at least use the landline to dial up security and/or his boss to try to get some answers about what was supposed to happen now. His habitual glance toward the coffee station brought him to a standstill.

"Oh, come on now. How passive aggressive can you get?"

There was exactly one French roast cup in the rack of coffee pods. It took a special kind of sociopath to load up a single cup after being called out for drinking the last one.

"Fine, Jerry. Two can play at that game."

He grabbed the pod and clicked it into the machine, then fetched his phone to kill the time with some social media nonsense. The connection had yet to reestablish. He made a mental note to bill the university for the cost of a new phone, then pocketed the phone again to seethe in anger while his coffee brewed. With nothing else to do, he found himself gazing around to take a mental survey of the surroundings: a torn sugar packet had yet to be cleared from the table; a few cups lower down in the rack were poorly sorted; the clock above the coffee maker was a few minutes slow.

He paused and eyed the clock suspiciously. It was new. Or, at least, it was new by university standards. Among other things, it meant it was networked, combined with the "change of session" chimes that let the professors know when their class period was up. He specifically remembered that, because it had always seemed like an awfully grade-school thing to have in a university.

His brain had yet to land upon what precisely bothered him about a whole university's clocks being off by a few minutes when the coffee machine started filling his cup. The compounding frustrations and distractions combined with the eager anticipation of his spite-coffee, took their toll on his concentration. In attempting to snag a cap, he dislodged a few extras and they tumbled to the floor. When he slapped one in place on his cup and turned to gather up the dislodged ones, he was struck by a dizzying bit of déjà vu.

The caps on the floor were precisely where they'd been when he'd walked by on the way down. And the caps that he'd spotted back then weren't there.

It probably didn't mean anything, his logical mind was quick to point out. Someone could have come by and cleaned up the ones that were there and he'd just knocked down a few more. Coincidence. And no excuse to leave a mess. He knelt down to pick them up.

A familiar whine echoed through the hallway, the stairwell alarm. It was cut short, just as it always was. Just as it was a few minutes earlier… right around the time that was currently displayed on the wall clock. The implications of this discovery weren't the sort of thing a sane person would be swift to embrace, but that didn't stop Damon from turning to the door down the hall and watching it keenly, coffee in hand.

He counted off the moments.

"I called Dr. Wells… She told me I had to go and do the program thing… 'A very big day, Mr. Robbins.' I griped about not knowing what to expect. And then…"

He heard the door click in the distance. He watched it open. And out from inside came… Damon Robbins. His earlier self locked the door behind him and marched down the hallway, more interested in his phone than the lobby ahead. Damon took this opportunity to take a brief survey of what he knew about time travel. A handful of works that he would have called science fiction until seven seconds ago had made it abundantly clear that encountering a time-displaced version of yourself was a bad, bad idea. Ideally he would have had more than a few moments to mull over the physical or logical underpinnings of that assessment, but with the fate of the cosmos at stake, he chose to trust Hollywood.

Just before his younger self could look up, he ducked into a side hallway.

"Frickin' Jerry…" Previous Damon muttered to himself. "Taking the last coffee and leaving a mess."

Current Damon backed against the wall of the side hallway as his predecessor pressed the elevator button.

"This isn't real. This isn't happening," he whispered to himself. "I'm hallucinating. I'm on the ground in the machine room right now, discombobulated by the activation of the device, and none of this is real."

He felt a wave of relief at the very reasonable explanation he'd come up with. Then a wave of fear at the realization that if it was true, he was currently experiencing the results of brain trauma. This was replaced by a fresh wave of relief as he reasoned that if he *was* experiencing brain trauma, then he wouldn't be thinking so clearly. But if *that* was true, then it meant he didn't get discombobulated, which in turn meant this was really happening.

He let his mind loop around that particular roller coaster for a few minutes before deciding there was a simple solution.

"I'll just go and talk to myself. Since I don't remember that happening, then it'll prove this isn't real time travel. Simple as that."

He took a breath and stepped quickly toward the elevators. Somehow, the sound of his *own* footsteps slapped him with a fresh wave of déjà vu. He *did* remember this part. He stopped short and looked to his coffee, then quickly retreated from the view of the elevator lobby.

"Jerry? I know that's you. You're the only other one who drinks that coffee."

Damon hurried away, now absolutely certain of the completely impossible fact that he was somehow a few minutes in his own past.

"You're supposed to refill the row when you finish it, Jerry!" Past Damon called.

Current Damon ducked into the side hallway again and tried to gather his thoughts.

"Social contract, Jerry!" his prior self announced before the elevator doors shut.

"Good *god,* I'm annoying," he hissed. "Wh—what does this mean, though? I should call the boss."

He pulled out his phone and was once again reminded that it was non-functional. In retrospect, that made sense. It was a "second" identical phone, and it was confused about the time. This whole thing was probably showing up as a spoof attempt on the network. Whatever happened next, he'd have to figure it out on his own.

"Okay, okay… So I'll go downstairs, I'll hit the button. I'll go back in time to be me. But now there's another one of me about to go down and go back in time. But *I'm* already the one who showed up back in time. If he hits the button and there's already this me in the location where that me will show up in the past, what does that mean? Is old me about to go back and try to occupy the same place and time as current me? That didn't happen *this* time, but this is only the second time through the loop. Am I about to telefrag myself? Or worse, start creating duplicates, one for each loop, forever and ever until I overrun the earth? I gotta stop this before it gets out of hand."

He dashed for the un-alarmed stairs. The last thing he needed was to be stopped by security on the way to stopping himself from creating a Damon-Apocalypse. Four flights of stairs shot by as quickly as he could run, but a few months of sitting on his butt for sixteen hours a day hadn't done his cardiovascular health any favors. With the head start created by his deliberation, it meant his earlier self was already inside the equipment room when he reached the final landing.

If he'd been thinking more clearly, he might have realized that what he was planning to do was precisely what had already happened. That point didn't dawn on him until he heard the words escape his lips.

"No, wait!" he yelped.

Again there was a crackling clap. Again the stink of electronics. Again the anti-flash. But this time, things continued differently. The light didn't return. Not in full, anyway. He could see the smolder of indicator bulbs and the dim glow of nixie tubes, but the lighting in the room was off. He felt around for the light switch. His hand struck something hot. He recoiled, finally dropping the coffee that had miraculously survived the trip thus far. A moment later, something glass struck the ground and shattered.

"Crap, crap, crap," he fretted.

When he finally found the light switch and turned it on, the room was *much* brighter than he remembered. The dark corner of the room was just as well lit as the portion containing the control panel. As the smell of spilled French roast filled the room, he realized that the weird chemical stink that had been mixed with it a moment ago was absent.

"Okay. Okay. Stop. Calm down. Assess," he said.

He peered around the room until he spotted the clock. It was a good two hours before he'd entered the room, and thus probably an hour and fifty-five minutes before he'd entered it the first time.

"Earlier. Good! That's good. Maybe a safety mechanism? If there's already a me in the arrival point, I go earlier?"

He looked around until he found some rags and started mopping up the coffee spill. As he did, he continued reasoning.

"So… this isn't some horrible, universe-destroying paradox. All I have to do is wait. I go lay low. I wait until this whole thing happens again. I press the button, go back, show up in time for the second press, then I end up as the current me and wait until after that and it's like nothing ever happened. Easy."

His cleaning reached a small pile of glass and the smashed innards of the vacuum tube.

"Oh… Right."

He tossed the coffee-soaked rags and the broken glass in a waste bin, then investigated the damage. It wasn't hard to find the socket where the vacuum tube had been.

"This isn't terrible." He glanced at the clock. "I've got at least an hour and a half. That's plenty of time to get to the equipment room for a replacement and look up how to install it in the manual. I plop it in, *then* I lay low until after. Easy. This is going to be fine."

He leaned on the door. It was locked.

"Right, I haven't been here yet."

He dug out his keys and unlocked the deadbolt. The door still wouldn't open. He fought with it for a second or two before he discovered something marked in red paint marker.

Automatic Purge Latch.

There was a keyhole beside it, but cycling through everything he had revealed he lacked the proper key for the lock.

"Calm… Calm… Assess…" he said, hands now shaking as he gave his assorted keys a third try. "It doesn't stink in here, which means the purge hasn't happened yet. But the latch is latched. Which means the purge is going to happen soon. There's a keyhole for the latch. Which means there must be a key. But I don't have it, so that doesn't help me."

He turned to the equipment, then felt his pocket. He still had the packet of punch cards.

"Maybe I can just run it again, jump a little farther back, to when there's no purge happening. Then I can just unlock the door and get out."

Damon stepped up to the control panel. He dumped the cards into the receptacle and pressed the load button. A bell chimed somewhere inside the system and a light illuminated.

Readings Not Entered.

"Of course. Of course," he said, gathering the cards again. "If it was as simple as just running the program they wouldn't have had me entering readings for three months."

Something in the ventilation system overhead produced a worrisome noise.

"Think!" he barked. "What tools do we have available to us? What do we know about time travel? Uh… Doc Brown… I don't think *Back to the Future* is going to solve this one. … *Primer?* I never saw that one. What's another one? Bill and Ted?"

He tilted his head aside.

"Bill and Ted. What if… What if I resolved to go back in time when I get out of here and let myself out? Everything else that was happening because of time travel already happened when I encountered it. I'll go back. I'll figure out how to fix it and where the key is. I'll *get* the key. But how will I know the right timing? I'll need a signal."

Damon stepped up to the door and gave it three quick knocks. On the third one, the bolt slid aside and the door opened, revealing a weary-looking duplicate of himself.

"Took you long enough," the future him said, pulling him outside.

"This is too weird," Current Damon said.

"It gets old fast," Future Damon assured him.

The new him snagged the bucket of rags, pulled the door shut, and locked it. On the other side, the potentially fatal gas flooded the resealed room.

"I… I guess I'll just run along then?" Current Damon said. "To get the spare and look up the repair?"

"Nope," Future Him said.

"What do you mean nope? That was the plan, and you're here as a result of that plan."

"There's no time for you to get the part or read up on the repair."

"How do you know?"

"Because I'm telling you now. I had to do it before coming here, rather than after leaving."

"But if you telling me is how I know, and me telling the *Past* me is going to be how I pass that information on, then where does that information—"

"Fine! Go and try," Future Him said. "Just get out of my hair. This is harder than you think it is, and I've got to do it between when this purge is done and when the first guy shows up. Now take the rags and bucket to empty them."

"Fine, jeez," Current Damon said.

It was impressive how a little bit of snippiness from his future self could manage to push the madness of *meeting* his future self into the back of his mind. He grabbed the bucket and marched upstairs.

#

Nearly an hour and a half later, Damon grudgingly admitted to himself that he probably should have just listened to his future self. The supply room was on the fourth floor, caddy corner from the monitor room and right beside the alarmed stairwell. It was supposed to be open twenty-four hours a day in order to provide support for the equipment in the building. The sign on the door suggested it was in the midst of a fifteen-minute shift change which, so far, had run for at least forty-five minutes. And here he was standing there like a dope with an empty wastepaper basket.

"Hey," someone whispered.

He turned. Unsurprisingly, he was looking at himself.

"Are you the repair guy?" Current Damon asked.

"No."

"Then who are you?"

"Don't ask. All you need to know is that you end up getting the spare parts from the previous shift."

"So what am I supposed to do now?"

"I'd recommend you find a spot in the Equipment room before it gets too crowded."

"Crowded? Just how many times do we end up going around on this thing?"

"I wish I knew."

"Frickin' great."

"Hey, I don't like it any better than I do."

He started to leave, but noticed that this new version of him was carrying very conspicuous thermal mug. "Where'd you find that?"

"The usual place."

"Heh. I guess I don't feel so bad about losing it, then."

Current Damon made his way in a roundabout route to the equipment room again, the better to avoid running into some other version of himself. When he reached the equipment room, it was empty. The stairwell alarm pealed through the hallway as he unlocked the door to slip inside.

"Okay… Gotta find a place to hide," he said, dropping the waste basket in place.

He looked around the well-lit room. There were a few alcoves he could tuck into, but none that would escape notice. Not while all of the bulbs were lit. He licked his fingers and gingerly unscrewed one of the bulbs. Darkening the room a bit.

"Do the other one, too," came his breathless voice from the doorway.

He turned. Another him was standing there, red-faced and winded.

"Which one are you?" Current Damon said.

"The repair guy. And you're the one who spilled the coffee."

The second him entered the room and locked the door behind him.

"So who's the guy at the supply room?"

"Me, in a minute. At least I hope, because there's not a whole lot more space for us to hide. But him being out there means I'm not going to get killed in the purge, which is nice to know."

"Hey, yeah, do we even know when you're going to get out of here?"

"*You* are going to get out like three hours ago, because that's when I did. I guess I'll probably end up getting out an hour before that. Seems like it tacks on about an hour each time except for the first."

"Man. You're going to have a lot of time on your hands."

"Yeah. I know. I'll keep myself busy."

"Oh, wait! Why are you back in here?"

They heard the sound of the original Damon approaching.

"You'll figure it out," Repair Damon said.

The door opened, in came the original Damon, who loaded up the program unaware of the pair lurking in the darkness. A second one showed up, startled him and again came the clap and the anti-flash.

Damon found himself alone in the dark. He fished out his phone and turned on its light rather than blindly fumbling around in a room that he was already going to have to repair soon.

"Okay… What's the to-do list?" he pondered, fishing out his keys to unlock the door. "I've got to get the keys for the emergency release. I've got to read up on repairing this thing, get the part… Wow. I'm starting to understand by 'Repair Damon' was so snippy."

#

The finding of the repair information was easy enough. All he had to do was slip into the monitor room, which he knew for a fact would be unoccupied since he wasn't due to show up for a few more hours. He didn't even have to waste time figuring out which binder had the info, since it would obviously be the one he'd noticed was "tampered with" earlier… Or later, he supposed. Point of view was becoming increasingly difficult to keep straight at this point.

It was, as he would suggest in a few hours, more difficult than he expected. He couldn't just plop a new tube in and be done with it. There was a whole power-down and power-up procedure. He made notes in his phone. He'd expected it to be functional again, since it was presumably the only one existing in the building, but all sorts of network complaints were still plaguing it. He put it in airplane mode to avoid any further confusion.

Once he was satisfied he could do the job, he stowed the book and marveled at just how perfectly he'd created the "crime scene" he'd noticed before this whole thing started.

Next, he hurried to the supply room. A rather sleepy young woman impatiently running out the clock on her shift was seated behind the half door that served as the customer service counter for the supply room.

"Hey… Wow, I'm not used to anyone being here this early except the security guy," she said after her brain booted up enough to be sociable. "What do you need?"

"I need… *this* tube. And also the bypass key for the equipment room in the basement."

He showed her his phone.

"Oh… wow. That's a weird one. I'll have to go to the back. And do you have ID? I can't give you the bypass key without holding onto your driver's license."

He dug out the ID and dropped it on the counter. She tucked it into some unseen folder on her side of the door and vanished among the shelves. In mercifully little time, she returned with the replacement tube in a brown paper bag.

"Here you go. And here's the key. Say, how long are you going to need that? The key, I mean."

"Oh, uh… At least until after nine, I guess."

She nodded. "Good. I'll leave a note for the next guy to give it back to you."

She stepped through the door, shut both halves, and hung the infuriating fifteen-minute sign.

"You're heading out now?"

"Yeah, man. No one else is even in here besides you. The next guy will be along in little while. Don't rat me out, okay?"

Tempted as he was to have a bit of proactive revenge for her current decision costing him forty-five minutes in the future, he decided punishing someone for something they didn't do yet was too much of a philosophical riddle for him to wade into, so he just nodded. He still had an awful lot to do.

#

A bit of stealthy movement and hiding in the basement burned the rest of the time before the coffee spiller showed up. He crept up to the door and waited for his signal. On the third knock, he unlocked it.

"Took you long enough," he said to his past self, pulling him outside.

"This is too weird," Past Damon said.

"It gets old fast," Current Damon assured him.

As before, he grabbed the bucket of rags, pulled the door shut, and locked it before the gas could turn on.

"I… I guess I'll just run along then?" Past Damon said. "To get the spare and look up the repair?"

"Nope," he said.

"What do you mean nope? That was the plan, and you're here as a result of that plan."

"There's no time for you to get the part or read up on the repair."

"How do you know?"

70

"Because I'm telling you now. I had to do it before coming here, rather than after leaving."

"But if you telling me is how I know, and me telling the *Past* me is going to be how I pass that information on, then where does that information—"

"Fine! Go and try," he said, impatient to get through a conversation he'd already had once. "Just get out of my hair. This is harder than you think it is, and I've got to do it between when this purge is done and when the first guy shows up. Now take the rags and bucket to empty them."

"Fine, jeez," Past Damon said.

His other self hurried away. Damon leaned on the wall and listened for the purge to end. He honestly wasn't sure how he would tell when it was done, but that turned out to be the least challenging part of the whole enterprise, because the lock they'd had to bypass clicked open on its own when the danger was past.

The repair itself was tedious but otherwise trivial, and when it was done, he found himself in uncharted territory. He knew that he *wasn't* here when the other him showed up to unscrew the bulbs. But he would show up shortly after, evidently certain he'd need to make another trip. He didn't know where he was until that time, nor did he know why he felt as though he should make another trip. With little else to guide him, he decided to head upstairs and keep an eye on himself from the sidelines. Chances were, if he was going to randomly figure out he needed to make another trip, it would involve one of his earlier selves, and they were mostly on the fourth floor.

#

He huffed a breath as he topped the stairs. From the way his legs were burning and his heart was racing, he was definitely going to have to get in better shape before doing another time hopping bit of shenanigans. Either that or save the trips on the elevator for later loops when he was running out of energy.

"Let's see…" he mused, marching through the floor. "It seems like the lobby is the epicenter of activity on this floor."

He glanced at the time. "Me yelling at me thinking I'm Jerry is coming up. I'm going to be over there, and over there, so I should probably watch from over here."

He strolled over to what turned out to be the security office door and leaned against the wall. No sooner had he started to recover from the stair climb, the door opened and the security guard paced out. He started to lock the door, then realized just who was standing next to his office.

"What, did you call from right outside my door?" the guard snapped.

"No! No, I just figured, uh… you might want to question me."

"I can do that in the monitor room," the guard said, stomping toward the lobby.

Damon's eyes shot open. There was already at least one Damon in the lobby, and this guy went there now, he would probably be present when a second one showed up. That would raise all sorts of questions he didn't want to have to deal with, especially because he already didn't deal with it. So somehow he must have stopped this guy from entering the lobby.

"Err, where are you going?" Damon asked.

"I've got a job to do."

"B-but I think I saw the guy! He ran this way!"

"What? Then why didn't you say that?" he said, turning just before he would have spotted Damon Number 2.

"Because I wasn't sure, but, I mean, who else would have been on this floor at this time except me, you, Jerry, and the perp."

"Don't say perp, you sound like an idiot on TV. What did he look like?"

"Uh… About my height and build."

"That as good as you can do?"

"You need more?"

"I suppose not. If there's someone to see, I'll see him on the cameras later. I'll check the room first."

He started to turn. Damon cast an agonized glance at the just barely visible clock on the lobby wall. He made a note of the time and, a heartbeat later, the stairwell alarm sounded.

"What the hell?" the guard barked.

He dashed down the hall, away from the lobby. Damon sighed.

"I guess I know what the next trip is about." He winced. "Which means I've got to get back downstairs."

He dashed for the stairs, trying to ignore the fact an earlier version of him would very shortly be following in his footsteps while *another* version of him was in the elevator.

He reached the door and opened it up to find himself loosening bulbs.

"Do the other one, too," he huffed.

The other Damon turned. "Which one are you?"

"The repair guy. And you're the one who spilled the coffee."

He stepped inside and locked the door behind him.

"So who's the guy at the supply room?"

"Me, in a minute. At least I hope, because there's not a whole lot more space for us to hide. But him being out there means I'm not going to get killed in the purge, which is nice to know."

"Hey, yeah, do we even know when you're going to get out of here?"

"*You* are going to get out like three hours ago, because that's when I did. I guess I'll probably end up getting out an hour before that. Seems like it tacks on about an hour each time except for the first."

"Man. You're going to have a lot of time on your hands."

"Yeah. I know. I'll keep myself busy."

"Oh, wait! Why are you back in here?"

They heard the sound of the original Damon approaching.

"You'll figure it out," Current Damon said.

The door opened, in came the original Damon. The event played itself out yet again. Startle, clap, and the anti-flash.

When it was through, he was once again in a dark room, alone. At this point he was familiar enough with the room to not have to worry about lights. He reached the door and headed to the elevator.

He had just two jobs to do, he knew exactly when he had to do them, and both were several hours from now. He briefly considered trying to figure out how to get into the security office and tamper with the surveillance footage on hopes of being able to deny this whole thing, but considering now many loops he'd had to do already, it was probably best not to take unnecessary risks. He strongly suspected this whole thing was going to get hushed up by some agency or another before the day was out. All he had to do then was keep from getting in his own way. The guard clearly hadn't been watching the footage, so he could just ignore it for now.

So how to spend a few hours?

"… I'm getting some coffee."

He left the building and waked across the quad to his dorm. While he'd left his driver's license behind, he still had this student ID, and thus could still buzz into the dorm. Very quietly, he opened his door and marveled at just how loudly he was snoring in his bed. He crept over to the cabinet and opened it up. He grinned.

"I had a feeling."

The big thermos was there waiting for him. He grabbed it and headed out. The next stop was the convenience store, where he filled his mug to the brim and used the last little bit of the store's non-dairy creamer.

"Boy, I'm really my own worst enemy," he muttered, dropping his money on the counter.

He picked a park bench not so far from the entrance to the research building and sipped his coffee, feeling pretty good. He decided it was probably best not to turn his phone on, so he just sat and waited. After the chaos of his last few loops, it was downright refreshing. Almost too soon, the clock on the bank across the street indicated it was time to go get in position. He slipped inside and made his way to the supply room. There was a previous version of him waiting there.

"Hey," he whispered.

The other him turned, and looked unsurprised to see him there.

"Are you the repair guy?" previous Damon said.

"No."

"Then who are you?"

"Don't ask. All you need to know is that you end up getting the spare parts from the previous shift."

"So what am I supposed to do now?"

"I'd recommend you find a spot in the Equipment room before it gets too crowded."

"Crowded? Just how many times do we end up going around on this thing?"

"I wish I knew."

"Frickin' great."

"Hey, I don't like it any better than I do."

The other him looked at the thermos. "Where'd you find that?"

"The usual place."

"Heh. I guess I don't feel so bad about losing it, then."

The other him walked away, and Damon took his place by the alarmed stairwell.

When the time was right, all he had to do was push the door, hide in the bathroom for the lobby to clear out, and slip back into his monitoring room. A few minutes later, there was a knock at the door. He answered it to find Dr. Wells, a decidedly professorial woman with an almost manic gleam of anticipation in her eye.

"Well?" she said. "Did it happen?"

"Something happened all right."
She shut the door and slapped a clipboard in front of him.
"I want a minute by minute breakdown."
He looked to the page. Each line had an hour and minute.
"You're going to have to give me a few more pages."

Dragons
in
Space
Joseph R. Lallo

Dragons in Space

For a long time I've wanted to document the nuts and bolts of how I write a book. This story turned out to be the focus of that project, or at least the dress rehearsal of that project. It slowed things down quite a bit, along with the holiday season, but I'm still glad I did it. As I write this (and most likely as you read it) there are a few additional steps left to share, but the story itself is done.

Some of my stories are full ideas that I get excited about. Others are vague notions. This story started as three words, Dragons in Spacesuits. I had no plot. I had no characters, beyond knowing there would be at least two and they would be dragons wearing spacesuits. Everything else developed as I wrote it. I'm happy with how it turned out, and there's likely to be at least one more story in this setting, if only to finish it up.

The searing sun was painfully bright today. Even a year ago, sun this bright would have been reason to stay below ground. But he had seen worse days. Many of them. For the last few weeks, the sun had sizzled the ground relentlessly. All but the heartiest or most foolhardy of creatures had sought shelter. The hunter was not hearty, nor was he foolhardy, but there was one more thing that could force even the wisely cautious from safety. Desperation. He could wait no longer. He'd not captured any proper prey in more than a month. If he did not eat today, it would be the end of him.

It was better to hunt at night, or at least when the sun was low in the sky. It was cooler then, but seldom dark enough for true stealth. It had been years since he'd seen true darkness. Even in the dead of night, the sky boiled with green and red auroras. It still gave the best chance of stalking a kill without being seen. Thus, it was when the others would hunt. This hunter needed every advantage. He had no choice but to hunt by day.

To spare himself the blinding light, he kept his eyes shut tight for minutes at a time. For now, scent told the tale. A small herd. They had been traveling for some time. Moving from dried, desiccated near the sandy stretches to the cooler, moister land toward the sea. He had to move quickly. If they reached the forest before he did, there was no chance he would have his meal. The forest was one of the last truly fertile hunting grounds left. And though the food was as plentiful as anyone was likely to find in this forsaken world, it was also home to far more formidable hunters. Creatures large and fierce enough to call him prey.

He crept low to the ground. Others of his kind stalked from the air. With the searing sky so bright no creature could safely raise its eyes for more than a moment or two without risking blindness. But this hunter was wise. There was more than one way to be revealed. He'd watched as far more able hunters had lost their prey when their shadow swept across the ground and gave them away. His mustard colored scales blended well with the sun-blasted rock of the low mountains. He moved by foot. What he lost in speed, he gained in stealth.

The herd was not far away. The wind was against him. Any closer and his own scent would give him away. His stout claws gripped the stone. He scaled the cliff side to gain a better vantage. A dozen lumbering beasts with dusty brown coats tromped along a well-worn trail. In this heat and light, there were precious few places to seek refuge. The hunter knew precisely where these beasts were going. A narrow, dried riverbed split the rocks ahead. It would provide shade, shelter, and cover from predators like himself. They would be safe there, perhaps until the sun set and they could travel more freely.

Or so they thought.

Now was the time to take to the air.

He spread his wings and drove his narrow, lithe body skyward. He'd been planning this hunt for days. Preparations had been made. A heap of stones awaited him, mounded at the edge of the cliff where it overhung the narrowest point of the valley. He touched down and trotted to the stones. Any single one of the beasts below would be meal enough to keep him alive for a month or more. But even if this plan worked, he would have to act quickly. Even far from the prime hunting grounds, he was seldom the only one in pursuit of a fresh kill.

Hooves clacked with steady grace across the gravel and debris at the bottom of the valley. The herd kept close. When moving as one, they were formidable enough to give even the largest hunter pause. He could see and smell charred sections of their dusty pelts, evidence of failed attempts by his kind to feed upon them. But this hunter was different. He wasn't strong, but he was clever. If the group could not be taken when whole, they must be divided.

The herd drew closer. Now he could not risk even peeking over the edge. A brief glance toward the searing sky brought its own painful punishment, but it was a small price to pay for a creature who might otherwise fall prey to a threat from above. He listened to the clacking and tromping as it echoed off the walls. Just a bit closer...

Now.

He scrabbled and heaved, butting his head against the mound of stones and tipping it over the edge. The heavy rocks crackled and bounced their way down the slope. Startled bellows blared from the valley. That was his signal. It was now or never. That sound was an irresistible call to any hungry predator that a meal was about to be served.

The hunter straightened his body and sprung over the edge. His wings would only slow him. Instead, he trimmed them sleekly behind him and dashed along the near-vertical cliff side. The panicked herd had indeed been separated by the tumbling stones. Some ran forward, others retreated. He set his steely gaze on a smaller member of the herd. Already the larger beasts were beginning to gather around it. A sharp inhale, a puffed chest, and a flare of flame startled them away.

He sprang, jaws agape and claws flashing. The force of his sprint heaved the beast to the ground. Stout, triangular teeth pierced its hide. Blood spilled. The others of the herd separated further, dim instinct informing them that it was too late to rescue the stricken creature. He did his best to make the struggle a short one, less out of mercy than out of fear. Time was running out. The moment the struggles subsided, he began to feed.

The first desperate swallow of his well-earned prey had barely reached his stomach when the telltale rustle of leathery wings put a sudden, urgent end to the feeding frenzy. He ripped away a final precious hunk of meat and dashed up the cliff side moments before another of his kind thumped down from above.

He scrambled into a tight alcove in the cliff side and turned to see a brute he knew all too well. Muddy brown scales, covered with deep gashes from battles with others of his kind. A maw of jagged, half-broken teeth, perpetually grinning. His piercing eyes were narrowed to slits as he lashed his tail. It was not fair to call this interloper a hunter. He was at best a scavenger. Always lurking nearby, he used his size to steal kills rather than gathering his own. For the last five hunts, this thug of a beast had stolen the fruits of the yellow-scaled hunter's efforts.

He clamped his mighty jaws on the meal and scaled the cliff, no doubt to take the hearty meal to the comfort of his lair to enjoy it. Meanwhile the rightful owner of the feast gulped down what little he had been able to salvage. The confusion of the landslide had passed. The herd had pulled together again into two groups that would soon reunite. There would be no more hunting today. With a belly still grumbling, he climbed from the valley and spread his wings.

#

A short flight into the mountains took the disappointed hunter to his lair. As with all things in his life, his size afforded him little choice in selecting a den. The low, craggy mountains had more than their share of caves and overhangs. Alas, only a handful of them offered proper shelter from the sun through the entire day. Those, of course, had been taken by any beast large and strong enough to scare off or kill its challengers. This left the little hunters to either wither in the sun or find ways to make up for what they lacked in physical strength. It had taken time and effort, but by cracking smaller stones against larger ones he had turned a narrow opening in the mountainside into something *just* wide enough for him to slip through. Like all things, he was able to keep this lair only because it was beneath the interest of his larger kin. It was a good thing that the entrance was too small for the others to properly investigate, because a vanishingly rare feature of this lair would have made it well worth almost any battle to claim it. Even as he wriggled his long, lean body through the opening, he delighted in the sound of a slow, steady drip of water.

The shade within the cave was a welcome respite. Though his eyes were sensitive enough to navigate by the faintest glimmer of light, spending even a few moments in the blinding sun was enough to burn away his night vision for hours. Fortunately, with surroundings as familiar as this he didn't need to wait for his eyes to adjust. Weary padding across the cool cave floor took him to the modest puddle of water accumulated from drops seeping through the pores in the stone. The flavor was bitter and harsh, and it offered only a few teasing mouthfuls each day, but it was a drink that didn't require him to venture across the countryside to a dwindling watering hole.

With the edge taken from his thirst, and a meager meal in his grumbling belly, he was ready for some rest to recover from the less than triumphant hunt. He'd eaten enough to get him to his next hunt, provided he saved his strength. That was enough. And enough was more than he normally got.

He crawled atop the mound of shiny, smooth river stones he'd gathered over the course of many years. Other hunters had other collections. For him, these glossy, rounded shapes were sufficient to satisfy some ingrained need to hoard. They slid easily across each other, forming a relatively comfortable bed that wouldn't rot or burn. Again, there were more desirable collections, but this was enough.

He slumped on his bed and flopped his head down to sleep. His thoughts became sluggish. The first glimmers of a dream of better things flickered in his mind. But his senses had been trained by survival instinct to remain sharp even at rest. Some half-noticed sound raised an alarm. The rustle and flap of great wings could faintly be heard beyond the mouth of his cave. He curled his lip in frustration and crept from his bed. The air carried the scent of another of his kind. A male, like him. He smelled well-fed. Large enough to be a threat. He kept himself low to the ground, legs tensed and ready to spring. The cave *should* provide proper protection, but he knew better than to fully trust anything. A large enough hunter could easily cause him trouble in any number of ways. Better to keep an eye on the invader so that there would be no surprises.

Crunching gravel and a snuffling snout confirmed that the stranger hadn't moved on. Already plans were crackling in the mind of the smaller hunter. How to escape? How to find shelter until the attacker was gone? What to do if this precious safe haven was destroyed? The light in the cave dimmed, blocked by the newcomer's bulk. Then, in what proved the most startling thing of all, a voice.

"Get out here. Let me get a look at you," rumbled the stranger.

The little hunter sprung backward at the sound. It had been so long since he'd heard one of his kind speak, he'd nearly forgotten they could.

"I don't want anything you have. And I don't have all day. Come out. This will be quick," the stranger said.

His voice was low and clear. The words were almost overly articulate, each word formed into a distinct and pristine statement.

"Go away," the little hunter said thickly. "You won't fit in here."

The words felt like mud dripping out of his mouth. His tongue had grown clumsy with disuse.

A rumbling growl of frustration rattled the stones on the floor of the cave.

"I have been watching you," the stranger said. "You are hungry. Get out here and I'll solve that for you. Food, I've got."

There was a meaty slap, followed by a tantalizing whiff of fresh flesh. The little hunter's claws scraped at the floor as the prospect of another meal eroded his better judgment.

He crept closer to the mouth of the cave and stopped when he was near enough to see a sliver of his uninvited guest. This new hunter was not the largest he'd seen. Indeed, the one who had chased him off and stolen his kill was larger. But the stranger was still entirely capable of bringing the little hunter's life to a swift end. He was stout and a bit plump, a far cry from the malnourished creatures who lived this far from good hunting. This hunter had been eating well. Well enough that he had food to spare. The offering was a strangely rectangular slab of flesh. The scent wasn't familiar. No telling what prey it had been torn from. But it was fatty and fresh, larger than his head, it was just sitting there, tempting him.

"What do you want from me?" the little hunter said.

"I want you to get out here and start eating so I don't have to shout into the darkness."

"Back away from the meat then."

A sigh powerful enough to kick up dust in the mouth of the cave followed. The stranger clutched the offering in one claw, hobbled back on three legs and dropped it again a few paces further from the mouth of the cave. He then trotted a fair distance further.

"There. Come and get it. But if you try grabbing it and running back into your cave, I'm going to be *very* angry."

The hunter poked his head out of the cave. His visitor was green with a yellow belly. Hardly the sort who would thrive here in the arid mountainside. A body like that was built for the forest. He must have come a long way. But his color was hardly the most out-of-place thing about him. An odd bundle was strapped across his chest, like a pouch that had been fashioned from a pristine sort of hide the little hunter couldn't identify. The stranger must have had quite a hoard of his own, as well, as he wore a curved piece of shiny metal on his head, smoldering in three places with glassy round gems.

"Oof," the large beast said. "You're even scrawnier in person."

"Others steal my kills," the smaller hunter said, squeezing out of the cave. "You are the first to offer one instead."

"Don't get too used to it. This isn't a gift, it's an advance for services rendered."

The smaller creature tipped his head in confusion.

"You use words I don't understand, large one."

"Something tells me you'll pick up the lingo quickly enough. A runt like you doesn't survive without being clever. Now eat, Runt. But listen close while you do it. This sun is diabolical, and I'm not used to dealing with it without my gear."

The smaller creature tried to pick through the statement and piece together its meaning from the bits he understood. While he puzzled over the odd manner of speech, he inspected the meal. The little hunter had never encountered this sort of flesh before. Nothing he'd found could have produced something this sizable without interrupting it with bone or sinew. The scent was fresh and clean, not tainted. He knew it was not the wisest choice to accept the offering from a stranger who in most other circumstances would sooner snap his neck and make a meal of *him* than offer one up. This knowledge didn't change the fact that a windfall like this was unprecedented and not to be ignored. If another hunt went poorly, he would curse himself for passing up a this free meal.

He sunk his teeth into the flesh to find it pleasantly firm without being tough. Flavor was seldom a consideration for a hunter, but the taste was bright and intense. Ribbons of nourishing fat threaded through it. It was precisely what he dreamed of when he envisioned the perfect meal.

"We'll get through this quick. Answer right and I might have something for you. Answer wrong and it's business as usual."

"Answer?" the little hunter said, unwilling to take his attention from the feast long enough to give the visitor an inquisitive look.

The larger beast shuffled aside and started to drag his claw across the dusty ground. He was tracing some sort of markings. The little hunter didn't give them his full attention until he'd finished devouring the meat.

"These shapes here," the visitor said. "What is the next one?"

After his first proper meal in ages, the smaller beast mostly wanted to slip back into his cave to sleep for the rest of the day. But an offering like that surely deserved some sort of consideration. He looked at the shapes. The first was a ring or circle. The second was half a circle, with a straight line closing the gap. The third was a trio of connected lines. He pondered the shapes.

"You want me to tell you which shape you would scratch next?" he said.

"Yes. And quickly."

"How should I know what you are thinking?"

The stranger thumped the ground angrily, prompting a startled backward scramble from the one he called Runt.

"The answer is in the shapes. You have to figure it out," the large beast said.

He nodded nervously and crept back to the shapes. How precisely he was meant to read the larger beast's mind by looking at some shapes wasn't clear, but he started to tug at the knot. He plopped his hindquarters down and sat up. With claws curled inward, he started rubbing them against each other, producing soft clicks. A few moments of thought brought him to an answer. It didn't seem to have any value, but it produced a pleasing sequence. He scratched two parallel lines, then two opposing ones to form a square. The stranger gazed at the fresh etching.

"And the next, to be sure," he said.

The small one, a bit less gracefully, managed to scrape a five-sided shape into the stone.

"Mmm…" said the visitor.

He sat on his haunches and raised a foreleg. One claw tapped at the strange silver crown. With eyes turned aside, he addressed someone who didn't appear to be present.

"Are you watching this?" he said. "He continued the sequence twice. … Yes… Well, you know how I feel about him. He's a little small, and he's old enough that he's not going to grow much more. Malnourished at a young age. Stunted him."

A churning anxiety was growing in the small hunter's belly as he began to piece together what must be happening. A creature, out of place for his home, had arrived. He brought the meat of a beast which could not exist, and he spoke to beings that others could not see…

"You are ascended…" the smaller creature said in a hush.

"Give me a minute before we start with that," the larger beast said before returning to his conversation. "… Yeah, I know the small ones put less of a stress on the engineers for suits and transportation, but they're also weaker. … I mean, I'm fine with it if you are. It isn't as though we're spoiled for choice. … All right. I'll get him up there."

He tapped the claw again and looked to the smaller beast.

"Come with me, Runt. Things are about to get a lot better for you."

#

The wind whisked over them as the two hunters flew north. If he were paying closer attention, the smaller one might have become concerned about their destination, but his mind was too seized with wonder to focus on anything but feeding his curiosity. After so many years of not using his mother tongue at all, he found himself stumbling over his words in his attempt to spit them out quick enough to satisfy his hungry mind.

"You *are* ascended, aren't you?" he asked, flitting beside the larger beast to steal a glance whenever he could. "You speak to the spirits! And you are a beast of the forest, but you are here in the mountains where life would be too hard for someone to be as well fed as you."

"Look, the easy answer is yes, I'm ascended. But you don't *really* know what that means. I understand what you're thinking. I used to think it, too. But you're about to get a lot of answers to questions you thought already *had* answers, so I'm not going to waste my breath on them now. Let's just say the 'spirits' have been keeping an eye on you for a while because they think you have what it takes, and it just so happens we need help and can't take the time to be choosy."

"An ascended!" the small one trilled, clutching his claws. "I never thought I would meet one. I doubted they were real! Tell me, is the land of the ancients as beautiful as they say? Is there a place where the searing sky does not burn? Is the burning a punishment? Please answer me, Ascended One!"

"Hey!" the large beast snapped. "What did I say? I'm not going to waste my breath on that stuff. You figured out the shapes. You'll figure this out the same way. The pieces are going to start lining up for you. But let's nip this one in the bud right away. Don't call me 'Ascended One.' Call me Brothin."

"Brothin. Yes. A fine name for an ascended one."

"And what do I call you?" Brothin asked.

"I don't have a name, Brothin," he said. "That is to say, I do not remember it. I was the smallest of the clutch. Food was scarce. It was easier to send me away than waste food on me."

"So you've been on your own since you were a hatchling?"

"Not quite that long, but nearly."

"Mmm… Well, I was right to call you a runt, so we may as well make it official. Until I change my mind, you're just 'Runt.' Got that?"

"So I have been deemed by an ascended one, so it must be."

Brothin shut his eyes tight and shook his head slowly. "This is going to try my patience if it keeps up…"

The freshly christened Runt turned his head to finally take stock of where they were headed. The sun was sliding from the sky, though the roiling red auroras kept the landscape well-illuminated. The sun-blasted landscape stretched out before. Only one speck of darkness amid the endless sprawl was in any way distinctive. It was precisely the place Runt least wanted to go.

"You're taking us to the Charred Lands," Runt said.

"We picked you because you are bright," Brothin said. "I'd have been disappointed if you didn't figure it out."

"That is a terrible place."

"It's just a patch of dirt. It can't hurt you."

"It is a patch of dirt that is blackened and jagged, like the black glass around the flaming mountains—"

"We call them volcanoes. You're talking about obsidian."

"But there are no … *volcanoes*… near the Charred Lands. And even the mightiest hunter's breath is not powerful enough to blacken the earth like that. It is a grim portent."

"It's just as well the locals give the place a wide berth. If you got too curious it could cause problems. But trust me when I say there's nothing spooky about the charred lands. It's just at a good spot for doing drop-offs and pickups."

"Drop offs and pickups?" Runt said.

They trimmed their wings and wheeled toward the speck of black.

"We've got a long trip ahead of us. We'll go over it then. Right now what you need to know is that you'll be working that brain of yours a lot harder than you're used to, but no one will be trying to kill you anymore."

"I'll be safe?"

"I didn't say that. We're 'ascending' you because your predecessor died. It's a dangerous job, but it's got to be done, and it pays well."

"I'll be ascended!?" Runt said.

"Yeah. It's not as majestic as it sounds."

The pair touched down at the edge of the charred lands. Runt had been here only once. There was something ominous about it. The ground crackled and crunched beneath his claws. The shards of shiny black stone were cruelly jagged and incredibly sharp. His scales were adequate protection for a few steps, but the slivers had a way of finding their way between them. More than a few minutes of trotting on this stuff would leave him hobbled and bloodied.

"Hold still," Brothin said. "I had them put together a smaller one, but it might take some tweaking."

He rummaged through the chest-mounted bag and revealed a silver band with its own jewels, a match for Brothin's own. Runt's heart fluttered in his chest. The gleam of the silvery metal set ancient parts of his mind alight with desire. This, he knew, was a proper treasure, something that even the mightiest hunter would be proud to have in his collection.

"Head down. And try to brace yourself. This is going to feel weird at first, but you get used to it."

Runt practically trembled as he lowered his head to be anointed by the ascended. He'd been on his own for most of his life, but he remembered the tales of the ascended. They could come and go without leaving a trail. Even the most skilled hunter could not follow them to their lair. The stories claimed that it was because their lair was in the Searing Sky itself. Imagine, a hunter able to fly that high? High enough to pierce the heavens. And how strong they must be to swim in the sea of fire and light that roasted the surface of the world. They were to be feared. To be admired. To be *worshiped*. And now, he was being *crowned* as one. It was all too much. It was above him. He was undeserving. But he dare not refuse.

The metal felt cool against his scales as the crown was pressed into place. He shivered a bit, not just at the light but undeniable sensation, but at the fact that it plunged far deeper than his scales. The coolness seemed to radiate inward. It wove like the roots of a tree, digging deeper into his mind. Odd, impossible sensations rolled over him. He saw flashing lights of red and gold despite the fact his eyes were shut tight. For a few moments he felt like he'd been plunged into a pool of water. Foreign tastes danced across his tongue, and his nose insisted a dozen different aromas were wafting through the field. Then came the tingling, needle-sharp sensations along his hide. He huddled down. His claws rose up to pull the crown from his head.

"Leave it. It's almost done calibrating," Brothin barked.

Runt froze. He was fearful of what this strange treasure was doing to him. The threat the larger beast posed was far greater, now that he knew him to be ascended. Sure enough, the phantom sensations faded soon after the reprimand. That is, all but *one* of the sensations faded.

"Okay, okay. It looks like we've got a good synaptic resonance," came a new voice.

Runt's eyes shot open and he whipped his head around, in search of the source of the voice. The words, when he first heard them, were nonsensical and random. But before even the first sentence had been completed, he could feel his mind tug and twist until they had meaning just as surely as Brothin's did.

"Easy big guy," the voice said. "Boy, he's real skittish, isn't he?"

"At his size, he's a rung further down the food chain than me. He's had to deal with the risk of getting eaten. It'll take a while to fade, if it ever does," Brothin said.

"Are those… are those the spirits?" Runt asked, eyes widening.

"That's Todd," Brothin said. "He's our tech guy. He runs the communications and handles the rest of our gear."

"I'll give you a crash course when you get up here. There's really not much to learn," Todd said.

"Tech guy. Communications. Gear. Crash Course. I don't know what that means," Runt said, face stricken. "Why can't I see him?"

"Because he's not here. He's up there. Don't worry about it," Brothin said. "Todd, how are we looking for a pick up?"

"Inbound. Seventy-five seconds."

"Great. Give us some privacy. This next part is going to really scare him and I don't need 'spirits' floating around in his head making it worse."

"Will do. See you when you get here."

Though he'd not noticed when the spirit had 'arrived,' so to speak, Runt found he was quite aware of the unseen entity's departure. The 'silence' in his mind had a different tone to it when the spirit was present but not speaking. And now it had vanished.

"This is all so much…" Runt said.

"It's about to me a lot more. But listen. Down here, it's every dragon for itself…"

"Dragon?" Runt squeaked.

"Yeah. That's you and me. They call us dragons."

"They?"

Brothin gave him a hard look.

"Would you cool it with the questions until I'm done? I'm trying to give you a pep talk."

Runt looked nervously at Brothin and wisely chose not to seek clarification on phrases like "Pep Talk" and "Cool it."

"Down here it's every dragon for itself. There's not a lot of food to go around and too many dragons trying to eat it. That's about to change. Up there, there's no competition. We've got enough, and no one is going to try to kill you to get at your share. But instead of focusing your mind and muscles on just staying alive, you're going to be working together on something much bigger and much more important. Do you understand?"

Runt paused. After a moment, he shook his head. Brothin shut his eyes and released a heavy sigh.

"This is going to be loads of fun…"

A low rumble drew Runt's attention to the sky. He squinted at the burning red aurora. A pinprick of light, like a star bright enough to show through the twilight and the aurora, drifted lazily through the sky.

"A falling star! A falling star!" Runt said excitedly. "Do the ascended travel on falling stars?"

Brothin gave Runt a weary, impatient glance.

"Yes. We ride on falling stars," he said flatly.

The roar from above was growing louder. Brothin flicked his eyes between the star and the charred land. He turned and bounded a short distance away, taking him to the very edge of the scattered black stone. Runt gingerly followed him.

"You will want to shield your eyes with your wing. It will be very bright and even at this distance we tend to catch some blown glass from the landing."

Runt shakily nodded and raised a wing. For several seconds, the sound grew steadily louder. Every time he thought it couldn't get any louder, that *nothing* could get any louder, it drew nearer and more intense. Soon a hot wind began to scour the landscape, kicking up dust and flakes of black glass. They flicked and clashed against his raised wing, prickling him painfully with little splinters but not doing much real damage. Had they not retreated, he would be bleeding from a thousand little gashes, he was sure of it.

The ground rumbled. Some sort of acrid-smelling smoke rolled across the field and then, silence.

Runt warily lowered his wing and shook the lingering bristles of blown glass from it. He was still trembling from the intensity of the sound, heat, and wind.

During many a long, hungry night, he had watched the sky. More than once he had seen one of the falling stars. Each time, he wondered what they must look like up close. Were they balls of flame? Were they gleaming jewels? Never in his wildest dreams had he supposed the chariots of the ascended would be so… boring.

The "star" was a dull gray block. Its sides were far straighter and smoother than anything Runt had ever seen before, for certain. The upper edge was slightly rounded like one of his pebbles. The bottom edge had sharp corners like a broken stone. The ground beneath it was radiant, blasted to a near molten state by whatever heat and flame had made it so brilliant during its descent. But that heat had vanished.

A strange groan grumbled from inside. Then, one of the smooth sides moved. Runt missed most of what came next, as the unexpected motion caused him to leap nearly double his own height straight up, then scramble for cover behind Brothin. He didn't look up until Brothin paced away, leaving him unprotected.

The larger dragon padded toward the strange relic from the sky. He stepped onto the lowered side, which had revealed the rest of the block to be mostly hollow. A few shakes of his legs and flexes of his claws shed the sharp stones that clung to his feet. Then he lowered his head and stalked inside. He turned and sat.

"Are you coming?" he called.

"… I have to get inside?"

"If you want to 'ascend', then yes, you have to get inside."

"… It was very loud, Brothin."

"It's not so bad from the inside. Come on."

"It does not look like a fallen star."

"It isn't. It's called a drop ship. But you don't know what that is, and we're on a deadline, so I figured I'd wait until we were inside to explain. So get in here."

"I am afraid, Brothin. This is strange. It roars and belches flame like a dragon. And now you want me to climb into its maw."

"Listen. You can stay here and fight for scraps until you starve or one of the bigger dragons eats you, or you can come with me, live a better life, and maybe even make a better life for the rest of us. But it's up to you to decide what you're going to do. I'm not going to beg, and there *are* other dragons who have shown promise."

A cooling stone popped, causing Runt to jump backward again. He trembled.

"You are sure it is safe?"

"The safest thing you'll do today."

"… And is there more meat?"

Brothin grinned. "All you can eat."

Runt steeled himself and scurried to the lowered platform. He imitated Brothin's ritual of shaking off the black stone, then slipped into the very limited remaining space within the block. Once inside, Runt could see that the interior walls weren't nearly as featureless as the outside. They were covered with odd protrusions and straps made from a material he couldn't identify. Here and there, more jewels flickered and glimmered with their own light. Many of them were marked with tiny black symbols. As with the voice of the spirit called Todd, these symbols had no meaning at first. But as he stared, they began to associate with thoughts, or at least sounds, that he already knew. It felt like the symbols were changing into something he could understand, but they were very plainly the same as they had ever been. It was his mind that was changing. Brothin's grin grew a little wider.

"What's it say?" Brothin said, pointing with a claw to one of the larger buttons.

"It does not say anything."

"What comes to mind when you see it?" Brothin amended.

"Oh-pen Hahch," he said awkwardly.

"And this one?" Brothin asked.

"Close hahch. No. Hatch. Close Hatch."

"You're taking to the translator well. Press the close hatch button."

Maneuvering his limbs in the close quarters was difficult, but he managed to raise a claw and tap the button. The same grinding rumble he'd heard before rattled around him, far more distinctly. The lowered side began to raise again.

His muscles tensed. He wanted to bolt, to run away. He'd been an ascended for scarcely a few minutes and already the world seemed like an unfamiliar and terrifying place. But he overruled his instincts. His belly was heavy with food. Brothin was a dragon large enough and healthy enough to challenge even the most fearsome of creatures that had made his life so difficult for years. Any other beast of his size would have had little more than a wordless roar and a swipe of a massive claw to offer Runt. Brothin gave him food. He gave him a *name*. He would have to be brave. He would have to see what life was like in the searing sky.

#

Moments later, Runt was desperately clawing at the door of the strange chamber as it rattled and roared around him. His courage had lasted until a few heartbeats after the door had latched. Every instinct screamed for escape, and everything around him built upon that terror. He suddenly felt heavy. Far heavier than he'd ever felt, even during dives and swoops. The rumble, as Brothin had suggested, wasn't nearly as loud. But it was *all around them*. He'd never been inside anything he couldn't scramble out of and it sent a bolt of anxiety like a hot knife through him. Even the fact he knew words for things like "door" and "knife" without ever having heard them spoken chilled him. All the while, Brothin sat with a stoic and sullen expression.

The rattling died away a few minutes into the journey, and with it, evidently, went Brothin's patience.

"Enough of that," he said. "You're curious, right? Curious about what's going on? That's fine. That's good, in fact. You've got a lot to learn and it'll go quicker if you're eager. But right now you don't even know what questions to ask and it'll take *ages* for you to get where you need to go without me holding your hand. So *listen up*."

The final words were a demand. They hit Runt like a blow to the head. The smaller dragon huddled in the corner of the chamber, tried to make himself as small as possible, and nodded fearfully.

"This is a drop ship. It is taking us up into the sky. We're going to something called a space station. Repeat that back."

"Drop ship. Up into the sky. Space station," Runt said.

Forming the words without interjecting a handful of yelps or whimpers took every ounce of fortitude he had.

"Good. Now, the things you call spirits are actually humans. They aren't from this world."

"Where are they from?"

"Their own world."

"There are other worlds?!"

"Many, though worlds with creatures are rare, and that's why the humans are here. They saw that we were here, and they knew that the searing sky was a threat. They want to help us."

"They can help us with the searings sky?" he said. "They truly *are* spirits of power and mystery."

"No. They have something called technology. This ship, that device on your head, and just about everything you'll see in the space station is technology."

"Where did they get technology?"

"They made it. They had to, because they are small and soft and weak. Without technology, dragons like you or I would have made a meal of them. That's why they like to keep an eye on dragons like you. Humans like to see a mind take up the slack for a lackluster body."

"… Then why did *you* ascend."

Brothin leaned low, poking his snout in Runt's face.

"What are you implying?" he rumbled.

"You're big and strong! You don't need the… the… technology."

"Mmm… Fair. Never mind how they ended up working with me. The important thing is that you and I will be working together to fix up our world."

"What will we have to do?"

"We'll get to that. But first, I want you to pay attention."

Runt waited.

"Pay attention to what?"

"You'll know soon enough."

The rattle and rumble had all but silenced. Most of what he heard was the rattle of the walls and straps themselves. The heaviness was starting to fade as well. In fact… it continued to fade, well past what should have been normal. His crouched body started to drift upward. He had the same feeling in his gut that he got when he was in a dive.

"We're falling!" he yelped. "We're falling! The drop ship is broken!"

"We aren't falling. … Well, we are, but we're falling so far and so fast we're missing the ground."

"What!?"

"Never mind. It's complicated," Brothin raised his wings to brace them against the ceiling of the ship, pushing himself back to his feet. "What you need to learn is that this feeling? This odd, falling feeling? It's just the first of an endless list of new things that might trip you up, foul your instincts and leave you unready for this threat or the next. Your instincts have kept you alive on the surface, but there's a whole new world outside this ship. If that door opens at the wrong time? Dead. The searing sky is as great a threat above as below. Once we left the surface, we entered a world where our every action must be careful. Measured. Our lives depend upon the technology that the humans have created. You need to learn to use it. You need to teach them how to improve it. And you need to pay attention. If it fails, you die." His eyes drifted aside. "It can happen to even the most seasoned workers."

"But I don't know how to do anything with this technology."

"We'll teach you."

"You and the spirits?"

Brothin glared at him.

"You and the *humans*?"

"Yes. Like I said, you won't be on your own anymore. You'll be part of a team. And we take care of our own."

Runt twisted his head. As dizzying as all of this madness was, he found grappling with the idea that someone else might actually look out for him was the most difficult of all.

"Before we get where we're going, a few ground rules. You don't touch any buttons if you aren't sure you know what they do. If you do that, you die and so does everyone else. You don't scratch at or pry at or dig through anything. If you put a hole in the space station, you die and so does everyone else. Don't breathe fire except under very specific situations. You do, you die and so does everyone else. There's more, but they are escaping my mind at the moment. I'm sure I'll remember. Any more questions?"

"… If everything can kill me and everyone else, why are we living in the searing sky? Surely there's a better place for the ascended to go."

"Because we have a job to do. And besides, the humans grow good meat."

"Meat doesn't grow. Plants grow, and things eat plants, and then *they* are meat."

"If there's one thing humans like to do, it's defy nature."

"They must be beings of terrible power."

Brothin snorted. "I'll be sure to tell Todd that you are awed by his might when he needs help opening his next meal pouch."

"If they can do such wonders, why do they need creatures such as us?"

"Because there aren't very many of them, and because the 'searing sky,' which they call 'elevated solar wind activity,' causes havoc with their technology. They are not wizards. The technology has very strict rules. And when the searing sky is acting up, this drop ship is the absolute most complex thing that can operate under its own power. They needed help. And we were the only creatures available. Now hold on to a strap. The docking procedure will begin soon, and it can jostle us around if we're not holding ourselves tight."

#

Runt was still dizzy with the instructions and updates he'd been given while the ship maneuvered itself toward the so-called "Space Station." Brothin spoke so simply and matter-of-factly, as though he was simply reminding Runt of things he should already know.

"… But what is an air lock?"

"You know what air is, yes?"

"Yes."

"Well, there's no air in space. An air lock is a couple of doors. You open one and close it behind you so that when you open the second one the air doesn't leak out and kill everyone. It's very simple."

"I only just found out what a door is! This crown you gave me is teaching me words but it doesn't tell me it taught them to me."

"You're going to have to get up to speed quick. You're fast-tracked, Runt. We've got a deadline and it doesn't care if you need to slow down."

A sudden hiss sent Runt flailing against the far wall of the ship. His wings propelled him backward and all four claws grasped straps or railings.

"Is that the air leaving!?" he yelped.

Brothin shook his head and simply turned to the door. It lowered, revealing a chamber slightly larger than the ship itself. A light flutter of Brothin's wings guided the massive creature inside with disarming grace. When he was able to coax his limbs into cooperating, Runt flapped his own wings and immediately slammed into Brothin.

"There's no gravity here," the larger dragon said. "Little flutters are all it takes."

"I'm sorry, I'm sorry," Runt said quickly, gathering himself.

The ship's door shut. Unseen mechanisms clanked and grumbled. The door ahead slid open and Brothin flicked himself forward at a slow, easy pace.

"Follow me," he said. "You'll need to see Todd."

Runt tried to duplicate his low-gravity motion, but very nearly slammed into the larger dragon a second time. Instead of risking another disappointed glare, he resorted to pulling himself along with the regularly spaced rails along the walls of the corridor ahead.

The station was quite spacious. It was much larger than his cave, for instance. And the walls were uncannily smooth and clean, made from some sort of highly reflective metal. The shine and gleam sparked the same ancient instincts to hoard and collect that the crown had. This place was like traveling *inside* a treasure trove. The corridor branched in four different directions every hundred yards or so, and small, gray-suited creatures scampered along the walls.

"Brothin!" said the three in the corridor in a single, enthusiastic shout.

"Boys," the dragon said. "And Deborah. Is the next meat slab ready? I fed Runt here in order to bribe him into coming out of hiding but I haven't eaten since yesterday."

"Should be done in five," said the creature with a slightly

different scent from the others and a high pitched voice.

"What's the meat of the day, Deb?" Brothin asked.

"Pork."

The dragon shut his eyes and threw his head aside in delight. "I love pork day. But where are my manners. Everyone, this is Runt. Runt, this is everyone. They're the humans you're so awed by. They're fragile, don't break them."

Runt turned his head aside, eyes narrow and expression doubtful.

"These are the ones who defy the rules of nature?" he said. "Who live in the sky and who seek to tame the searing sky?"

"I also play poker on Thursdays," Deborah said. "Swing by and I'll teach you the rules."

"Don't trust her. Her poker face is diabolical," Brothin rumbled. "Bob! Is Todd on duty still? We've got to get the new guy sized up for his suit."

"He's in the cupola, waiting for you two," said one of the other humans.

"Perfect! Runt ought to get used to the view. This way. And again, give the humans some space."

"Welcome aboard!" Deborah said brightly.

"T-thank you," Runt said, shrinking away from them as he hauled himself after Brothin.

They passed three intersections in the seemingly endless anthill of a space station before turning and drifting down a fresh corridor. With the humans no longer in line of sight, Runt felt confident enough to speak, albeit quietly.

"The humans are very small."

"I told you they were."

"They have no scales, no wings."

"Runt, we picked you because you seemed smart. I'm not sure if observations like that prove us right or wrong. I told you they were little, fragile, and smart."

"I expected them to…"

"Look like us?"

"Well, yes. Every other creature in our world is smaller, but not nearly as wise as a dragon. I thought, if something is *wise*…"

"You're going to have to get used to the notion that what you've always assumed was true probably isn't in the same ballpark as the truth."

"… Ballpark?"

"It's a human thing. It just means it isn't even close."

"How can creatures so small and insignificant build something as grand as this place?"

"Teamwork. It's what they do best. No one thought up any of this on their own. And they *sure* didn't build it on their own. Lots of them, working together, can get just about anything done."

"But how can they…"

Runt's voice trailed off as he allowed himself, for the first time, to focus on what lay ahead. While the other corridors were lit with some sort of cool white bars recessed between panels on all sides, this corridor was darkened. The only light came from a large, dazzling display at the end of the corridor. It took Runt's mind a few moments to make sense of what he was seeing. He'd flown high before. In the old days, when the searing sky was not so intense, and on those rare more recent days when it briefly relented, he would soar as high as his wings would take him. At those heights, the land below lost its definition. It reduced to swaths of blue, yellow and brown. Here there was green. There, sometimes, there was white. What he saw before him were the same blotches of color, but they were smaller still. He realized he was seeing a radiant, red-bathed swath of his world that it would have taken him days of travel to cross.

"We truly are in the heavens…" he said, transfixed.

"Yeah. But, anyway, that bald guy down there admiring the view is Todd. Go talk to him, he'll size you up. I'm going to get some pork. I like it best when it's fresh out of the lab."

Runt looked to Brothin, suddenly stricken.

"You're leaving? But what should I do."

"What did I just *tell* you to do, Runt?"

"Talk to Todd."

"Then why don't you go do that? We're going to be working together, and big as this place feels, it's not usually open for travel like this. So just get sized up and give me some privacy for now, understand? We'll see each other enough to get sick of each other."

"I understand. But what do I do after?"

"He'll tell you what to do. Humans like telling people what to do. Dragons, other humans. Giving orders is their lot in life. Now go."

Brothin thrust his wings and daintily vanished around the bend of another intersection. Runt turned back to the cupola and pulled himself carefully along. The closer he came, the more windows became visible. This section of the station must have bulged out beyond the rest. When he reached the end of the corridor his vision was filled with the sight of the surface of his world impossibly far below, with only the thin lines of struts to interrupt his view. Directly below was a sea of green. It faded to brown and gray around the edges, except to the south where the ocean twinkled.

"Is that the great forest?" he uttered.

"Sure is!"

Runt flinched and scrambled, briefly forgetting he'd allowed himself to drift out of range of the railings. His reflexive flap sent him headlong into the window. He bounced painfully off.

"Whoa, hey! Easy there, newcomer!" said the bald man Runt had forgotten was there. "These things are rated for grade-three micrometeor impacts, but I'd really rather not test them."

"I am sorry. I am sorry, this is new for me."

"It'd be a little weird if it wasn't. Name's Todd. I think I heard Brothin call you Runt?"

"That's right. He has named me."

"Well, I'm going to hold my hand out for what we call a handshake. It's a sign of friendship, so when I hold it out, you just put your claw out and I'll grab it and shake it, okay?"

"… Is this necessary?"

"It's neighborly, which in my book makes it as close as you can get to necessary without being written down in the rule book."

Todd held out his hand. Runt crept forward and presented a claw. Todd grabbed him around one digit, about as much as his little hands could manage, and gave it a largely symbolic attempt at a shake."

"There you go. Your first hand shake," Todd said.

Runt tried to ignore the vaguely unsettling softness of the barely-felt grip. Fortunately, there was a ready-made distraction in the form of the view out the window behind Todd.

The dragon carefully pulled himself aside and maneuvered to the window. The world seemed to curve away as he looked along its edge, and high above the ground, higher even than the clouds, dancing and shimmering veils of red light coiled and churned. It was the searing sky, the red scars that painted his sky and broiled the ground. They seemed to reach up, to radiate away from the ground into crimson waterfalls. It seemed almost cruel that something so horrid, so destructive could be so beautiful.

"Oh, yeah. The aurora. It's really something, isn't it? Charged particles in the solar wind, deflected and precipitated. I've seen them on three different worlds and I've *never* seen them so strong, so violent. On most worlds, they're just a wondrous display. But your star is a troublemaker. It's trying to do you dirty, and those auroras are *angry*. But you'll be getting plenty of looks at them. We've got three weeks to get you ready to do twelve-hour EVAs, so let's get you sized up for a suit."

#

Todd led the way through a long sequence of twisting and turning corridors, moving with remarkable ease and speed considering his small size. After the majestic vista Runt had been treated to in the cupola, it was something of a letdown to discover their destination was a boxy, cramped space lined on all sizes with cubbies and compartments. Two larger than average doors were centered above and below. The upper one had a long gash along its metallic surface, the one thing in the entire station thus far that wasn't perfectly pristine.

"Do me a favor and hold onto those rails there with your fore claws, and those there with your hind claws. I've got to take some measurements," Todd instructed.

Runt nodded and did as he was told. Todd fetched a small silver device and started navigating the chamber, lightly tapping points on the dragon's body as he went.

"I want to thank you for being so mellow about this. Brothin was a real handful when we got him up here, but then, he wasn't recruited by another dragon. That was… what, six years ago already? Time flies on these long-haul missions. Has he been treating you okay?"

"He gave me food and a name. He has treated me more kindly than even my parents."

"Woof… It's getting rough down there, I guess. We're working as fast as we can. The next array should be up in eighteen days. Sooner, if your training goes smoothly. Wings out, please. As far as you can spread them."

Runt obliged. He squirmed a bit as Todd pulled himself hand over hand along the wing outstretched to the left and continued tapping his device.

"You critters are *made* for this, you know that? If all goes well, this mission will be done in another three years or so. When we're all done and ready to head out, I really hope at least a few of you will come along. You're kind of big for most space habitats, but between the resistance to muscle atrophy and the wings, you're better equipped than humans to handle longterm space habitation."

"I… don't know all of those words…" Runt said.

"Oh, yeah. The synaptic interface… the crown, it gives you the vocabulary but doesn't always associate it with meaning right away. You'll figure out the important stuff soon enough."

Todd nudged off Runt and drifted to one of the walls.

"The good news is, you're a lot smaller than Brothin, so your suit will be a quick manufacture."

"Suit?"

"He didn't tell you what sort of job you'd be doing?"

"He said many things. I don't know. It is happening so fast."

Todd tapped a few more buttons. A startling metal-on-metal grinding began to vibrate the walls of the chamber. Runt clutched tight to the rails.

"You're going to be heading out into space to do the exterior work," Todd explained. "It takes a couple inches of shielding to keep us safe from the solar output when the star is acting up. Even more to keep the electronics working in tip-top shape. It's just not feasible to use drones to…"

Todd must have noticed the glassy look in Runt's eyes.

"We need someone who can withstand great heat, someone with great strength, and someone who is smart enough to do the job. That's you. But you can't live out there without protection. So, hold still, and we'll get you suited up."

"I do not understand… and I do not understand why Brothin would not explain all of this to me before he brought me here."

Todd shook his head and tapped at a panel of flashing lights. "You'll have to give Brothin some time. He worked with his partner from day one. Between the grief of losing her and being used to having someone who knew everything he did, he's liable to have a quick temper and no patience. I'd prefer to have given him a few weeks off, but the timeline won't allow it."

"What happened to her? His partner?"

"Freak accident. The stellar wind isn't perfectly consistent, and…" Todd seemed to sense he was traveling down a linguistic dead end. "There was an unexpected event and she was killed. No one's fault. Couldn't be avoided. But Brothin took it hard. Anyway, brace yourself. It's time for a test fit."

The doors that dominated the ceiling and floor of the room slid open, revealing dark interiors with the telltale glint of metal within. Strange mechanical arms emerged from above and below, each clutching a dull gray shell. The two pieces clamped around his chest, neatly missing his wings and legs. They latched together and the arms withdrew. Almost instantly the arms emerged again with additional components. Piece by piece, a suit was assembled over Runt's body, enclosing him more and more. Sleeve-like sacks pulled over his wings. A maddeningly complex set of interlocking shells clamped around his tail. A glass-topped helmet pulled tight over his head, pressing his jaws shut like muzzle.

Thirty seconds of mechanical chaos left him fully suited up. It was easily the most terrifying part of this bizarre journey thus far. The soft hiss of his own breath in the helmet was rapid and harried, but he'd managed to keep from panicking and trying to escape.

"Give me a test of motion. Move your legs, move your tail, move your neck, move your wings," Todd said, counting off the lines on a list he now held.

Runt shakily obeyed. The hard shell constructed over him did surprisingly little to restrict his movement. His wings felt a bit stiffer. His tail couldn't curl quite so tight. But outside of the most extreme limits of each extremity, he was unencumbered.

"Good, good. Voice test. Say something."

"How? My mouth is sealed shut," Runt said.

He paused. The words had come through loud and clear, despite the fact he'd scarcely been able to twitch his lower jaw.

"The synaptic interface works fine for communication," Todd said. "Dexterity check?"

Runt stared at him, awaiting clarification. Todd raised his hand and waggled his fingers.

"Go like that."

Runt did so. The astoundingly complex gauntlets around his claws rendered them a bit more clumsy, but not so much that they would hinder him.

"Okay! That's the check. Training starts tomorrow. Hold still again, we've got to get this off you."

Runt shut his eyes tight and clenched his armored gauntlets around the rails as the mechanical arms descended upon him again.

#

"Here you go! This is where you'll be staying," Todd said. "Sorry it's not larger, but we've got regulations. Sleeping accommodations need maximum shielding, and we haven't got the materials to spare."

Runt curled his neck to peer inside the lair they'd prepared for him. It was indeed quite small. Smaller than the sleeping chamber in his lair on the surface. The place was perfectly round, an odd little node dangling down out of the bottom of the space station, he supposed. Soft, flame resistant cushions lined the floor. He pawed them and found them to be tough enough to resist his claws.

"Zero-G, there's really not much use for cushions," Todd said. "But there's elastic bands there that hold you firm against the wall when you're sleeping and a little something soft to lean against is always nice. But, anyway. Light controls are there. They're also voice controlled. Just say 'computer, lights off.'"

The cool light within the chamber faded.

"Computer, lights on," Todd said.

They swelled to full brightness again.

"We'll be in touch in…" he checked his watch. "Nine hours. It'll take us that long to do the full pressure and safety test on your gear. Until then, you're on your own. Enjoy!"

Todd drifted away. Runt curled himself into the chamber and, with some pawing and nudging, discovered there was a thin curtain which he could tug across to attach to the far side of the opening, providing a degree of privacy.

His heart hadn't stopped hammering in his chest since he'd arrived. Being encased in the suit and then peeled out of it had been easily as startling as the last time he'd nearly been torn to pieces by a dragon displeased with him trespassing on its territory. Even now, the fact that he felt like he was in constant freefall, the unnatural light, the presence of the small, soft-skinned creatures who had somehow created this place… if this was the fate of the ascended, they were clearly made of tougher stuff than he.

"Runt!" barked a familiar voice.

He scrambled to pull the curtain open again. Brothin was drifting just beyond his door.

"You all set?" the larger dragon asked.

"Y-yes."

"How'd you do? When they put the suit on you, that is."

"… I don't know what you're asking me."

"Did they talk about the crack in the ceiling?"

"No. I saw it, but they didn't say anything about it."

"The first time they tried to clamp my suit on me, I bolted. Tore three arms out and nearly cracked the hull." He gritted his teeth and rumbled. "I still don't like those arms… Point is, if you held your ground, good for you."

"Thank you," Runt said meekly.

"I didn't see you come by the lab for your meal."

"I already ate, Brothin. Your generous gift."

"Bah!" Brothin said. "A morsel. Here."

He curled his head out of sight. It returned with a huge slab of synthetic pork. He opened his jaws and nudged the drifting feast with his snout so that it bopped Runt in the face.

The smaller dragon clutched the hunk of meat and sunk his teeth into it. An entirely new flavor danced across his tongue and his eyes rolled back in his head. As ravenous bites and tears made short work of the meal, he felt a flutter of calmness and serenity, and even excitement at the prospect of meals like this that he didn't have to risk his life for.

Perhaps ascending wasn't so bad after all.

Brothin flicked his folded wings and darted along the corridor, presumably to his own chamber. As he departed, he called back.

"Eat hearty. Training starts tomorrow…"

The
Dwarfendam
Run
Joseph R. Lallo

The Dwarfendam Run

What follows is part of the "Shorts of Dubious Canonicity" project I started in 2018. In an attempt to keep my mind sharp and fresh, I started taking votes on short stories to write each weekend. Some of them stayed short. Some of them grew into full novellas. But almost all of them were the result of my fans and followers casting their votes to give them support.

If you are a particularly dedicated reader of Joseph R. Lallo output, you will be familiar with *The Dwarfendam Run.* This was one of two stories written for something called *The Lone Wolf Anthology.* I believe the anthology is still available, but this is my first time releasing the story on its own. Here's a fun fact: This was originally envisioned as a section of a Book of Deacon story. It would have starred Ivy, but as the idea took form, it felt like too much of a technological departure from the Book of Deacon world, so I split it off into a standalone.

The Dwarfendam Run

Dwarfendam was at once the most impressive and most shameful spectacle one was likely to see. It was built across a wide, deep river, and was by any measure a wonder of engineering. If it had merely been a bridge, it would still have been an astonishing achievement. The span arched taller than the tallest building in the admittedly modest nearby town of Bremberg. Stout planks of wood still green from the construction traced out maddeningly complex trusses, arches, and platforms. From a distance they looked as though they should be delicate as lace, but Dwarfendam barely creaked or swayed against the flow of the mighty Bredst River. Near its center, two massive waterwheels harnessed the flow and used its power to run what made the structure nothing short of a wonder: The Run.

It was a gauntlet of machinery—thrusting walls to shove men aside, swinging clubs to beat them down, jabbing spikes to skewer them, and lurching platforms to fling them. Narrow paths, walkways, and ladders taunted would-be champions of The Run, leading them through devilish twists, looping back to the same hazards again and again. Dwarfendam was a monument to humiliation, a mechanism designed to batter, bash, douse, and toss anyone foolish enough to challenge it.

And therein lay the shame. There was no shortage of such fools.

"Forward all! Press close to see the next noble champions to face The Dwarfendam Run!" barked a brightly dressed man standing atop a platform to one side of the entrance to the devilish device. "Each year the Dwarfs of Grindstone Mines climb from the dark bowels of our world to put their grim ingenuity to work on a mechanism so complex, so ingenious, that only the fleetest of foot, the burliest of brawn, and the sharpest of intellect can hope to surmount it! By Royal Commission, this year's Run is the most magnificent yet! Bones have been broken, pride has been bruised, *hundreds* of challengers have been sent sprawling into the water—and none have made it past the halfway point of this monstrous machine. With just days left in the season, *you* can still be the first to best The Run—*if* you have the mettle!"

The announcer reached down into a bin beside him and pulled out an overripe head of cabbage. He lobbed it down the walkway into the workings of the machine. A heaving floor panel launched it into the air and a whirling club bashed it to fragments. The crowd cheered as the shredded leaves rained down.

"Why, you may ask, should a man or woman of sound mind risk so cruel and unforgiving a foe?" He thrust his hand out, pointing at a caged platform high above the very center of The Run. "Why, nothing short of the King's Chalice!"

Again, the crowd cheered. It was easily the twentieth time today they'd heard the enthusiastic announcer give some variation of the same speech, but it never failed to stir them into a frenzy. The chalice, and what it represented, was too tantalizing to be ignored.

"The King's Chalice, passed down from champion to champion from time immemorial. Heavy as a well-fed pig ripe for the slaughter. Made from solid gold and engraved with the names of those lucky enough to hold it in bygone years, the King's Chalice is more than a cup. It is a symbol! A symbol of greatness! It is the proof that those who retrieve it from its perch are worthy of all the glory their people can heap upon them, and, of course, the King's Bounty! Your weight in silver and a rarefied place among the champions of the chalice!"

The crowd roared again and the announcer signaled Allemande. As the musician hired to spice up performances such as this, and to keep the people occupied and in high spirits between challengers, she was quite accustomed to what was called for at this time. She raised a horn to her lips and trumpeted out a spirited fanfare that stirred the crowd further.

"Step forward, oh brave and hearty challengers, and be recognized!" the announcer proclaimed.

Two thickly built men stepped from the crowd and climbed atop the announcer's platform. They dressed in rough-cut bear skins and carried weapons and shields that had clearly been part of a tree that morning. The clubs were simply branches, still jagged and green from where they had been torn free. Their shields were little more than two layers of bound and lashed sticks.

"Ah-ha! Unless I've missed my guess, these two gentleman are from the Frust region. Mighty warriors from the north!"

The men raised their clubs and bellowed war-cries that sounded somewhere between a warthog's mating call and a hungry bear.

"Now, gentlemen, you know the rules. If you work as a team, the victors share the spoils. You can traverse The Run in any way you see fit. Evasion, defense, or," he tapped the larger man's club, "try to bash the whole thing to bits if you like, though I wouldn't waste my time. It's dwarf-made. You won't hurt it. Are you ready to test yourselves against The Run?"

Again the men bellowed, this time with a dash more bear than hog in the cry.

"So be it!" The Announcer glanced to Allemande.

She set down the horn and replaced it with a lute. He raised his hand.

"And... *begin!*" he proclaimed, dropping his hand.

Allemande strummed the lute into a rousing, heroic tune. She thumped one boot, jangling bells on a loop hooked over it to keep beat as the burly men rushed forth.

They began well enough. Both were the very definition of burly, mounds of fat and muscle hardened by a difficult life in the icy mountains at the northern edge of the kingdom. Navigating the frozen paths of their homeland had taught them to adopt a low, wide stance and favor boots with plenty of grip. For the first dozen paces or so, they simply charged forward. Here, the walkway was wide enough for them to move shoulder to shoulder. The first few hazards were floor panels that tipped and jumped, but their combined weight was enough to make them more of a nuisance than a threat. When they came to great wheels with clubs and flails attached, they were ready, raising their shields from each side and enduring a few heavy whacks before moving on.

Each crack and thump brought a new cheer from the crowd. Perhaps there were some in attendance who truly wanted to see these men succeed. Far more wished to see them fail in an epic and entertaining manner. The Dwarfendam Run was an annual tradition, and brought spectators from all over the kingdom. First, there was the spectacle of the construction of The Run, each year from a new design lest champions learn its secrets from season to season. Then there were the summer-long trials, in which hundreds of hopefuls would take their lumps and, for most, end their attempt being fished out of the river by the boats floating on either side of The Run. In few weeks, when the temperatures began to fall, there would be the demolition of The Run before ice became a concern.

The men reached the first bottleneck, a ladder not nearly wide enough for the two to scale side by side. They pushed and shoved, solidarity giving way to the desire to be the first to reach the chalice despite having not crossed a tenth of The Run yet. The winner was the scrawnier of the two. He mounted the ladder, climbed six rungs, and found himself hurtling through the air after it suddenly shifted to the side and dislodged him.

As rescue boats rowed up to the floundering failure, his partner looked warily at the ladder and gripped it tightly. Three more times it tried to buck him free, but he held firm and reached the top. When he was free of the ladder he turned and raised his hands. The crowd roared. They roared louder a moment later when the landing pitched to the side and sent him sailing into the water.

"An admirable showing, but The Dwarfendam Run will not be so easily conquered." The Announcer pointed eagerly to the crowd. "Step forward, would-be challengers, if you believe you can best them..."

#

Allemande sighed and took a seat at the bar. It had been a long day—a long *season,* in fact—keeping the frothing crowd occupied between humiliations at the hand of dwarfish engineering. The Tavern, like virtually everything else surrounding Dwarfendam, was clearly temporary. Something of a boomtown sprouted up at the beginning of each summer, a whole community with the singular focus of watching the festivities of the beloved tradition. The cluster of tents and rickety buildings appeared overnight and lasted only until the claiming of the chalice or the first sighting of ice in the river, whichever came first. The tavern, dubbed the Dwarfendam Draft, was a canvas and wood construction knocked together quickly and cheaply to serve food and drink of similar speed and quality.

She brushed her short black hair out of her face and inspected her dish for any unpleasant surprises before beginning her meal. The meals offered as a supplement to her pay for the entertainment tended to be swept together from the remnants of proper meals. This one, though certainly not a banquet, at least appeared to have been prepared for her. As often as not, she received a dish rejected by a paying customer. She sawed into what was ostensibly a beef steak and let her mind wander.

Almost immediately, her daydream was brought to an end by the creak of the seat beside her. She cast a sideways glance. It was a young man barely out of his teens. He looked horribly out of place. In a room stuffed to capacity with aspiring adventurers who lived and died on their strength, this boy looked like a stiff wind would sweep him out the door. He had a chipper, enthusiastic look to him that was somehow undiminished by the telltale weariness of a long journey. Rather than dripping with cockiness and bravado, he was beaming with interest and curiosity. In other words, he was sure to be a talker. Lovely.

She shifted her eyes back to her plate and took a sip of her ale, adopting body language that fairly screamed her wish for solitude. As luck would have it, this young man lacked the perception to interpret that particular message.

"Hello there!" he said brightly. "You're the musician, yes?"

She glanced to him and offered the barest of nods before stuffing a leathery bite of beef into her mouth as a conversational deterrent.

"You play beautifully, Miss, if you don't mind me saying."

She raised her glass in a silent toast of the compliment and took another swig. It was a tad bitter, but better than she'd expected—and badly needed to wash down the dry meal.

"My name is Tristan. And you are?"

She glared at him and forced the mouthful down. "Allemande."

"That's a beautiful name. I--"

"You can turn off the charm, Tristan. I'm not interested in anything but filling my belly, slaking my thirst, and shaking off the weight of the day."

He recoiled slightly. "I apologize if I've been unduly forward, ma'am, but I assure you, I had no intention beyond polite conversation."

"All the same, as unappetizing as the menu is in this place, conversation isn't on it."

"Oh... I... Um... I'm sorry."

He fumbled with his hands and looked vaguely about. She tried to keep her eyes on her plate, but seeing him fidget and not know what to do with himself was almost painful. She'd met the type. This was a boy who didn't take a breath if it wasn't to have a chat. He turned to the man to his other side, a brute easily twice his weight and layered with what was in the *best* case was a thick coating of soil.

"Hello, sir! I'm Tristan. Are you here for The Dwarfendam Run, too?"

The man glared at him.

"What's that supposed to mean? You don't think I'm good enough to be doing The Run?" the man snapped, his breath a cloud of cheap ale and cheaper meat pie.

"I meant nothing of the sort, sir, I just--"

"I got as much a chance as anybody, you little rat!" He thumped the table with one fist and tapped the conspicuous handle of a holstered knife with the other. "Anyone who says different'll get a belly full of blade!"

Allemande sighed again and picked up her plate and tankard. Unless the scrawny young man chose his next words wisely, he was half a sentence away from a beating. In her experience, tavern keepers were slow to replace complementary meals that were ruined by brawls.

"I didn't-- I don't-- I just wanted to--" Tristan stammered.

"You just wanted to *what?*" the man rumbled.

She muttered under her breath. It would have been nice to suggest that what Allemande did next was out of charity, or concern, or even general principle. In truth, it was because she'd glanced about the tavern and failed to find another open seat, so keeping this one free of collateral damage suddenly became a priority.

"The boy here just wants to buy you an ale," she said.

"Eh? Is that so?" the man said.

"Oh! Yes, yes, certainly," Tristan said. "For, um... For luck!"

"You think I need luck, do you? I ought to--"

"I mean as an early toast to your forthcoming victory!" he blurted. "And we'll make it two! A future champion shouldn't have to go thirsty, right?"

This appeased the beast. "'S right!"

Tristan fished two small coins from a notably meager coin purse and dropped them on the table. "Barkeep! Two tankards of your best ale for this fine gentleman!"

The promise of drink shifted the ogre of a man's attention to the bar. Tristan shakily took a breath and turned back to Allemande.

"Thank you," he breathed.

She shrugged. "Learn to keep your eyes open and you won't need another rescue like that."

He nodded and dropped a third coin on the bar. The barkeep quickly replaced it with an ale of his own.

Allemande looked him up and down. She knew she would regret it, but her curiosity got the better of her.

"You're not thinking of trying The Run, are you?" she said.

He looked to her with the same look as a hungry dog being tossed a ham bone. His answer was a gush of words. "As a matter of fact, I am! It is truly a fascinating event and all of my life I've dreamed of attending. This year I realized if ever there was a time to do it--"

She raised her hand. "Fine, fine. 'Yes, I am' would have done it."

"I apologize. It's just that I've always been a bit loquacious."

"That much I gathered."

"If I read your tone correctly, Miss Allemande, you are of the opinion that my attempt at The Run is ill-advised."

"It isn't an opinion. That is a cold, hard fact."

"What brings you to this conclusion?"

"Because *any* attempt at The Run is a waste of time, but at least this lot are thickheaded enough to take their lumps and laugh them off. You're liable to be snapped in half out there."

"I've got as much a chance at succeeding as any of these fellows."

She gave him a doubtful look.

"Well, perhaps not as *much* of a chance, but I've got a chance!" he defended.

She took a sip of her ale and gave him a more thorough looking-over. "You are *not* foolish enough to believe that."

He frowned and took his ale in both hands. "If it is foolish to believe in oneself, then call me a fool."

"Once again, you're a fool." She speared a hunk of potato and stuffed it into her mouth, forcing it into her cheek as she spoke. "Look around you, Tristan. This little exercise in lunacy attracts an awful lot of people, but they all fall into three types. First, there's idiots who don't know any better. We've already met one of *those* today. Then there's the sort like that one in the corner."

The man she indicated was very likely not a man at all, but some breed of lesser giant. He was taller sitting down than the people standing around him, and had the better part of a full hog set on a tray before him.

"Brutes who think they're strong enough to push through any obstacle they come across. And, finally, there's *those* sorts."

This time she motioned toward a man in a decorated military uniform holding court at the end of a table. He was surrounded by men and woman hanging on his every word.

Tristan turned back to her. "Do you know who that is?" he scoffed.

"Some military blowhard."

"That is Captain Mefrit! He is a decorated war hero!"

"That's what I said."

"You don't honestly mean to suggest that *he* is a fool for attempting The Dwarfendam Run!"

"I certainly am. Him above all others."

"Why?"

Allemande muttered briefly and pushed her plate aside, resigned to the fact she'd not be finishing her meal any time soon. "What do you get for the chalice? Fame and fortune. That man, as you've said, is a decorated war hero. So fame he's got. And he's a captain. An officer. That means he's a noble. So fortune? He's got that, too. What sort of a man risks his pride and his health for something he's already got? A fool. Tell me I'm wrong."

"I can certainly see your point, and perhaps he has less of a reason than most, but for those who lack his wealth and notoriety, there is *much* to be gained from The Dwarfendam Run. Plenty of excellent reasons to test one's wit and agility against the mechanism out there."

She shook her head and turned to her plate, spearing a slice of meat. "I suppose there's liable to be some excellent reasons to do it, but that's not what brought any of this lot."

"How can you be so sure?"

She smirked, then hiked a thumb at the flap of a window. "Look out there and what do you see?"

He looked. "That's Dwarfendam."

"Anyone taking a run on it?"

"No."

"Why not?"

"I suppose it is... closed for business?"

She snorted. "It's a mechanized gauntlet, Tristan. They don't have business hours. You win by handing over the chalice to the King's representative, who happens to be that finely dressed gentleman in the private booth over yonder. There's still light enough in the sky, and the moon's awfully strong this time of month. No reason people couldn't be running it right now. But no one's out there. And that's why no one's doing The Run."

"Because no one's out there?"

"Now you're getting it."

"I don't understand."

"It's all glory to these folks. Plain and simple. Captain War Hero? A battle tends not to have much of an audience, so he's never had the pleasure of hearing the crowd roar over his great deeds. And most of these folks haven't heard the crowd cheer at *all*. You can ask each and every person in this tavern why they're doing The Run and get a different answer from them all, but deep down, if they *really* wanted it for the money or for the challenge, they'd be out there right now."

He sipped his ale. "Well, not me."

"Of course not you," she said. "Never you. All the problems of the world are with other folks. Never us."

"You seem bitter."

"Call it what you want."

He stared at The Run through the window. "First thing tomorrow... When I've had my rest... I've got my date with destiny."

"For some reason other than fame and fortune."

"That's right. Maybe you're right about all of these people, but I've got a noble cause. The noblest."

Allemande took a bite. "And her name is?"

"How did you know it was a woman?"

"I'm a musician. There are only so many stories in this world, and I've sung them all. Whenever a foolhardy young man starts crowing about being noble, it's always a fair lady's heart that he's after. As though there is something inherently noble about needing one another."

She glanced at him. Tristan looked unsteady, like someone had pulled the rug out from beneath him.

"Tell your story, Tristan," she said. "A good song is always worth another listen."

"Her name is Mariska," he said eagerly. "I've known her since we were both children. There's never been another woman for me, and never another man for her. But her father's older brother died a few years ago. He inherited some land, and then he went on to marry a widowed noblewoman. Now he's a man of means, and he's decided I'm not good enough for his little girl."

Allemande nodded. "Yes, I've heard this song. It's an old one."

Tristan continued as though she'd not spoken, too deep into the tale to be interrupted. "But out there, at the top of that run, there's a simple golden cup that can make me into the man he'd give his blessings to. I'd have the—"

"The gold and the glory, which you said you weren't after."

"Yes, fine. Glory is a part of it, but glory in the name of love has got to count for something. And it all begins with the rising sun when I make my run."

"Best not to get your hopes too high, Tristan. Granted, your cause is nobler than most, there's still the matter of getting your hands on the cup."

"With a cause like mine, how can I fail?"

She finished her ale and looked evenly at him. "With a cause like yours... Look back at The Run, would you? Describe what you see."

"It's... It's The Run. Lots of iron and wood. Planks and clubs and ladders."

"You see a heart in that mess? A conscience, maybe? I know dwarfs can work wonders, but I'd wager even they can't knock together a contraption that'll go easy on a boy because his intentions are good."

"Not The Run itself, certainly. But *fate*..."

She laughed, almost choking on the last of her veggies. "*Fate?* You think fate is going to shed a tear if you don't get your girl? Fate has its own plans, and you may have a part in them, but your happiness certainly doesn't. If your future depends upon fate being kind, you haven't got a future at all."

"If a man can't rely upon fate and righteousness--"

"And he can't," she said.

"--then what can he rely upon?"

"There's only one thing you can be sure you can rely upon, Tristan, and it's also the only thing you've got any control over: yourself. Forget this girl."

"Perish the thought."

"Fine, then forget her father. Forget the blessings. The two of you run off together. But don't set foot out there on that run if you think that anyone but you has an interest in seeing you through safely to the chalice and back. We're alone in a crowd, the lot of us. You'll live a lot longer and be a lot happier when you learn that."

Allemande dug into the meager remains of her meal, taking advantage of the merciful silence that such bluntness typically inspired. When she looked up to him again, expecting to see a stunned or angry expression--another common and not altogether undesirable result of speaking her mind--she instead got something entirely new. Pity.

"I don't know what sort of a life you've lived to believe such a thing, but I mean to prove you wrong. You just watch for me tomorrow."

He drained his tankard in one defiant swallow and stood to leave. It was at that moment that Allemande got her first glimpse of his gait. It was subtle, but each time he put his weight down on his right foot, he did a bit of a stutter-step to shift quickly back to the left. Allemande pushed her empty plate away and hopped to her feet to catch him by the shoulder.

"Just one moment now. What's this limp?" she said.

"Took a spill from a horse. Ages ago. I've had it ever since."

"And you're fool enough to set foot on that run?"

"The worst I can do is fail."

"The worst you can do is fail? Haven't you seen the cornerstone?"

"The cornerstone?"

She took his arm. "Follow me."

Her firm guidance navigated the pair through the shoulder-to-shoulder crowd of the tavern and out into the cool air of the riverside evening. Now away from the din of the crowd, the grinding, thumping cacophony of The Run filled their ears. Though it was an intimidating sight during the day, without the crowd and the announcer and the overall thrill of the daily festivities surrounding it, the massive device seemed downright menacing, looming unnaturally over the river and gnashing its hungry teeth while awaiting its next meal.

There was a stone at the base of the platform from which she'd been performing and the announcer had been whipping the people into a frenzy. It was smooth, white, and unassuming, so much so that though it had been visible to every challenger, not a single one had looked down to it before tackling Dwarfendam.

"Read it," she said, thrusting a finger at the stone.

Tristan knelt down and brushed some dust away. "*In memoriam. This stone commemorates the noble--*"

"There's that word again," she remarked.

"*--challengers of The Run who sadly lost their lives in pursuit of the King's Chalice.* There's... there's a very long list of names..."

"Is that so surprising?" she said. "Look at it. Those aren't toys out there, Tristan. Those are clubs and flails. And armor sturdy enough to protect you from that his heavy enough to drag you to the bottom if you get thrown aside. According to the announcer, he expects to lose at least one challenger a year. And the people do, too. Give a listen tomorrow. See when the loudest cheers come. It isn't when someone gets close. It's when they finally fail. We haven't had our blood yet this year. Are you really eager to be the first to be claimed?"

She tapped his thigh. "You go out there with a bum leg like

yours and that cup isn't where they'll be carving your name, it's this stone right here. Is Mariska worth that?"

He looked up from the stone and stared at the chalice. Its polished rim caught the final rays of the setting sun, gleaming like a beacon. He turned to Allemande.

"Yes. I'll take any risk if it means I can be with her."

Allemande tapped his head. "Think, Tristan. You *won't* be with her if you get killed. And what'll happen to her? What's the best case? Does she mourn your loss for the rest of her days? Curse her father for pushing you to such lengths? Or does she shed a few tears and forget about you, marrying out to a man who meets her father's standards and living a happy life without you?"

"What would you have me do?"

"Live your own life, Tristan. Worry about yourself—because in the end, you're the only one who will."

He shook his head, the look of pity even more heavily in his expression. "What happened to you that would put a thought like that in your head?"

"*What did I just say?*" she growled. "You worry about you, I'll worry about me, and we'll both be healthier and happier."

"Everyone needs someone, Allemande. I need her. And she needs me. No force in this world or the next will stop me if it means we have even a chance of being together. And *that* will carry me to my reward. Thank you for your concern, but--"

"I'm not concerned about you. I'm giving you advice you're too thick to take!"

"Thank you for your advice, then. But if setting such wisdom aside is what you'd call thick, then I am the thickest man you'll ever meet. Good night to you. I'll see you tomorrow, when I face my destiny."

He marched toward the hastily built inn, leaving Allemande beside the cornerstone.

"Your destiny... *that* much you're right about..."

#

Night fell, and Allemande retired to her cozy little cart. For one who spent so much time traveling, and who carried as much from place to place as she, the wisest thing she'd ever done was take the time to convert a little corner of her cart into a shelter of sorts. It wasn't much-- the whole *cart* wasn't much--but it served her purposes. A small bedroll covered a long patch of clear floor tucked behind the crates containing her harp and drums. She'd hung a lantern on a hook to one side and cut a small, latching window on the other. On fair nights such as this, she seldom needed anything else.

She'd set a small handheld harp in her lap. It was a far cry from the large, stand-up model she used for weddings and funerals, but it helped her compose without doing an awful lot of hauling and unpacking. Her delicate fingers danced across the strings, plucking out tinny, thin chords that refused to come together into anything catchy. She'd not expected this night to be a fruitful one. That idiot from the tavern had lodged himself too deeply in her thoughts for that.

"Foolhardy, willfully dim *child...*" she muttered under her breath.

At the moment, her little window framed the thrashing machinery of Dwarfendam. She didn't bother looking away, merely letting the images of swinging weapons and turning wheels filter into her mind as she strummed. Her foot tapped out a beat, the ring of bells jangling in time.

"Listen, my friends, to the tale of Tristan. He suffered from that greatest folly of man. He thought with his heart instead of his head. A fool like that is better off dead..." she sang. "Pathetic. Not even any good for inspiration, that one."

She set the harp aside, though her foot continued to tap. For a time, she focused on the simple little loop of bells as it rattled to a rest between beats. It wasn't anything special. A bit of twisted metal with a few brass chimes affixed. By now she'd had to replace nearly all of them, but the loop was the same one she'd used since she was a little girl. Back then, she'd held it in her hand. Now it fit firmly into little divots on either side of the toe of her boot. A few letters, worn by the years and poorly rendered when they were new, were still visible. *Mande.*

A scowl came to her face as she glared at the little band.

"Oh, shut up," she muttered, reaching down to tug it free and stow it in a cubbyhole beside the window.

For a few minutes, she sat, harp silent in her fingers as she gazed out the window, but even without the tapping of her toe and the jangling of the bells, the same beat kept time in her mind. She tried to set it aside, dreaming up rhythms faster or slower, but sooner or later they always slid into the same *Rum Tum Rum-Tum-Tum-Tum* that had served as the beat for her aborted ballad of the lovelorn fool sleeping blissfully through what was likely to be his last night. It wasn't until nearly an hour had passed with the rhythm still solid in her mind that realization finally dawned.

Allemande glowered at the cubbyhole for a moment, then tossed the harp aside to cross her arms.

"You *would* do something like this, wouldn't you," she muttered, evidently to the inert little timekeeper she'd stowed. "This is precisely the sort of cause you'd take up. Well, I won't. Not this time. If he's fool enough to throw himself at *that* monstrosity for love, then what's he liable to do when things start to go wrong? Hmm? No life is perfect. People certainly don't stick around forever. *You* of all people would know that."

The beat rattled through her mind for a few more bars as the workings of Dwarfendam continued to grind and slam. Finally, she'd had enough. She ran her fingers through her hair and snatched the time-keeper.

"Fine, have it your way. But this is on *your* head, not mine."

#

Allemande marched along the gravel walkway leading to Dwarfendam. It was a full moon and a cloudless sky, leaving the mechanical gauntlet well-lit in the silvery glow. She walked with purpose, eyes locked on the stunningly intricate workings. Only when she came to a figure seated beside the start of the wooden walkway that led to the to the official entrance of The Run did she pause. He was the Dwarfendam scribe. Along with the king's representative and the announcer, he was one of the three individuals that officiated The Run. His job was a simple one. Record the names of the challengers, such that when the time came they would know what name to add to the chalice or, more likely, the cornerstone.

Like most scribes, he was quite elderly, and had managed the rather impressive feat of dozing off despite the constant din of Dwarfendam itself. She briefly considered waking him and sending him to bed, but she thought better of it. Considering what she had in mind, it was better that no one know she'd come along.

She stepped onto the walkway, giving a cursory glance to the cornerstone, and continued on her way. After a short distance, she could hear the steady gurgle of the flowing river beneath her feet. Five paces from the riverbank, a crude line had been carved into the planking of the walkway. The safe line. Prior to that line, the ground would stay beneath one's feet. Past it? Nothing was certain.

Allemande lingered with her toes at the line for a few minutes, watching the motion of the countless mechanisms. They seemed horribly random, like the dwarfs had conjured up a beast of wood and metal, a thing with a mind of its own. She rummaged in her pocket and found the little bell-clad loop and clicked it into place.

Dwarfendam was built. It was assembled. And though nature had a way of defying expectations, she'd made her living based upon the simple fact that a mechanism, when built properly and used skillfully, could be trusted to behave itself. If she plucked a string, it would give her the note she required. If she blew into a horn, it would blare out in just the right tone. She tapped her toes. Dwarfendam was the same. It had a rhythm. She'd heard it, tuned her ear to it. *Rum Tum Rum-Tum-Tum-Tum*. Allemande took a breath and shut her eyes, letting the beat flow through her. Ever since she was a girl, music had kept her fed. It kept her warm and safe. All she'd ever needed was a beat. And Dwarfendam had given her one.

Rum Tum Rum-Tum-Tum-Tum.

She stepped out onto the walkway, leaving the safe line behind. Her strides were slow, sure. Each foot struck the sturdy wooden boards on a beat. The bells jangled, and their ringing meshed perfectly into the chorus of clanks and creaks, just another instrument in the orchestra. Ahead, a section of walkway lurched up and tipped aside. She did not stumble, she did not slow. It locked back into place an instant before her foot came down. Next, a wheel of flails whipped through the air. She could hear them whistling their contribution to the melody. A graceful pivot and sweeping sidestep brought her between two blows.

With each step forward, with each iteration of the constant beat, she saw the truth of The Dwarfendam Run reveal itself. It wasn't an obstacle course or a collection of traps and trials. It was a dance. The machine was at once the band and her partner, demanding precision and rewarding it with safety. The ladder flipped forward, presenting itself to her. Rum Tum. She climbed three rungs and braced herself. Rum-Tum-Tum-Tum. Pitfalls and weapons sprung and slashed, but she didn't slow. There was nothing to fear from them, they were in their place and she was in hers. The beat rolled on and she moved forward.

As she approached the waterwheel, the thrashing of the current began to swallow the subtle beat, drowning out even the jangling of her bells. She hummed along and kept her pace. In two minutes she had traveled as far as any challenger had made it in the whole of the season. Ahead lay traps that she was the first to encounter, but there wasn't room in her mind to be frightened. She was a part of the dance, and though the steps were more complex, they were precisely in time with the melody.

She dipped and pirouetted, skipped and pranced. Slats slipped into place in time for her foot to land atop them and swept away again the moment she was on to the next. Trap doors fell away from her feet and shifting walls stopped a whisper from her face. Some weapons swung so close she felt her hair flutter in the breeze.

At the midpoint of The Run, as she approached a waterwheel from the other side, something seemed wrong. Water sprinkled down upon her from the paddles and flecks of oil spritzed from the heavy axles, but her steps remained steady. She trained her ears. Rum Tum Rum-Tum-Tum-Tum. Rum Ta-ta Ta-ta Tum Rum Ta-ta Tum. Her chest was already heaving with the task of keeping up with the choreography, and now the tempo was accelerating.

A moment of hesitation would throw her out of sequence and the Dwarfendam would chew her up and spit her out. She caught only fleeting glimpses of what this new twist in the melody held for her. Parts of the mechanism itself thrust in and out of her path. Hinges and struts swung and lurched. Sections of the roof over the walkway dropped down like hammers. She let the stirring of fear slip from her mind. It was simply more percussion. The better for keeping the beat. She counted off the final steps and, with a double tap, launched herself into the new routine.

The hazards came closer now, here tugging at her shirt, there, snagging her pants. Water kicked up by the wheels and pulleys splashed in her eyes, but she pressed on.

Allemande had long ago resigned to the fact that fate had no interest in anyone as insignificant as a woman like her, but what happened next would, for the rest of her days bring doubt to that belief. She finally blinked away the last of the water. With the first clear look she'd had of the whirling machinery for longer than she cared to consider, she beheld a great cogwheel rotating swiftly in the flurry of motion over her head. It was a single wheel amid a thousand others, but this one was unique. This one had three broken cogs.

The Dwarfendam Run

She didn't know much about devices, least of all dwarfish ones. But she knew music, and she knew dance. A broken string would spoil a chord; an injured dancer would miss a step. It didn't matter how precise she moved and carefully she stayed in rhythm now. It was her partner in this duet who would let her down. Already she could see moving conveyor belts stuttering and sweeping blades falling out of sequence. From this point forward, the heartbeat of the mechanism meant nothing.

Allemande whipped her head about, seeking some means of escape, of abandoning this foolish endeavor. It was no good. She was deep in the machine now. Chopping, thumping, swinging, tipping, and lurching hazards surrounded her. Each were off her current path, dancing to a different section of the song. She spun on her heel and felt a spiked wall prickle against her back. Before her now was the sweeping paddles of the second waterwheel.

A grin came to her face. These days, like in all other aspects of life, she preferred to play solo, but she'd spent a fair amount of time in larger bands. Sometimes another musician would hit a sour note. When that happened, it fell to the more skilled members of the ensemble to improvise. She'd always been fine at that.

The proper dance had her stepping forward. She chose instead to step to the side, planting a boot firmly atop one of the rising paddles of the waterwheel. A toss of her head and a hook of her arm took her out of the range of a swinging pole. She spun to the side, around the frame of the waterwheel, between the spokes, and into its center. She locked her legs and steadied her arms, holding herself in place as the wheel tipped her steadily upward. As she neared the top, she tucked her legs in, then thrust them out, hooking the toes of her boots over the paddle as she flipped entirely upside down.

This maneuver dislodged the bells from her toe, but she reached out and snatched them from the air as though it was just another part of the dance.

"Oh no, you don't. You're seeing this through to the end, same as me," she muttered, tucking the jingling bauble into her shirt.

As the wheel began to descend back toward the water, she grabbed a spoke and spun to the outside. With knees hooked over the waterlogged wood, she reached out and clutched a leather strap running between two pulleys. It hauled her up, pulling her away from the rushing river and back into the workings of the device. She dismounted, touching delicately down atop a horizontal wheel and matched her pace with it such that she was stationary.

Allemande took stock of her surroundings and got her bearings. The impromptu shortcut had left her a stone's throw from her prize. The cage containing the chalice wasn't ten paces away, though the space between was the *outside* of Dwarfendam, a collection of rolling axles, scything counterweights, and grinding gears. As treacherous as it was, the pathway through the heart of Dwarfendam was supposed to be difficult but not impossible. This part wasn't even supposed to be part of the trial. But all the same, it was far from the cogwheel that had thrown off the rhythm. The choreography was even more exacting here, but it was at least harmonious.

She reached into her shirt and retrieved the loop and bells. After threading her fingers through it and tapping them lightly on her side until she'd found her place, she took a breath and stepped off the horizontal wheel.

Never before had she stepped so lightly, so surely. A shuffle here, a skip there. Balancing atop rotating pinions and tiptoeing across the peaks of gears. But all of it made sense now. All of it *worked*. Before she knew it she'd caught the edge of the cage and pivoted herself onto the platform at its door, slipping right back into the gauntlet for the last few steps.

The designers of Dwarfendam had done the challengers the small kindness of leaving the chalice plinth and the platform surrounding it free of hazards. Allemande suspected it was more about protecting the chalice from damage than showing mercy to the challengers, but she wasn't about to look a gift horse in the mouth. In this brief moment of peace, took some time to admire the chalice. While the cornerstone listed a dozen names, the golden cup bore only three.

A few thoughts drifted in and out of Allemande's mind. Her own name would make a fine addition to the chalice... but no. She already had a plan for the priceless chunk of gold that had inspired so much foolishness, and the last thing she wanted was a crowd of worshipers and grovelers hoping for a glimpse of the latest challenger to claim the honor of champion. Along the same lines, she had just put on what may well have been the finest performance of her life, flawlessly executing what was certainly the most complex dance ever devised. And she'd done it without an audience. It was her little secret.

Allemande smiled. She wouldn't have it any other way.

She lifted the chalice from its stand. A hatch hinged open to reveal a ladder leading into the bowels of the mechanism. Just visible in the dim innards of the beast stood a lever. She followed it to small strut that in turn supported a large gear. No doubt this would shut down the machine and allow the champion to return to shore without endangering the prize.

With the chalice in one hand and the bell ring in the other, she clucked her tongue.

"Seems an awful way to end such a fine performance, doesn't it?" she said.

A few graceful twists and turns gave her a sense of the heft and balance of the chalice, and when she was satisfied, she affixed the bells to her boot again, tapped out the rhythm, and stepped back into Dwarfendam for a proper return trip...

#

Allemande made her way through what amounted to an inn in this place. Far from the small, comfortable, *private* rooms she'd always found to be the absolute minimum for proper lodging, the inn was little more than a huge tent filled to capacity with cots, bedrolls, and bunks. Some were stacked five high. The whole place smelled strongly of the inevitable results of pressing that much humanity into so small a place. Alcohol and sweat were the *most* pleasant of those scents.

She held her breath and stepped lightly through the dim interior. One of the nice things about an assembly of drunkards mounded atop one another like a basket of puppies was the sheer depth of their fight or drink-induced slumber. Though she moved with care, she probably could have clambered atop the snoring mounds and not woken a single one. And that was just as well, because there were a few notable things about her person at present that would raise their share of justifiable questions if they were to be noticed.

Her search eventually turned up Tristan dozing in the corner of the tent. He either had arrived too late or with too little money to claim one of the beds, so he was sitting on the floor, back to a tent pole, with his arms wrapped tight around his belongings. She leaned low and gave him a tap. He didn't stir beyond a grinding snore as his head flopped aside.

"Useless..." she muttered.

Allemande executed her next maneuver with a practiced level of grace and precision. She delivered a sharp kick to his ribs, then clapped her hand over his mouth to stifle the startled cry. Tristan struggled briefly, eyes sweeping about until they came to rest on Allemande.

"A word, outside, now. Quietly," Allemande instructed.

Tristan blinked away sleep and tried to focus on her. "Why?"

"Because what's about to happen is the sort of thing that requires privacy."

"Allemande, I've told you, I'm promised to another woman."

She visibly shuddered with anger. "*Outside. Now.*"

Anger robbed her of a bit of caution as she thumped back through the crowded tent, stepping on some toes and fingers along the way. She stormed through the cloth flap that served as a door and stood at the corner of the tent. A few moments later, Tristan stumbled sleepily through. She flagged him down and led him to a secluded alley between two of the three stables.

"Do we have to stand *here?*" he asked, holding his nose.

"Horses are good at keeping secrets. And trust me, this isn't much worse than that tent you were sleeping in."

He looked her up and down. "What happened to you?"

Allemande ran her fingers through her still-damp hair. She'd not had time to change after her little performance, so she was soaking wet. Her bodice was streaked and flecked with the greasy sheen of oil from the gears, and she was overall exhausted and disheveled. She lightly shifted an awkwardly bulging sack strapped across her back.

"Never mind me. This is about you. Let's say you wake up tomorrow and get your hands on that chalice. What happens then?"

"I marry Mariska."

"*How,* Tristan? That's not a plan, that's a goal."

"I'd use the prize to buy myself a nice plot of farmland to work. Her father has denied me time and again, saying I can't have the hand of his daughter because I wouldn't have the means to support her. As a landowner, I'd have that. He couldn't argue that any longer. And the fame and glory that comes with collecting the King's Chalice? The man would surely be *eager* to have me as a son-in-law."

"And this Mariska. Is she a good woman?"

"The finest woman I've ever met. Sweet and kind. Brilliant with a loom. You should see the tapestries she makes for--"

"Fine, fine. Just so long you weren't after a pretty face. Looks fade, and I'll be damned if I'm going to do this favor for a couple that will part ways after a few rough seasons."

"Favor?"

She swung the sack around and began to fiddle with the strings.

"Now, I want you to keep quiet when you see this. You'll want to whoop and holler, but you keep your mouth shut, you hear me?"

"What's this all about?"

Allemande tugged the sack open. At the first glimmer of gold, his eyes widened and he drew in a breath.

"*That's the--*" he began, but his outburst was cut short by a hand to the mouth.

"What did I just tell you? Keep your mouth shut or at least keep your voice down, and don't you dare say the name of this thing out loud. Now here. Take it."

She foisted the sack upon him, glancing about as she did as though she were delivering contraband. He nearly toppled forward at the weight of the thing.

"How?" he breathed.

"Never mind how. That's not the important part. '*What next?*' is the part you should be worrying about. You take this, you find the King's Representative, that'll be him in the tent near the river there. You hand him the chalice and you get your prize."

"But I didn't earn it. I didn't complete The Dwarfendam Run."

"Nowhere does it say you need to complete The Run. All it says is you need to deliver the chalice, and that's what you're about to do."

"But *you* got the chalice. Even if you would be generous enough to give me the prize, *you* at least deserve the honor and glory of--"

"Honor is worthless and glory is more trouble than I need. I'm a musician and a dancer. What good would that sort of a reputation do me? Have you ever seen how someone treats a hero? All hushed tones and reverently bowed heads. How am I going to get people dancing and having a good time if that's how people are treating me? Take the cup and get out of here. If you don't give it over before the crowd starts lining up, people are liable to ask questions."

Tristan gazed down into the bag. Tears welled in his eyes. Allemande deflated somewhat and looked aside.

"Please don't. There's no need for that," she said.

"You don't know how much this means to me," he sniffled. "To *us*. You've created a family today. You've made two lives complete!"

"Fine, fine. Just go and claim the prize."

"How can I thank you? I can't just let this kindness go without reward!"

"You'll be having a wedding, right?"

"Of course! The grandest wedding I can afford." He hefted the sack. "And even after I've bought the land, I can afford *quite* a grand wedding now."

"You'll be needing a musician, won't you? Any proper wedding needs music."

"Of course."

"Then keep me in mind. I spend most of my time out west, in a little town called Wendt."

"For as long as we both live, your music shall be present at every celebration and every gathering our family holds."

"Much obliged. Now off with you."

She turned, already thinking of where her first stop would be on the way back to Wendt.

"Wait," he said.

"What is it now?"

"Why?"

"Why what?"

"Why help me like this? You made quite clear you thought it foolish to care about others."

"Good advice isn't always easy to take. And this wasn't about you. This was about me. I wouldn't be able to live with myself if I sat there playing a spirited little jig as you limped your way to an oblivion I'd failed to warn you away from."

"I might not have been killed."

"I'm sorry. Which of us did The Run?"

"You."

"Then I think I'm in a better position to make that determination than you. Now run along! And so help me, if you so much as *mention* my name, there will be trouble for you."

Tristan nodded. He looked to be struggling to find the right words of farewell, but she saved him the trouble by not waiting around to hear them.

#

Allemande sat at the reins of her little cart, watching the

proceedings from afar. If things went sour, there wasn't much she could do to improve them, but having done this much, she felt oddly responsible for Tristan, and was determined to see this ridiculous enterprise to its end.

She needn't have bothered. After some initial confusion from the representative at being awoken by a man bearing the chalice--it *was* the sort of thing that normally had a greater pomp and circumstance around it--the announcer showed up and hastily spun it into a suitably remarkable story. By the time she was snapping the reins to move along, the crowd was gathered and in the palm of his hand as he slapped Tristan on the back and lauded him for not only his skill, but his stealth.

Allemande hit a bump on the poorly maintained road leading back to the main thoroughfare. It jostled the whole cart and brought a faint jangle from her bodice. She fished out her bell band.

"I hope you're happy with yourself," she muttered, threading her fingers through the loop. "I could have milked that job for another three weeks, easily. But you *had* to have your way."

She shook her head.

"When I think about all of the lousy lessons you taught me that I've not been able to shake, it's a *wonder* I've gotten anywhere at all..."

The Front Way

Joseph R. Lallo

The Front Way

A few years ago, I wrote a short story called *The Back Way.* It was intended to be part of a time travel anthology that fell through. The person organizing the anthology was quite enthusiastic about it, and suggested I shop it around for publication. I did, and no one was interested. This, I should say, has been my observation with all traditional publishers. Not terribly interested in my work. But, once I had Patreon, I had a place to put it out there, and it turned out to be quite popular with you folks! Popular enough that it was frequently listed among the stories that people most wanted a sequel for. Well, the time has come!

A typical day in an antique shop was fairly unremarkable. With one rather significant exception, this was doubly true of Yesterday's Tomorrow. When the front door of a store is at the top of what seems to be a fire escape, tucked into a poorly labeled side alley of a flood-prone street in New Orleans, foot traffic is the exception rather than the rule. As it so happened, the exception to the "unremarkable" rule came in the form of customers entering through "the back way."

"Where are we on appointments, honey?" called Ms. Thomas, the wizened owner of the establishment.

Claire flipped a key up from her chain and unlocked a drawer on the antique shop counter. She pulled out a meticulously kept ledger and flipped it open. Everything about this was inefficient. These days she'd be better served by an app on her phone. But there were two things working against the forces of efficiency. One, there was Ms. Thomas herself, who had been running the shop her way for more than fifty years and was impressively capable of shutting down any well-reasoned argument to change or update things. The other was the nature of the business they did, which was quite vigorously focused on security. A ledger locked in a drawer couldn't be hacked, leaked, or otherwise compromised unless someone physically got their hands on it.

She ran her finger down the page.

"Looks like we've got two appointments. One just before closing, and one in just a few minutes."

"Help me get this display from the 1970's fixed up. Dang lookie-loos got the whole wallet and watch display jumbled up."

Claire locked up the ledger and hurried from the back of the store. She swept past displays for the 1890s through the 1940s, decades ticking upward as she moved toward the front door. Along the way, she snagged a set of cufflinks that were incorrectly placed in the early 1950s. It was impressive how just a few weeks of working in this place had given her the eye to spot fashion trends and technological quirks on a year-to-year level.

She stepped up beside Ms. Thomas and started straightening, sorting, and arranging the watches while the owner worked on the wallets.

"Oh. I got the call back on those wingtips. He said we can pick them up on Thursday," Claire said.

"Thursday. That's two full weeks. I don't know what that man's doing with his hands half the time, but it's probably making the angels cry, because it *isn't* fixing shoes."

"Ms. *Thomas*," Claire said, hand to her chest. "I am scandalized."

"You be scandalized. I'm going to find myself a phone book and start looking for a new shoe guy."

"I can do the research for you," Claire said as she walked toward the counter in the back of the store.

"You can get some names and numbers. But I'll be doing the research."

A soft knock rattled the door to the back way, just beside the counter in the rear of the store.

"Right on time," Ms. Thomas said. "At least some people know how to stick to a schedule."

She turned and unlocked the door. Out stepped a portly older woman wrapped in a fuzzy white robe.

"Oh! Vanessa. I didn't expect to see you through here again so soon," Ms. Thomas glanced up to Claire. "Claire, order Ms. Vanessa a bowl of tomato soup and a pint of sour kraut."

"Right away," Claire said.

One of the many things that had become "typical" in this place was the strict adherence to a short list of rules created by Ms. Thomas. An odd lunch order like tomato soup and sour kraut, a few weeks ago, would have seemed like a perfectly innocuous thing to ask about. But rule number 1 strictly forbid asking questions to folks who entered through the back way. Given the consequences of her *last* violation of the rules, she wasn't going to risk violating any of them right now.

Over the course of a few hours, Ms. Thomas assembled the young woman's requirements. First and most important was the proper wardrobe. In her case, she requested a rather ostentatious pizza delivery uniform for one of the larger chains. It should have surprised Claire to discover that they had one in stock, but she'd learned that surprise was a wasted reaction in Yesterday's Tomorrow. Things had a way of lining up perfectly when it came to inventory. That is, until they *didn't*. The bulk of this young woman's order was gathered up for her in just a few minutes. The oddball requests required the rest of the day. Items that needed to be fetched included a bottle of a specific brand of mouthwash (available locally), a library book insert card between 15 and 19 years old (surprisingly accessible via online auction), and a TI-83+ graphing calculator (available via a Goodwill shop one town over). Once the research was done, their customer was nearly ready to be on her way.

"Now, before you go, do you have any other questions?" Claire asked.

The customer glanced at Ms. Thomas, as if seeking permission.

"She works here, honey. She knows the rules," Ms. Thomas said.

"Err… So, 'boomers,' 'gen x,' 'millennials,' and …"

Claire nodded knowingly. "Don't stress to much about it. Everyone is fast and loose with that. Boomers just means old, Millennials just means young."

"But…" she glanced at the calendar on the wall. "At this point Millennials are between 18 and 38 years old. Young seems to be an overly broad interpretation."

"Boomers don't update their mental picture of the generational demographics very often."

"And where does Gen X fit in?"

"Just forget about Gen X. Everyone else did."

"Ah. Well, that will simplify matters. Thank you for the clarification. When will you have the other items?"

"Everything but the library card will be ready tomorrow before lunch. The card will take another week or so."

"Excellent. Thank you, ma'am."

She marched out the front way without a word of explanation regarding the reason for such strange items and questions. Such was as it should be.

Claire glanced at one of the many clocks. At present they had seventy eight wall clocks on display and nearly two hundred watches. It didn't matter which clock she looked at. They displayed the same time, as synchronized as could be achieved with weekly adjustments. Said adjustments were the reason Thursday remained her least favorite day of the week, but if nothing else they ensured she knew each of the clocks inside and out, which had given her a special appreciation for the cuckoo clock on the back wall. Its delightful little tweet let her know when quitting time had finally arrived, and presently it was just seven minutes away. She liked working at the antique shop much better than her previous career, but she was still eager to head home after a day of researching authentic 1920s headwear or haggling for a better price on a tv tray with a forgettable western screen printed on it.

"You said that calculator was $6, is that right?" Ms. Thomas asked.

"That's right. Should I pick it up on my way out?" Claire asked.

She flipped to the next page in her ledger and marked something down. "No. I'll need you here. Right until closing today."

"Need help with the final appointment?"

"I've got a mark to that effect," she said. "That or the pen was leaking."

The chime drew her attention to the front door. In general, someone coming through the front way made for a simpler transaction. The moment she saw this particular gentleman, with his oddly spaced eyes and his ramrod-straight posture, she knew she was in for trouble.

"You…" Claire said.

He grinned. His face seemed poorly suited for the expression. Like holding a pen in his off hand, it didn't quite seem natural.

"You know this fellow?" Ms. Thomas said.

"He came via the back way," Claire muttered to her employer. "Right before the, uh…"

"What we would call a Type Seven interaction: pseudo-manipulated continuity maintaining displacement incident," he said. "Tell me, did you end up purchasing the lotto ticket or did you merely consider it?"

"Hup, hup, hup," Ms. Thomas said, tottering toward them. "Don't go running your mouth just yet. Gotta button things up proper first."

She walked the length of the shop and personally locked the front door. When the placard for the door was flipped from open to closed, she turned back.

"This fellow asking you about something that already happened?" Ms. Thomas asked.

"Yes."

"Go ahead and answer, but don't you go getting cavalier, Mister. What sense is there in me keeping to the rules if you just wander up and start talking all willy-nilly."

"My apologies. And I'm sorry I didn't get the opportunity to meet you upon my arrival. I was somewhat untimely and—"

"I know it. Burns me up when you boys and girls can't keep to schedule. But Claire, what's this about the lotto ticket?"

"This is the guy who gave me five dollars and said I should buy a lotto ticket. I *didn't,* by the way."

"A shame. You did a fine job and you deserved the tip."

"Oh, don't pretend like things didn't go exactly how you planned," Claire snapped.

"They did! Things went swimmingly, as I knew they would. But they could have gone that way with more money in your pocket."

"Then it wouldn't have gone the way it did, right?" Claire said.

"Nonsense. You'd still have become fixated on the nature of my knowledge of the unpredictable event, you would have indulged your curiosity and things would have unfolded as required."

"But… but there'd be an extra five dollar bill circulating. And… and the money would probably change things later, right?"

He shrugged.

"Don't shrug at me!" Claire said. "Butterfly effect, right? A butterfly flaps its wings in Africa and we get coastal flooding in New Orleans."

"Right, right, right," he said. "Chaos theory. It's true, that any sufficiently complex closed system with a high degree of interaction between individual components is bound to be sensitive to small changes in initial conditions. However! This system is not closed. Temporally speaking there is little in the way of unpredictable interactions, and these are not the initial conditions. Yes, a butterfly flapping its wings can cause all sorts of perturbations, but you aren't the only butterfly, and most of the others are much larger and flapping much harder. Things get lost in the mix more often than you'd think."

As they'd been verbally sparing, Ms. Thomas had trudged back to the back of the store to check her ledger.

"From the way you're talking, I get the feeling today's the day," Ms. Thomas said.

"What day?" Claire said.

"Debriefing. You didn't think you'd be sent back in time and not have a debriefing, did you?" he said.

"I didn't think I'd be getting sent back in time at all!"

"A fair and sane assessment. But you did, and thus your experience shall need to be chronicled. I would have preferred to have the debriefing happen closer to the initial event, but one of the primary means by which the aforementioned butterfly effect can be kept under control is limiting time crosstalk to ensure eras are isolated directionally. So, we must stick to predetermined temporal displacement windows and utilize them to maximum effect."

"Chatter, chatter, chatter. You won't be long for this job if you keep with the chatter," Ms. Thomas said.

He laughed. "The tightness of the ship you run has not been exaggerated, ma'am."

"So you're going to debrief me. How long is this going to take? It's a few minutes until quitting time."

"Oh, no. I am afraid that is not an area of expertise for me. And more to the point, your displacement was not isolated to yourself. You interacted with Ms. Thomas, so she will have needed debriefing as well."

"So someone will be along to interview both of us?"

"If I wasn't pleased with a few weeks of delay before your own debriefing, it should come as no surprise at all that I would prefer not to wait decades for Ms. Thomas' interview."

"I don't like where this is going," Claire said.

"It should be familiar ground for you. 1970. Specifically, two weeks after your departure. The entire ordeal shouldn't take more than seven hours, thirteen minutes, eleven point seven-three-seven-eight-eight-four seconds when measured contiguously along your world line. And you'll be pleased to know that for this trip, not only will you be showing up with foreknowledge of your destination, I can provide you with instructions regarding your behavior. Specifically, when asked any personal questions about your own activities that have already occurred—which are coincidentally the only activities you can speak of with any degree of confidence—answer honestly and thoroughly. And for clarity, I am specifically referring to things chronologically in the past of your relative position on your world line and not—"

"What is world line? You keep saying that."

"It is the path you take through spacetime. The sequence of 4 dimensional points in space and time that you trace as you live your life. Most people have a continuous, unbroken line. You happen to have a loop back to prior to your own origin and a *second* loop to the same pre-origin point before returning to the present. Such bilocation is—"

"I am already sorry I asked. Just tell me what I need to do."

"Travel back, be debriefed, and return."

"Be debriefed by whom? Is there an office I should be heading to?"

"You've already gotten far more answers than I am typically permitted to provide. Enjoy your trip. And if you wouldn't mind holding on to this, Ms. Thomas, I would be quite grateful for its safekeeping."

He handed a thick, document-sized envelope to her, then turned to leave.

"You aren't leaving through the back way?" Claire said.

"Heavens no. My task is unfinished, and requires a degree of freedom regarding travel, so I can't delay."

"This better be your first trip, buster," Ms. Thomas said. "Because you're letting slip all sorts of stuff you oughtn't. If you're going to go, go."

"So I shall. I'll return when my job is through, though there may be some fairly specific props I'll require before I make my official departure."

"You know our number. Drop a dime before coming here and stirring up the new hire."

He nodded, provided a wooden wave, and marched out the door. Claire turned to Ms. Thomas.

"Do you remember any of this?" she asked.

"I'm old, I'm not senile."

"But because it's my future, even though it's your past, you won't discuss it."

"I knew I hired the right girl. Head on out. You'll be through before closing."

"Closing is in four minutes." Claire squinted her eyes. "But this could take *years* and I'd still be done before closing…"

"I'll make sure of that. Now get."

Claire sighed. She was inclined to protest, but if she did, she knew she would be reminded that she was being paid $2000 a day for what, 99.95% of the time, was a run of the mill customer service position. Instead, she slipped behind the counter and checked the ledger. Sure enough, on the intended arrival time in the past, there was a faded line marking it as an appointment. She was expected. There was nothing for it but to step through the door to the Backway and get started.

For such an incredible device, the mechanism in the back room of the shop wasn't terribly impressive to look at. Some mundane plumbing pipe erected into a sparse framework to support the three key components. A reflective dish, a bundle of crystals, and a plate with assorted knobs and sliders that Claire had spent most of the first week learning how to operate. She carefully worked her way through the settings until she honed it in on May 7th, 1970. When triple checking the settings failed to turn up an error, she pulled the activation lever. The reflector dish shifted up to catch the light of the single naked bulb. The crystals smoldered with a subdued glow. Then came the flash.

Being prepared for it didn't do much to rob it of its uncomfortable effects. Her whole body tingled, and her inner ear revolted, insisting she was tipping over forwards. She reflexively overcorrected backward and stumbled against the far wall of the very same dim room. She braced herself against the wall until the dizziness subsided, then raised her eyes to the door.

"Great…"

If the time transfer had failed, she'd be looking at the very same white robe her recent visitor had been wearing. If the transfer was successful, she *should* have been looking at a somewhat tacky robe from the seventies. As the first sign that things hadn't gone precisely to plan, the hook for the robe was empty. Ms. Thomas was just as much of a stickler for the rules in 1970 as she was in 2018. The robe should be there. That it was missing wasn't a guarantee that things weren't as planned, but it was a bad sign.

She glanced up and shifted the curtain to ensure the device wouldn't activate again, then crept into the light of the naked bulb. The absence of the robe on the hook was unfortunate for a more mundane reason. Shifting through time, with rare exception, sent *only* the traveler. No equipment. No jewelry. No clothes. The occasional visitor through the back way arrived with a case or a bag, but as far as Claire had been able to determine, the techniques for achieving that feat required either expertise or resources that didn't exist yet.

Claire crept up to the door and gave it a knock. No answer. She tried the knob. Unlocked.

Her jaw tightened. Again, nice as it was to know she wasn't trapped in the back way, the door should *never* be unlocked. She took a deep breath and opened the door enough to peer through the crack. The store was dim. What little light there was came through the windows at the far end of the floor. She crept out of the back way and crouched behind the counter. No keys. Wherever Ms. Thomas was, she'd taken them with her… or someone else had taken them.

She glanced at the small electric clock on the counter, and the day planner beside it. Precisely the date and time she'd intended to arrive. It wasn't yet closing time. Ms. Thomas should be right here.

This was wrong. The right thing would be to head right back, to explain that there was no one there. But something deep in her gut told her that this was a bad sign. A part of something bigger than she'd been told about. And in her limited but *very* notable dealings with time displacement, anything she encountered in the past was something that she was supposed to encounter. Or, more accurately, something she had already encountered by the time she'd stepped into the back way to come here. If she felt as though she had to do something, she'd better do it, because she'd already done it, and thus…

She shut her eyes and tried to push the confusing thoughts from her head. *Why* she was going to do what came next didn't matter. What mattered was what she was going to do and how she was going to do it. She needed to find out where and how she would be debriefed, but far more importantly, she needed to make sure nothing had happened to Ms. Thomas. Before any of that could happen, she had to find some clothes.

The racks and shelves nearest to the counter were the oldest items in stock. Mid-to-late 1800s. The women's fashion of the time was profoundly uncomfortable and would probably get her more strange looks than if she just walked about nude. She crept through the store until she got to the late 1940s, which struck the perfect balance between "near enough to modern clothing to pass for normal" and "near enough to the front window that she was afraid she might be seen naked. Finding undergarments that were tolerable turned out to be an exercise in frustration, but a hasty shopping trip on the clothing racks found her a blouse that would fit. She picked a pair of men's trousers rather than having to deal with a skirt, and topped it all with a trench coat. But when the ordeal was over she was dressed in a way that wouldn't get her arrested and *probably* wouldn't draw too much unwanted attention.

Now that she was decent, she crept toward the front of the store. Men's pants and a trench coat meant she had pockets, so she didn't have to worry about a purse, but she still felt naked without the watch that had become an indispensable part of her day to day life in the shop. She lingered in front of a display near the front of the shop to select a watch. The moment her fingers touched the timepiece, a thump on the front door nearly stopped her heart.

She turned. A thick, rugged man in a sweat stained dress shirt and suspenders was hammering on the door.

"How did you get in there!" he demanded, with the authority and entitlement that could only belong to a police officer.

Sure enough, as one hand went for the knob, the other went for his pocket to retrieve a badge. Claire didn't even bother trying to run. There was only one other way out of the shop, and she hesitated to imagine what sort of a mess she would cause if she were to use the back way with a witness. She held her hands up. He thundered up to her.

"Answer me! How did you get in here, and what are you doing here?"

"I was already in the shop. I was hiding until everyone else was gone."

Claire wasn't sure why that particular lie, or any lie, came tumbling out of her so readily, but it was the best she could muster in a situation where the alternative involved the sort of stuff that didn't even exist in science fiction of the day.

"Why?"

"I… needed clothes," she said.

"Who are you? Let me see some ID."

She reflexively reached for a wallet which she realized wouldn't exist for another few decades.

"I don't have any ID," she said.

He curled a lip to reveal cigarette-yellowed teeth clenched into a grimace.

"You're coming with me."

He grabbed her by the upper arm and hauled her toward the doorway.

"Am I under arrest?"

"Shut up and get down the stairs."

"Why are you standing outside the shop?" she asked as he shoved her roughly toward the steps.

"I'm the cop, you're the suspect. I ask *you* the questions."

"But I just…" She glanced at him. "*You* ask *me* the questions…"

"That's what I said."

She brushed down the front of the trench coat and hurried down the steps.

"You could have been a lot more straightforward about this, you know. There's such a thing as being *too* subtle."

#

A short, uncomfortable ride in the cracked vinyl seats of a cop car brought them to the police station. A few things pressed upon Claire's mind as she stepped out of the car and once again found her arm in the tight grip of the man she presumed would be debriefing her. First, there were few times of the year that a trench coat was in any way reasonable attire for New Orleans, and this was decidedly not one of them. The second was how easily one can take for granted something as small as not having to breathe cigarette smoke every waking moment of every day.

The moment she stepped through the doors of the police station, the air had a tobacco sting, and when she was plopped down in a small office for her questioning, there a visible film of decades of high-tar smoke on the lamp shade. A thick glass ash tray had the remnants of a half-dozen butts, and a pot of coffee on a hot plate had been boiling long enough to produce a stink to rival the smoke.

Her debriefer sat in a well-worn chair behind the desk and, predictably, pulled a pack of cigarettes from his pocket to light up a fresh one.

"Now, start talking."

She coughed lightly. "Is there a form I should be writing this in? Some sort of a structure? I imagine you'll want to be thorough so that—"

"*Start talking.*"

"*Fine!*" she said, more forcefully than she'd intended thanks to his startling tone. "I arrived the first time two weeks ago. The circumstances of my arrival were initiated by someone--I've been thinking of him as an agent--who made a few purchases and offered a five dollar tip and the advice that I buy a lottery ticket..."

She recounted the details of her first, and technically second, temporal jaunt. She tried to be comprehensive. Presumably, no detail was too small for the kind of records these people would want to keep. Which made it seem particularly odd that he didn't start taking notes of any kind until she got to the part about the warehouse where the thieves had taken the crystals stolen from the back way. He seemed to check out again when she mentioned the second copy of her arriving. After one full cigarette, he was through listening, though she didn't finish talking until the end of the next cigarette.

"Is that sufficient?" she asked.

He stubbed out his butt and rubbed his face.

"What was your name again?" he asked.

"Claire Daniels."

"Have you been drinking, Ms. Daniels?"

"No, sir. I don't drink."

"If I were to place a call to the county psychiatric hospital, would I find them with an empty bed and a broken window?"

"Look, I didn't make a jaunt through *time* to be insulted and belittled. I'm trying to help you do your job," she said. "Now, if we're through here, I'd like to be on my way. It was nearly quitting time and I was looking forward to bingeing on a season of something or other on streaming tonight."

He stood.

"Come with me. We're putting you through processing."

"But I've been debriefed! That's what this was about, wasn't it?"

He stepped up beside her and once again clamped his hand around her arm. Over the next few minutes she was treated to the state of the art of criminal justice in 1970. Fingerprints were taken. Phone calls were made. Records were checked. She repeatedly requested some sort of an explanation and received, in response, incrementally rougher treatment until she was placed in a holding cell. A few minutes later, she was joined by a young woman with an unmistakable look of sharpness and intelligence in her eye. The same look that persisted after fifty years running a front for a time travel operation. The Ms. Thomas of this era. Elenore. For some reason despite intellectually grasping the fact she and her future/present employer were one and the same, Ms. Thomas and Elenore occupied two very different places in Claire's mind. The young woman's afro was pulled back from her face, and she was dressed in what Claire knew from her prior visit were her work clothes.

The officer locked her in the cell with Claire and wandered off. Claire assumed he was headed for a cigarette break. It seemed like smoking was 85% of their activities these days. Both women remained silent until the guard was out of earshot. Then Elenore turned to her.

"We've got to stop meeting like this," Claire said.

Elenore jabbed her in the shoulder with her finger. "We've got to stop meeting at *all*."

"It wasn't my idea. The guy with the weirdly spaced eyes sent me back and *you* told me to go along with it. It was supposed to be a debriefing."

"A debriefing. Of course," Elenore said. "You didn't tell them anything, did you?"

"I told them everything," Claire said warily. "That's what a debriefing *is*."

"What? You… how could. *Didn't I tell you the rules?* Or were you just ignoring them again?"

"I was told to come back for a debriefing and I ended up in your shop, naked and alone. It threw me, okay? And I was worried about you. And then a guy comes and he tells me I'm supposed to answer some questions and that's the whole reason I was sent back here. What was I supposed to think? This whole foolishness would be an awful lot easier if you'd quit being so coy about what's going to happen when we go back to the past."

"It isn't supposed to be a routine thing. It, frankly, isn't supposed to happen at all. It's not our job to use the back way. It's our job to make sure the people who *do* use the back way are served with discretion."

"*I was following instructions*. What few instructions I was given, anyway. Why weren't you there to meet me? And why wasn't there a robe?" Claire asked.

"When the police arrested the guys in the warehouse they about you, and *you*, and where they stole the crystal from, and eventually it came to me. They took me for questioning because… well…" She gestured vaguely to herself. "It's what you do when someone who looks like this isn't willing or able to answer all of their questions on the spot. I had been heading out the door to pick up the robe from the laundry when they picked me up. They left the officer with the teeth that look like Indian corn to keep an eye on the place."

"He's the one who brought me in."

"And you told him everything. The existence and purpose of the back way. The fundamentals of time travel."

"A man from the future told me I should!" Claire shut her eyes. "Listen to me… Is this what I sounded like to him? I'm going to be in a mental asylum for this. I'm going to be a *woman* in a *mental asylum* in 1970!"

"Calm down. Calm down. Things will be fine. Just… Things will be fine."

"How can you say things will be fine?"

"Because there are people whose job it is to *make sure* that things will be fine."

"So someone's just going to come and let us out at some point?"

"I very much doubt that."

"Then how exactly are things going to be fine?"

"I said *things* would be fine. I didn't say *you* would be fine." Her expression sharpened. "The back way is always supposed to be about the big picture. The people who come and go through it are also supposed to be about the big picture. An awful lot of stuff can change in the small picture and not make a lick of difference in the big picture."

"A woman cannot just *appear* in the past, with no history, and not change things."

"No. Not for long."

"Not for long…"

"Right now you exist as a few sets of fingerprints and the testimony of a few eyewitnesses. If you vanished, it would be strange, but ultimately dismissible as a curiosity. A processing error. Either it would become an urban legend or someone who looks enough like you would be spotted and arrested and that would be that. So long as *you* don't exist anymore."

"So they would have to rescue me."

"They don't have to rescue you. They just have to get rid of you. There's a million ways to do that. It's been done before, it'll be done again."

"What!? There are people traveling through time, terminating people who are a danger to the timeline?"

"*Most* of the time, a person who ends up displaced into the past did it on purpose and for nefarious reasons, or else did it for *good* reasons but botched it and knew the price of failure. And I'm not even supposed to know that, by the way. But sometimes someone comes through and gets chatty."

"Oh my god… Oh my god, oh my god…" Claire muttered, hands on her head.

"Calm down. Calm down," Elenore said. "We'll figure something out."

The door at the end of the hall swung open and the chain smoking officer trudged irritably toward them.

"Well, well, well," he said. "Seems we've got a couple of master criminals, and with some *real* bad timing," he said. "I just got a call from the FBI. Apparently there's an ongoing investigation. Month's old. And guess whose name and description matches their files."

"What?" Claire squeaked. "That's impossible. It's literally impossible. Months? I only showed up a couple weeks ago."

"Save your breath on that nonsense. The point is, you're going in for more questioning, and your little friend here is an accomplice. An agent is on his way from the local office. He'll be here in a few minutes. You two are his problem now. Present your hands for cuffs. Let's get you trussed up for him."

"I'm sorry, officer," Elenore said. "But I have been in questioning for hours. I need to use the restroom."

"This isn't grade school. You don't get bathroom breaks. Let's go."

\#

Twenty five minutes later, they were being helped out of the back seat of another boat of a vehicle with uncomfortable seats. The FBI office was different from the police station in ways that were difficult to articulate. The station felt like a stack of complex forms and worksheets haphazardly tossed on the corner of a desk. The FBI field office felt like that same stack of forms, but tapped into a tidy pile and neatly placed in a wired basket labeled "In." The same work was being done here, by broadly the same sort of people. But everything was more precise, more careful, more professional. Claire found herself calming somewhat as she found herself surrounded by such expertise and care. Elenore was visibly more vexed.

The pair were separated for additional questioning. For the second time since her arrival, Claire gave a detailed account of her prior visit. This time the words were recorded on reel to reel tape, and overseen by a mousy older woman who jotted down key points. After three hours, she and Elenore were reunited in a small, sparse office with a name plate bearing the name "Agent Connolly."

He was a lean man with a neat, white-collar cut to him. He wore a solidly middle of the road suit in terms of quality and tailoring, and though the air conditioning was considerably better in this office, he had a glaze of sweat on his temple that Claire suspected was there in the dead of winter.

"Ladies, sit down. I'm afraid I've only just been assigned to this case, so I'm not as familiar with the details as I could be, but I'm told by my colleagues and our associates in local police that you have been broadly cooperative, if perhaps not entirely honest."

Claire rubbed her face. "The issue isn't honesty, it's credulity. Sometimes when people don't believe you, it's because what happened is unbelievable. It doesn't mean it isn't true."

"Mmhmm," the agent said.

Dispassionate didn't begin to describe his tone. The man wore a look of interest and civility like a poker face.

"Now, I've gone through your statements. Have you been made aware of the charges of which you are accused?"

"No. And frankly if this is going to turn into a legal challenge I think you are going to have some significant trouble, because we have been denied some very basic rights and the arresting officers have neglected some standard points of procedure," Claire said.

"I'm sure if and when you actually request a lawyer, that will be a point worthy of discussion. For now, you should know that several months ago, we received a series of anonymous tips that there was a money laundering operation and a small scale fencing operation in the city. Normally something of this sort wouldn't be of much interest to us here at the bureau, but the tips were quite detailed, quite thorough, and seemed to indicate a deeper, underlying link to a related operation with the potential to smuggle people into and out of the United States with no possible means for tracking them. You can see how you, Ms. Daniels, are thus a person of interest for us, as we have not been able to turn up any firm records of your existence prior to the incident in the warehouse."

She looked to Elenore. Elenore's eyes were shut and her head was slowly shaking.

"Ms. Thomas, Ms. Daniels. We are going to get to the bottom of this, and we will have as close to the truth as is available. The question is whether it will be because of, or in spite of, your testimony. I assure you, it will make quite a difference when the time comes for sentencing."

Elenore opened her eyes and glanced at Claire.

"Honey, if we're going to do this, we're going to do it like you did last time. But that means one of us is going to have to talk and one's going to have to listen. I think we both know which of us he's liable to listen to," she said.

Claire nodded and took a breath. "Right. Fine. I'll talk."

She cleared her throat and turned to the agent.

"Agent Connolly, you say you want the truth. And we say we have given you the truth. What will it take for you to believe us?"

He tapped the typed pages before him.

"Extraordinary claims have been made, Ms. Daniels. Those call for extraordinary evidence," he said.

"Extraordinary evidence," she said.

She crossed her arms. If whatever was happening really had been happening for months, then it had to have been put into motion by a time traveler. And since their only way out of this mess relied upon being in control, she had to operate on the assumption that either she or Elenore had set it in motion. If she was in the middle of a scheme she'd cooked up with Elenore, what would she have done…

"How about knowledge of your informant?"

"We can begin there."

"You've been receiving anonymous phone calls and hand delivered messages from couriers from around the city."

His expression didn't change.

"The description of myself was uncannily detailed, but there was never any mention of Elenore or her shop. *That* connection came from the testimony of the thieves in the warehouse."

He crossed his arms.

"You have an unopened dispatch waiting for you. It arrived during this conversation."

For the first time, he offered up a visible reaction. His expression hardened slightly and he reached for his phone.

"If you are going to make bold claims that can't possibly be true, you would be better served by staying away from specifics." He dialed a number. "Ms. Kelly, I don't suppose you have any direct addressed, non-postal messages for me? … I see… Skip standard processing and send it in."

He hung up the phone.

"All right. So far what you've established is that one or both of you may have been responsible for the tips being given to the bureau. If they are true, your situation has not changed for the better, save perhaps the fairly bizarre means of providing a confession. If the claims are false, I'm afraid lying to the FBI carries its own penalties."

"I need you to think of something. Make something up. Before the message arrives. Something I couldn't know. Something you couldn't know. Something that didn't exist until this very moment. Write it down."

"My salary is paid by the government, Ms. Daniels. I don't waste tax dollars on parlor tricks."

There was a knock at the door. An intern provided him with a sealed envelope. He ripped it open and unfolded the contents.

"My salary is paid by the government, Ms. Daniels. I don't waste tax dollars on parlor tricks," he said slowly, this time reading from the page. "Now answer the phone. It is your wife. There is a burst pipe in the basement."

The phone rang. He gave the women a wary look, then answered.

"Agent Connolly. … Y-yes. I… It's fine, honey. The main shut off is by the washing machine. Good. Will you talk to the plumber or should I? … Good. Good… No, it's fine I'm… there's something at work." He hung up the phone and leaned heavily on the desk, glaring at Claire. "Explain this."

"I've explained it twice already, Agent. Wouldn't want to waste tax dollars on a third time."

"You don't honestly expect me to believe you are visitors from the future."

"If you'd been listening, I'm the visitor from the future. Elenore is local."

He sat down and knocked his knuckles on the table, jaw tight and eyes intense.

"Agent, there are a few things you need to realize. First, the mere fact you received that message proves we *do* walk out of here. Maybe not today. Maybe not tomorrow. But eventually. That's how this all works. We get out, we send the information back in time, and you get it. So the fact of our release is established."

"But that doesn't make sense."

"It does, honey," Elenore said. "I've been at this for a while. It takes a bit to get your head around, but once you do, the math checks out."

"Now you need to make a decision," Claire said. "Here's what I propose. You let us go. Once you do, I'm gone. Hopefully for good. You close the investigation, and you make a note that Yesterday's Tomorrow is off limits for future investigation."

"I can't just do that. Making broad proclamations of policy and resource management is above my pay grade."

"You of all people should be able to appreciate the concept of information security," Claire said. "There are some things which must be kept in strict confidence. Information from the future is very much at the center of the sphere of sensitive data. You know better than I do how the FBI will proceed with this investigation if you take this testimony as truth. Now imagine an organization with the resources you've just seen demonstrated. What lengths do you think they would be willing to go to in order to keep things from spreading too far?"

He knocked his knuckles a bit harder and shifted his glare to the desk.

"If you don't have the imagination for it, you can just wait a bit and find out the hard way," Elenore said. "Like Claire said, we come out of this just fine, or else you never would have got that message. Doesn't say anything anywhere about you coming out of this fine. Who knows about this? Me? No one cares about what a black lady says. A couple of crooks? Who'd believe them? That cop back at the station? He took us for cranks and probably forgot all about it. Claire's headed back where she came from just as soon as she's out of here. And then there's you. You're the only one here with proof. You can just crumple it up, throw it away, and forget you ever saw us. It isn't like you've got any proof of a crime. Matter of fact, Claire led the local police to that warehouse, didn't she? It's you. You get to decide if this stops here or if things get more complicated for everyone. Seems to me you've got a lot to lose and not a lot to gain."

"… Look, this just isn't enough evidence for me to effectively falsify records and—"

The phone rang. His eyes flicked from it, to Claire, to Elenore, and back to it. He picked it up.

"Hello? … Thursday? That's… listen honey, I'm busy. Wash the clothes at your sister's house. I'll deal with it when I get home."

He hung up. Elenore reached forward and flipped the envelope from the message over. *Wash the clothes at your sister's house* had been scrawled on the back. His nostrils flared. After a smoldering moment, he picked up the phone again.

"Get me the regional director."

#

Two hours later, Claire and Elenore had been dropped off by a highly irritable Agent in front of the alley leading to Yesterday's Tomorrow. The moment the car pulled away, Elenore pulled out a pad and pencil and started furiously taking notes.

"My salary is paid by the government, Ms. Daniels," she muttered, scribbling it down. "Was it magic tricks?"

"Parlor tricks," Claire said.

"I can't believe I'm going to have to take a trip through the back way. I was hoping to avoid that, you know. My father never had to do it."

They paced along the alley and climbed the steps.

"It isn't so bad. The physical experience I mean," Claire said. "It can be a little jarring psychologically."

The door opened as they approached. Elenore, in somewhat more casual clothes and with visibly longer hair, was there to greet them. She jabbed a finger in Claire's chest.

"You're a troublemaker," she said. "Do you know where I've had to be and what I've had to do for the last couple months?"

"I've been thinking about that," the current Elenore said. "I'll have to pick a time when I'm likely to have left the door to the backway unlocked. I don't do that often. Keeping my head down for *months*. Not looking forward to it."

Both Elenores turned to Claire.

"You better turn out to be a real asset in the future," said the current Elenore.

"For sure, honey, because you are getting to be a pain," said the other.

"Don't shoot the messenger," Claire said marching toward the back way. "I'll see you in a moment. Hopefully you won't see me for a few decades."

"I'm not going to hold my breath. You're a bit of a bad penny," said one of the Elenores. Claire didn't glance back to see which one.

A careful setting of the controls and a tingly flash of light left her disoriented and standing on a pile of clothes that were still warm from when she'd been wearing them prior to her departure. She got dressed and knocked on the door. The knob turned and the wizened but still sharp elder Ms. Thomas opened the door.

"Right on time for closing," she said.

Claire reset the machine to its default state and stepped out to the counter.

"Two things before you punch out for the day. First, I need you to file that folder so-and-so dropped off in the cabinet."

"I was kind of looking forward to heading home. An awful lot of time has passed in the last few minutes."

"Won't take a second," she said, handing over the folder.

Claire sighed and accepted the old intra office mail envelope. Faded pencil markings on the grid of to and from lines marked off whose hands it had passed through in its time. The last line was *secure records storage*. The line before that: *Agent Conolly*. There was no doubt in her mind that this envelope contained the detailed record of her visit to the past. The very debriefing that was the supposed reason for the trip. She shut her eyes and let a tremor of irritation come and go, then opened the bottom drawer of their file cabinet and slipped it inside.

When she turned back to Ms. Thomas, she was marking down the final appointment of the day, Claire herself, off the list.

"You wanted one more thing?" Claire said.

She nodded, shut the ledger, and slipped it into its drawer.

"Been a while since I went out for a drink. Care to take an old lady out for a few drinks? My treat."

"… Yeah. I think we could both use a drink or two."

The Pencil Hoarder
Joseph R. Lallo

The Pencil Hoarder

People frequently ask me where I get my ideas, or how I start writing a story. I don't have any one answer to that question, but quite often the process is a stunningly simple one. I will sit down, think of some basic concepts, and pick one that tickles my fancy. At times like these, comments from friends or fans will pop into my head. Which leads me to the story I need to tell before I tell you this one.

The pandemic hit New Jersey particularly hard in the early days. After my brother was twice exposed to people who later tested positive, the whole household decided collectively to quarantine for two weeks. During that time, I stopped trimming my beard. It got puffy, and I decided to see how far I could push it. Once it got bushy enough to be annoying, I wanted to test just how substantial it had gotten before it was time to trim it. So I grabbed a handful of golf pencils and managed to stuff thirteen of them into my beard before I ran out. Then I recorded and shared a video of me pulling them out.

I will remind you, I am a professional author.

This eventually led to someone making a joke about hoarding pencils. Weeks later, this story came tumbling out of my head.

Behold, the grandeur and majesty of the creative process.

Dragons were supposed to be enormous. Great, terrifying creatures. They were supposed to tower over their foes, to make lairs of whole mountains. They were supposed to be fierce.

Scritch was none of those things. But he was still a dragon.

Scritch… A name his father had given him. His sisters were named for the elders who came before them. His brothers had names fitting of the cunning and might they would grow into. Scritch was named for the sound his claws made on the eggshells of the rest of his clutch. Whatever fickle fingers of fate poked and prodded the world into shape had seen fit to mold this little beast not into a hulking threat, but into a scampering pipsqueak. His egg had been no larger than a chicken egg. Now, ages after he'd hatched, he was still no larger than a rat. His form was long and lean, almost serpentine. At a glance, one would hardly imagine he was a dragon at all. It was his curse, but in time, also his blessing.

In the old times, Dragons ruled. No weapon could pierce their hide. No armor could withstand their breath. The greatest threat was the human race, but they were hardly a threat at all… at first. Time marched on, and with it marched an irritating new magic called 'science.' The wizards were bothersome, but their skills were rare. Science was available to all. Even those unable to learn or uninterested in learning could taste the fruits of science for a few coins. Slowly, bows became crossbows, then rifles. Horses were replaced with jeeps and tanks. Once impenetrable scales gave way to increasingly potent weaponry. And the massive size that had served to intimidate now only served to make dragons easy targets. One by one, the beasts were plucked from their place at the top of the heap, punished for untold centuries of toying with the humans and making meals of them.

But Scritch was too small for that. Barely a dragon at all. He didn't need a mountain or a cave. A hole in the wall would be sufficient. And so, as the humans built their cities, Scritch skulked in their alleys. He survived. If it could be called survival. But a dragon still had needs. The same deep compulsions that had driven his brethren to ruin still broiled in his brain. And right now, it was practically screeching at him.

He needed a hoard. It was maddening. These humans built great, towering palaces of stone and glass. They clearly still had the same drive toward wealth and glory that they always had. But they'd somehow left behind the one worthwhile part of it. Gold. Now their greed took the form of bits of paper with etchings of dead leaders. Gold still existed, but it wasn't in handy sacks hanging from belts anymore. Some merchants still carried the stuff, but under lock and key. It was frustrating. But instinct was instinct. He needed a hoard. And gold was the best thing to hoard.

The last one had taken him *years* to amass. Three cufflinks, two rings, and even a *coin*. But he'd made the error of making his lair in the space behind the cupboard, and when they'd decided to do something called 'renovation' they'd found it. Now the carefully chewed holes were sealed up and his precious hoard had been traded for something called a 'television.' He was so disgusted, he'd decided to find someplace fresh to start over.

He sniffed the air. He was after very specific, very pungent smells. Sharp, chemical odors. Paint and plaster. The smells of construction. If he'd been chased from his last home when they decided to paint the walls and patch the holes, naturally the thing to do would be to find a place that had just been painted and patched. Then it would be a good long time before they moved any furniture or tore into any walls.

The building he found was certainly not a home. Humans made different shaped buildings for different purposes. This was too square, too big, and had too many rooms to be a home for even a very wealthy person. This was a place where they did business. Or so he thought. When he scrabbled through a grate and worked his way up through the basement, he found room after room of desks. Not the big, paper-strewn desks he'd found in places with far too many people and far too little food. Offices, he'd heard them called. These desks were small. An office for children?

Regardless of the purpose, it quickly became clear this was an ideal lair for him. Great metal tunnels ran through the ceilings and through the walls. They were cooler than the rest of the building, but a puff of flame here or there to warm him up was a small price to pay for freedom of motion without the risk of being spotted. And then there was the *food* room. A great big place scattered with bigger tables and stinking of the burnt meats and simmered vegetables that humans seemed to love. The room with the actual food was a bit harder to get into, but some fluttering of wings and heaving at handles popped a door open and revealed a feast of small foods. They were even carefully wrapped and easy to carry. Yes. This would be an ideal lair. But a hoard was still on his mind.

Scritch scrabbled from room to room. There were no humans here. That would surely change. They didn't leave places like this empty. But for now it meant there was no danger in searching thoroughly. The larger desks at the front of each room were the most promising. If all he was looking for was *shiny* things, a single drawer would have been more than enough for him. Little shiny bits of bent wire by the dozen, gleaming tacks, and a hundred other metal doodads were in ready supply. But they weren't *gold.* The innate sense for the precious metal meant that even the things that *looked* like gold weren't enough to fool him. Sheets of waxy paper with little gold stars. Sweet smelling bricks with gold foil wrappers. None of the *real* stuff. By evening of the first day, he had given up on finding any true wealth here, so he was willing to settle for a facsimile or two to start things off. He could always replace them later when some proper treasure came along.

A few small wooden spears stood tall in a cup. Wrapped around one end was a gold something-or-other that, if he squinted and tipped his head, looked something like a crown. It would have to do. A fought with it for a moment or two, but it was too firmly attached to the spear to pull free. He gave up on separating the two and just took the whole wooden rod along with him as he fluttered through the ceiling grate and found a comfortable, easy to miss chamber to begin his new horde.

Dragging his first acquisition along was easier said than done. It was longer than he was, and he couldn't clamp it in his teeth and tote it along because it wouldn't fit though the grates. It meant he had to clutch it in his forepaws and totter along on his hind legs like a human would. He plopped down in a place high in the building, where the handy metal tunnels led to the roof. He plopped the purloined object on the ground and grinned. A fine start. The metal walls were rather pleasant. And it was all so clean… Except for the odd black line.

He scampered over and investigated. He felt certain he would have noticed that he was waddling past such a distinctive feature. It certainly couldn't have been there when he'd passed through. But, just as certainly, it was there now.

Scritch narrowed his eyes. This could be a trap. This could be something nefarious. One didn't live as long as he had in the world of the humans without working out that they were a devious lot. Leaving tasty treats in bent wire contraptions meant to ensnare him. Finding ways to place all of their most precious items inside containers that were impossible for him to open. They were fiendish. He needed to investigate.

A quick sniff suggested whatever the line was, it wasn't poison. A lap of the tongue produced a strange, somewhat bitter flavor. He sniffed around until he realized the only other source of the odd, sandy scent was the tip of the spear. Experimentally, he scraped the edge and made another mark.

Strange… It was pointy, and when humans made things pointy it was almost always to poke holes in their enemies. But the way it made such a clear, sharp mark hardly seemed like a mistake. He shook his head and set the spear down. I didn't really matter what it was or why they'd made it. All that mattered was that it was shiny and it was his. Humans were strange, there was no sense trying to figure them out now.

With a belly filled with stolen food and the first addition to what would hopefully be a towering mound of riches beneath him, he dozed off.

#

The following morning, he was rattled awake by a clanging bell. Scritch shook his head and stalked angrily through the metal tunnel. The air that was so heavy with the smells of paint and adhesive was now layered with a thousand new scents. Humans, young and old, but mostly young.

He took care to keep from making too much noise as he navigated the tunnels and found his way to the first room with activity. He must have been correct. This *was* an office for human children. Each desk had a child seated at it. He would have left them to their strange, pointless little tasks but something piqued his interest. Each of the children was holding one of the little spears he'd stolen.

Scritch flopped to his back and inched his head between the bars of the grate, careful to keep as well hidden as he could while still getting a good hard look at what was going on.

The one adult in the room was prattling on about "words" and "sounds" and "the alphabet." He kept pointing at a row of symbols above the black board along one wall. Then, one by one, he traced the shapes onto the board. The children dutifully followed suit, scratching their little spears onto bits of paper to make marks.

It was a curious sight, and one that held his interest at least

162

until his belly started to rumble. Evidently the odd strings of symbols had meanings. They were signs that represented sounds. That certainly explained why they were so prevalent everywhere in the human world. The blasted creatures were always talking. Why *wouldn't* they find a way to decorate their objects with things that allowed them to talk even when they weren't there?

Scritch snuck down to the food room. It was a bit more difficult to navigate, now that there were humans there putting heat to the various pouches and patties, but he'd gotten rather skilled at sneaking around without being seen, and in no time he was back in the tunnels with a well-wrapped bit of food that he now realized was entirely covered with those sound-symbols. He twisted his head searched his memory. He'd seen two of the three symbols that dominated the front of the wrapper, and two of them were the same.

"M," he recalled. "And another M. With a squiggle in the middle."

He tore at the bag and nibbled at the colorful treats within.

"Mmm… I like these M-squiggle-M things," he crunched through another. "I bet the humans make sure to label all of their best things."

He swallowed.

"I ought to learn a few more of them. Could come in handy…"

#

That year was quite interesting indeed. For one thing, he was very well fed. Children could always be depended upon to drop the tastiest treats on the ground and make so much noise and distraction Scritch could risk snatching them up in broad daylight. On the rare day that they weren't so messy, it was easy enough to scurry out into the places where food was kept and grab some. Humans were lousy hoarders. They never seemed to keep careful count of their treasures. So long as he didn't leave crumbs or wrappers to hint at what he'd been nibbling on, they would never notice a few purloined snacks.

All that food meant he didn't have to spend much time foraging at all. Though most of his life he would have spent any free time searching for gold and silver, but for once he had something that captured his interest even more. There were things to *learn* here.

It seemed it was no coincidence that he'd first noticed what those symbols meant only after he'd come to this place. This was a place meant to teach those very lessons. It was a "school," according to the one adult in the room he'd chosen to observe. That person was called a "teacher," and her role seemed to be assigning words to things. The odd little spear was called a "pencil." The list of shapes was called the "alphabet." The little ones in the room were having a hard time grasping the lessons, but Scritch was quite old and quite clever. In less than a month he'd committed the twenty-six letters to memory and worked out how to make sense of most of the words they formed. Some of them didn't make sense. Through, tough, thorough, thought, and though seemed like they ought to make mostly the same sounds, but they *seemed* to make completely different ones, based on how the teachers spoke them.

Before long he'd grown weary of the lessons taught to the younger children. He sought out other rooms with older children. More difficult and fascinating lessons were taught there. In some rooms they told themselves stories about history. Most of them weren't as Scritch remembered them, but he supposed the world looked awfully different when one wasn't busy hiding in attics and scrambling in the shadows. The science classes were every interesting indeed. It seemed science was so much more prevalent than the old magics because, they didn't jealously guard their secrets like the old wizards did. Yes, the knowledge was still scrawled on the pages of books, but they passed on the knowledge to any interested in knowing. Judging by the attitudes of the children in the class, they passed on the science even to those who weren't terribly interested in learning it.

In time, he realized he'd learned enough of their reading and writing to skip waiting for them to say things he was interested in and instead seek them out on his own. A large room in the school was *filled* with books and was mostly empty even during the day. The library. The books were massive, compared to him, but he was stronger than he looked and a bit of effort was sufficient to dislodge even the largest of them from their places on the shelves. He could read them from their place on the floor and simply leave them there. The adults had no problem blaming the children for misplacing the books and grudgingly replaced them without a second thought. For a dragon his size, a school was the best domain one could hope for. He was going to make himself at home here for a good long time.

#

At the end of a long day learning about something called "The Renaissance," he swiftly navigated to his place high in the school and looked upon his chamber.

All of the good food had given him the robust physique usually reserved for the finest hunters. That he had free run of a massive lair meant that his territory had grown as well. The only thing that hadn't grown was his hoard. Seven bottle caps he'd quite liked the look of and twenty-three pencils were all he had been able to gather.

He climbed atop the mound of pencils and tugged a tasty little concoction called a "Slim Jim" from his pile of stolen goodies. He chomped on the salty, meaty, greasy stick and put his cunning mind to work.

"I have everything I need here. Everything except a worthwhile hoard," he mumbled through a full mouth. "I just need some gold, but these humans seem to have forgotten its value. All they collect are bits of paper and coins made of common metals.

He glared at the single "Gold Dollar" he'd found. Even a hatchling could tell it was a thin layer of gold atop a worthless metal disc. He'd set it aside rather than sully his hoard with something that seemed to have been designed to *fool* someone into believing it was a proper gold coin. At least the other bits of gold-colored metal weren't acts of deception.

"It is like they are *purposely* avoiding things of real value."

He chomped at the Slim Jim again.

"Though I suppose humans have always been more interested in creating things than finding them. They probably think they can create *value* somehow."

His eyes lingered on the ersatz gold coin for a moment. A stray thought shifted his attention to the bottle cap in front of him. *That* had made it into the hoard in spite of its clear lack of value. He simply liked it better. He valued it more.

"They *can* create value, can't they?" he reasoned aloud. "The books are far more valuable with the words in them. They took a tree and made paper. Paper isn't half as nice as a tree. Value lost. But then they and made a book, with words in it. Words with useful meanings. And suddenly it has more value. Maybe even more value than a tree."

He closed his eyes and scrunched his face in an attempt to wrack his brain.

"They have a name for it. E… con… omics. Economics." He straightened up and pushed the rest of his snack aside. "Well, if a human can do it, a dragon can."

\#

Scritch started small, as tended to be necessary, given his size. He already had pencils, and paper was easy enough to find in a school. He started to write. Mostly he wrote about things the humans couldn't. things were more valuable if they were rare, and a dragon's thoughts were very rare. It took weeks before his writing was precise enough that *he* could read it. Weeks more before it was precise enough that someone else might be able to. But dragons were patient.

May sheets of paper later, he had recorded a brief memoir, a single anecdote from long ago. The time he'd stolen his first gold coin from a larger dragon ages ago. Then came the greater challenge. Figuring out how much value he had given the pages, and furthermore, figuring out how to increase that value. He read more books. Books about writing books. He found out there were things called agents. And things called publishers. They were the ones who assigned value. Getting the story to them required all sorts of new skills. He had to find envelopes. Stamps. He had to find something called a "phone book" and look up and address. And he had to have a name. A name other than Scritch. That simply wasn't a human name, and humans wouldn't do economics with dragons, he felt quite certain. Thus, S. C. Ritch was born. That was a human enough name.

Mailing the letter was as easy as dropping it in the right place, the box marked "Out." But after many weeks, each morning carefully crawling through the mailbox in search of a letter in reply, the agent did not respond. He wrote the story again, this time with more care, and picked a new person to send it to. This time there was a reply, but it was an awful lot of words that may as well have just been "No." No matter. There were other names in the phone book. Again and again he wrote the tale. Each time it grew longer, more colorful as he remembered more details. He began tracing out pictures of the other dragons involved. Most times there was no reply at all. Other times more rejections, seldom even mentioning his name. If this was how humans treated people they thought were other humans, it was a very good thing he hadn't claimed to be a dragon.

More than a year passed, and by now the story had grown to twenty carefully written pages, both sides. There were little, intricate images, and he even worked out how to operate the "Stapler" which seemed to be an important part dealing with any stack of pages.

The Pencil Hoarder

He'd taken to doing his writing in the library, where the big table (and the stapler) made things easier. Unfortunately, he'd gotten a bit too invested into the most recent writing and lost track of time. The distant sound of a key startled him. He dashed for the safety of the top of a shelf and huddled down. There hadn't been time for him to collect his manuscript. At his size, and at the size the story had grown to, moving it was something of an ordeal for him.

The librarian took her place at the desk, frustratingly close to where he'd left the manuscript. He couldn't risk fetching, but it was the work of an entire night. He couldn't just leave it either. Instead, he nestled himself in the dim corner of the room, stone still atop a shelf, and watched over his manuscript like a Gargoyle.

Classes came and went. Most lingered in the portions of the library where the books with pictures could be found. It seemed he might just be lucky enough to have his stack of pages go unnoticed, and he might be able to stuff it in an envelope and send it to the next likely person. But then a little girl wandered up to the table. At the first glimpse of the dragon Scritch had etched onto the first page, the manuscript seized her attention. She climbed onto the chair and flopped the pages open.

Scritch stood rigidly in place. The same instincts that drove his larger cousins to protect their hoards screeched in his ears. Fortunately, he had the resolve to resist the rather self-destructive urge to fly down from this hiding place and belch flames at a creature several times his size protected by dozens of other, even larger creatures. So he watched and waited. The bell signaling the end of the period should have been his saving grace, but the vile little creature, swept the manuscript into her bag and took it with her.

The dragon clenched his teeth and scrabbled into the vents. Long disused tracking and hunting skills surged to the front of his mind. He followed her scent, and searched the different rooms until he spotted her. Like so many children, she wasn't well equipped to the rigors of paying attention for forty minutes at a time. At least, not to the teacher. Mere minutes into class, she had already let her mind wander from the lesson and straight into her book bag. She fetched the manuscript and sneakily started reading again. As Scritch watched from the vent, he saw her lose herself in the words. She was infinitely more invested in the tale than the "social studies" lesson the teacher was delivering.

As she flipped through page after page, Scritch found himself strangely proud of the little expressions of interest and excitement that graced her face. After rewriting it a dozen times, he'd grown rather weary of story, but it was new to her. It *mattered* to her. It was valuable to her.

By the time she'd finished and stowed it back in her bag, Scritch's attitude had changed. He'd gotten what he needed from the story. He knew that his words had value. At least to her. And that was a start. He'd need more papers, and more pencils.

There were *many* more stories to tell before he had his hoard.

Soft Summoned
Joseph R. Lallo

Soft Summoned

What follows is part of the "Shorts of Dubious Canonicity" project I started in 2018. In an attempt to keep my mind sharp and fresh, I started taking votes on short stories to write each weekend. Some of them stayed short. Some of them grew into full novellas. But almost all of them were the result of my fans and followers casting their votes to give them support.

Sometimes I plan out a project from the start. I sit down with a pad and pen and jot down ideas, then move to the computer in order to type out an outline. Once that's done I get into "writing mode" and do 3,000-5,000 word chunks until the thing is finished. *Soft Summoned* is not an example of that particular pipeline. In the case of this story, I got an itch to write a specific sort of story, something where a creature had to grapple with being stripped of all of its power and status and having to come to terms with how it would pursue its goals. A few hours later, I had this story about a demon who doesn't quite get the journey to earth that he was hoping for. I hope you like it!

A crooked, yellowed trio of six-sided dice rattled across the cracked ground. They struck the coarse black bricks of a wall and rattled to a stop. On each die, six gouged divots blackened with grime rather than paint faced the sooty sky.

The creature who had pitched the dice peeled his lips back to reveal a jagged grin. His name was Vord, and he was a walking nightmare. He was hulking in size, such that he nearly filled the alleyway where his little game was being played. Tufts of brown-black fur bristled irregularly from his leathery hide. Tattered, bat-like wings, a bestial muzzle, the talons of a raptor. He was the most horrid, frightful parts of the creatures that lived above. And, worst of all, he was *very* lucky at dice.

"Hah!" he hacked. "Three sixes. Pay up."

"You're cheating," croaked a smaller but no less wretched creature sniveling beside him.

Vord leaned down, snout to beak with the lesser monster.

"You're calling me a cheater?"

"Yeah, I'm calling you a cheater."

"You would dare malign the integrity of the mighty Vord? Seventh Lord of the Darklands? Baron of Blackpool? Ninth in line for the Agony Throne?" he rumbled, brimstone stench belching from his maw.

"I *know* you're cheating," the smaller monster croaked.

Vord snatched him from the ground. And shook him. "You know *nothing*."

"We're playing with *my* dice, and the third one ain't got a six on it. It's got two fives."

Vord narrowed his eyes. "You cheated, too…"

"I cheated *first*."

The massive creature dropped him.

"Then we are even. You cheated, I cheated. The two balance out. And I still win."

Evidently, the logic was more than the beaked imp could counter. He rummaged in a small satchel and pulled out a pair of rubies.

"Fine. Take your bloody winnings."

Vord hacked out another laugh. He curled his fingers around the pot he'd won and willed it away in a swirl of flame and smoke.

"Double or nothing," Vord said, gathering up the dice.

"I've lost enough to you already. What's a baron doing fleecing lesser demons in back alleys anyway?"

"What are you, ignorant? You should know better than to ask that."

"I should know better than to play dice with you, but I did that."

Vord sighed. "How many times have you been to the surface?"

"Three. If the moon's right tonight, I'm hoping to have my fourth chance."

"I have been to the surface one hundred sixty-eight times. Each time feeding on sin. Each time confounding those who would bind me. That is how you become a baron. That is how you become a towering figure in the Darklands."

"Fine, fine. But it doesn't explain the back-alley thing. Or the cheating at dice, or the--"

Vord snatched the imp up again and slammed him against the brick wall.

"Do I interrupt your sniveling idiocy while you are prattling on?" Vord snapped.

"You… just… did…" the thing wheezed.

He dropped the imp and palmed his face. "I suppose you wouldn't be down here if you had the sense to treat your betters with proper reverence… I was coming to a point. Each summoning, if you feed well, makes you stronger. But to summon a more powerful demon takes a more powerful spell. Thus I am at the mercy of those above to craft my summoning circle with incrementally greater precision in order to ascend the ladder. It has been *decades* in their time since someone last traced out the runes with sufficient skill to draw me forth. I have not *fed* since 1947."

"What's that got to do with anything?"

"On the thirteenth summoning of the thirteenth cluster, a demon may walk the halls of agony. *One more time on earth* and I shall have my place among the other lords. Until then, I am here with you wretches, locked away from the inheritance of my bloodline and locked away from the power I have so rightly amassed."

"What do you want? Sympathy? You want me to shed a tear that you'll be rich and living the easy life once someone can trace out a couple shapes properly during a full moon?" He cracked his neck and spat on the ground. "I hope you choke on those gems."

The imp scampered away. Vord rumbled with anger. Raw power rolled off him. The ground beneath his feet crackled and sizzled. The wall fractured. By the time the flare of his temper had passed, it looked as though a bizarrely precise earthquake had struck the back alley. He reined in his temper and turned to the street.

He could have mashed the imp to paste. He could have torn him to pieces. He could have seared him to his skeleton with arcane power the little scum couldn't hope to harness. But there was no point. He would be back the next day, none the worse for wear. He was as low as a creature could get, and thus nothing could bring him any lower. It was a cruel irony that those with the least to lose had the least to fear from someone like him. But then, everything was cruel here.

As he stepped out into the main thoroughfare, he cast a glance toward the Ashen Gates. They separated him from what was rightfully his. His lineage didn't matter. His power didn't matter. In this lawless place, the gate was the one rule that could not be broken. All he could do was wait.

#

Vord thumped into his home. While he was not permitted to join the other nobles on the far side of the ashen gate until his final summoning, he at least was able to make a comfortable life for himself here. Using his knowledge and power to fleece the local imps and lesser demons was a remarkably profitable enterprise. He shut the door and layered a particularly vicious ward of protection atop the myriad other curses he'd applied, then heaved open the lid of a black iron coffer. Deep trays lined the bottom, each divided into different compartments into which gems had been fastidiously sorted into size and type. He daintily plucked each ruby and dropped it into the appropriate cubby.

"Plenty for bribes, provided they ever let me through the gate."

He slammed the coffer shut and cast another potent spell of protection. With that, unless he felt inclined to find another neighborhood filled with imps not yet familiar with his particular brand of gambling, he had nothing left to do that evening. He pulled the dice from his pocket and poked at them until he found the one he'd swapped during his last throw.

"Huh… he was right. Two fives." He tossed it into a bowl beside the door. "Might come in handy."

Vord paced into his reading room. For a room in a demon lord's lair, hidden away in a land of darkness and sin, it was disarmingly cozy. The same horrid, torturous flames that crackled in irregularly spaced pits all around the city had been tamed into a tasteful little fireplace. A leather chair built to suit his hulking frame had been set before it. He

175

paced past the chair and stood before a wall of bookshelves.

He was still scanning the spines of tomes bound in unspeakable leathers when he heard a distant, distinctive sound. At first he ignored it. It had been so long since he last heard it, the sound could have been a trick of his mind. A moment later, it came again. Something like a piece of chalk dragging across an old plank of wood. He raised an eyebrow and glanced up. A pattern of baby blue lines hung in the air above him.

"Can it be?" he murmured, a terrible smile wrinkling his snout.

Another line etched out from the shape, completing the complex rune that was as near to a mortal could render of his true name. Someone was at least attempting to summon him.

Vord tried not to let his hopes get too high. This was just the first in a full *ring* of symbols, each of similar complexity. A single errant dash or point could render the entire summoning powerless and he would have to wait until another attempt. But slow care from someone in the world of light continued to work at the invocation. Like numbers on the face of a clock, the symbols traced out a circle.

"Vord. Lord of the Darklands, eight take one. Baron of the pool of black. Third of the third in the line of the throne of agony…" He read as the final few runes formed above him. "By these offerings, I give you substance. With this drop of life, I do bind my fate with yours. To do my bidding…"

His clawed talons split the stone beneath his feet as he flexed them in anticipation. He spread his wings and lashed his tail, knocking his chair to the ground.

"One more rune, you blasted mortal. Trace it out and bring me to the fate that has waited so long!"

The last rune appeared one stroke at a time. Finally, it was done.

"I summon thee!" he crowed.

The ring above him gleamed with painful brilliance. A faint glow filled the space between, until a ceiling other than his own became visible. Above, fragments of matter drew together, an earthly body for him to inhabit. The time had come. At long last he would have his final journey to the world of light. One last time he would twist the desires of a mortal to his whims. He would sow chaos and misery. And when the opportunity arose, he would use some twist of logic or some letter of the unwritten law to break his binding and return, fully empowered, to the Darklands.

The form completed itself. Flickering and indistinct as it was through the other side of the portal, he couldn't quite focus on it, but that was of little concern. The summoner had followed far more complex instructions to trace the circle. Gathering the assortment of materials necessary for his body was a comparatively simple task of fetching and scavenging.

He reached up through the portal. His claws felt horrifically cold, like he'd plunged them into icy brine. When they touched the form awaiting him, the cold was whisked away, replaced with a warmth and an almost painful tightness.

Decades of waiting had robbed him of his patience. He flexed his mighty legs and launched himself upward. The leap thrust him through the portal and subjected his whole body to the flash of cold, followed by the snug warmth of a fresh form. His senses were briefly taken from him, replaced by a cacophonous blast of new sensations his mind could make little sense of. Bit by bit, new connections within him formed. This was light. That was sound. This was touch. That was scent. New eyes focused and blinked. Unfamiliar limbs wrangled and straightened. He hauled himself to his feet.

Clumsy as he was in his newly crafted form, he refused to allow himself to totter about like a newborn foal. Somewhere around him was the person responsible for giving him flesh in this world. That person, for the time being, held sway over him. It chaffed at him to be, even briefly, an underling of any other creature. He'd spent his time as an imp. He'd been the servant of over a hundred other humans. It was important he get the relationship started on the right foot. A little intimidation should make it clear where the *true* power laid in this arrangement.

He spread his legs into a wide, powerful stance. He spread his wings and puffed out his fearsome chest.

"Foolish mortal," he roared. "You have summoned Vord, the… Vord, the… What is wrong with my voice?"

Something was off. His tone didn't have nearly the command and terror that he'd anticipated. No matter how much effort he poured into it, it sounded soft. Delicate. He blinked his eyes again and, for the first time, allowed himself to process what his eyes were telling him.

He'd been summoned into a bedroom. That alone did not bode well. His massive body should have been far too large to comfortably form inside a human dwelling. Though this dwelling *was* quite large.

The roof over his head was towering in height, like something he would have expected in a cathedral or palace. Except in a palace it would have been vaulted and ornate, not plain white. The place was decorated with gigantic mockeries of human furniture. Chairs larger than he was, built stout and painted in pastels. A bed the size of the courtyard outside his own manor stood against the wall. And then there was his master.

It was a human male, thrice his height at least. Like the furniture, the proportions seemed wrong. His head was too large, as were his eyes. His limbs were stubbier, fingers fat and grasping. Was he some manner of ogre? Some terrible giant? But those should not have existed here. He almost looked like a child, but a titanic one.

The alternative, which until now he'd not allowed himself to believe could be true, finally asserted itself in his mind. He worked his wings. Rather than the apocalyptic leathery flap that usually accompanied his flight, he was treated to a rapid, pathetic, fluttering pitter-patter. As he flitted into the air with ponderous and ungainly swoops, he saw the summoning circle from above.

"Why did you draw the circle so *small*!" he squealed.

The circle was barely two feet end to end. He, the mighty Vord, was barely the size of a housecat.

"Wow…" the little boy said.

"Answer me! Why did you draw such a tiny circle! The instructions are quite clear. You must draw the circle at a size suitable for the demon's full grandeur."

"I don't know what grandeur means," the boy said.

Vord glared at him, now at least able to hang in the air at eye level so as to avoid the indignity of looking *up* to a child.

"Grandeur means… it means *bigness* and *fanciness*," Vord translated.

"Oooooh… Well, that's all the room I had to draw anyway."

Vord looked down.

"You could have *easily* moved the little desk there and made it twice as big."

The little boy shook his head. "No, 'cause that'd wake up Dad and he's got work soon."

"I don't understand. How did you even get the bull carcass in here, and the…" Vord glanced aside.

Fluttering in the air as he was, he was level with the mirror above the colorful dresser. His reflection told a sad, sad story. Gone was the brown-black mane of stinking pelt. Now there were downy vermillion tufts. Claws that could rend flesh from bone were now blunt pink nubbins. His hirsute hide, matted with the blood and gore of his trampled foes, was fuzzy and pleasant. Eyes that burned like embers were glassy black points half-hidden under a tousled and unruly head of hair.

He felt himself with his little hands and found that he wasn't even *flesh*. He was some manner of cloth and stuffing. He was a toy. His gaze shifted to the ground again. The components of his earthly form should have been placed at precise points around the circle. Instead, stray bits of fluff and thread suggested each position had been occupied by a plush.

"You could not have… The summoning invocation was extremely clear."

"It was hard."

"I know it was hard, but… show me the tome you read this from. I will stain this pathetic maw with blood from the throat of the sage who penned it."

The little boy reached up to the dresser, which was still a shade too large for him, and groped about until he found a sheet of paper. Vord snatched it from him. At his size, handling the sheet was like wrestling with a poster. The text was faded and streaked. This wasn't the actual page from a tome. Rather it was the *image* of one, transcribed onto this page. Nevertheless, it was quite readable and quite accurate.

"Look, here! The carcass of a bull. A goblet of viper venom. A coil of thorn vine, its barbs flavored with the blood of virgins. It is all spelled out for you! And here, right here, it warns 'a terrible fate will result from the failure to provide all of the offerings precisely.' You should have known better."

"I didn't have a caucus."

"*Carcass*," he snapped.

"I didn't have that. Or the other stuff. But it worked, didn't it!"

Vord ran his petite claws through his hair and tried to steady himself. It was a well-kept secret among demons that only the runes of the summoning circle required any degree of precision. Everything else from the size to the materials from which the earthly form would be crafted were extremely flexible. The reason this secret was so well kept was for situations precisely like this one. If people knew they could invoke a mighty archfiend but render him toothless through some strategic replacements in the invocation ritual, they could have all of the power of a demon with far less risk of the demon overcoming mystic safeguards with raw force.

There were stories of imps and the like being summoned by inexperienced wizards and being forced to spend their time on earth composed of wood and stone, or with feline features thanks to the lack of suitable calves. But this… nothing like this…

Things had been worse. In ancient eras, magic was everywhere. Powerful mystics could raise a potent, and even *dangerous* defense against him. Creatures more powerful but less cautious than him had been bound to weapons and mechanisms to fuel them until freed, even in more recent years. Somewhere in California something called a light bulb had been fueled by the soul of his least favorite cousin since 1901. But even in the forties when he'd last been summoned, magic was being set aside as quackery. It meant that his kind had fewer opportunities to be summoned, but those who *were* summoned were in a world with virtually no defense against them.

If what had happened to him today had happened in the Dark Ages… He shuddered to think of where he might have ended up. But even *they* didn't end up as a toy… Even so. He had the benefit of his "master" being a child. Children were greedy monsters with simple demands. They were simple to corrupt, and lacked the cleverness to overcome even the most basic manipulation. A child's soul wasn't a terribly valuable one. Like a fine wine, a bit of age and experience tended to season a spirit sufficiently to be desirable, but it would be a simple thing to use the boy as leverage to get a more favorable soul, and that would be that.

"You have summoned me. I am bound to you, to do your bidding. What do you want, oh wise… What is your name?"

"Billy."

He grumbled. "Oh wise Billy."

"I just want a friend."

Vord dropped to the ground. He produced an undignified squeak when he landed.

"A *friend?*" Vord said. "I am not summoned to be a *friend*. I am Vord! The blood of legions stains my claws. I am not a friend! I am a *fiend*. I am your sword of vengeance. I am the woe of your foes. I am the shadow that haunts the dreams of your rivals."

Billy frowned. "You're supposed to do what I say. It said on the internet that you had to do what I say."

"What is the internet?"

"On the computer. In the library. You look things up and stuff. It's always true, most of the time."

Vord did his best to release a fearsome roar of frustration. Instead he produced buzzing grumble.

"I am bound to serve you. But *surely* you did not summon a greater demon to serve as your *friend*."

Billy nodded.

"There is *nothing* else you want?"

"Uh… I wanna play a game?"

A devilish smile flashed across Vord's temporarily adorable muzzle. This was as near to ideal as he could hope for out of a child. More souls had been lost in wagers over the outcome of games than in any other way. He still didn't want a child's soul if he could avoid it, but laying temporary claim to one was a steppingstone he could tolerate.

"I will play a game with you. What shall it be? Chess?"

It was always chess.

"Dr. Mario."

Vord's lip curled. "I don't know what that is."

"It's real, real fun!" Billy proclaimed. "I'll show you how to play, but you have to promise to be quiet, okay?"

Billy stood tapped at the button of a large brick of a piece of furniture. It took Vord some time to recognize it as something called a television. They had been rather rare when he'd last come through.

"Dad brought this TV and this game home from Mamaw's house. It was in the closet, but it still works good. You just have to blow in it sometimes. Dad played it when he was little."

"Televisions are not for playing, they are for watching."

"Shows what you know," Billy said. "TV is where you play everything. Except computers. And phones. But I don't have a computer except the one they let me use at the library. And I don't have a phone except sometimes when Dad lets me play with his, but I have to be careful."

The screen lit up with a dazzling array of eye-searing colors. It was like some manner of animated stained-glass window. A far cry from the muted blacks and silvers he remembered from televisions a scant few decades earlier.

Billy set a badly worn device with colored buttons and a wire snaking out the back end. Vord eyed it distrustfully.

"You hit this button to turn it, and you move it around like this. Stack up the colors over the little germ things to make them disappear. You need four, up and down or sideways. You gotta make them *all* disappear to finish."

Vord pressed a button. The image on the screen seemed to react.

"Curious…"

It took the demon a moment to realize that the frenetic twirling, bleeping, dropping, and blinking on half of the screen was Billy's doing. He tried to gin up the coordination necessary to match the boy's feats, but it was maddening. A tower of colors reached the top of the screen and the device proclaimed Billy to be the victor.

Vord's lips pulled back and he trembled in anger.

"You did pretty good for a first try, especially because you're so little."

Vord snapped his head in the boy's direction. "Again!"

"Sure! I told you it was fun!"

#

For an hour, Vord made steady progress. His thousands of years of life had taught him endless skills, all for the purpose of either serving or besting his masters. He could weave a rug to perfection. He could play every instrument from the pan flute to the fiddle. This vid-ee-oh game would be no different. He had only just discovered its existence, and already he had reached the point that he could clear three germs. If he was lucky. And if Billy was not lucky. Which the blasted child *always was*.

After the latest in a string of victories Vord had long since stopped keeping track of, the boy yawned.

"That was lots of fun, but it's bedtime. It's a school night."

"Another game. I demand another game!" Vord squealed.

"Tomorrow," Billy turned off the TV and the game. "Come on."

"Where would you have the—*yeek!*"

The boy scooped the demon up like some manner of overfed housecat and tottered over to bed. He threw Vord onto the mattress of what was clearly a bed intended for an adult and scrambled up after him.

"Now listen, Billy. You have invoked the ritual, and thus I am bound to serve you, but I absolutely will *not* have you—"

The boy threw an arm around his tiny form, compacting his plush body with a playful squeak. He madly slashed and gnawed at the arm pulled tight around him, but his blunt claws and smooth teeth did little good.

"Good night, Vord."

Billy clicked off the lamp beside the bed and did something which had not, in the entirety of the untold centuries of their dealings with the human race, ever occurred to a demon. He snuggled him.

As the boy drifted blissfully to sleep, Vord simmered with fury and set his mind to the task of concocting some wretched punishment that he could inflict upon the mortal world to make up for this injustice.

#

The next morning, Vord was standing on the center of the kitchen table while the boy poured sugary nuggets into a bowl and doused them in milk.

"Do you eat?" the boy said.

"You saw fit to craft this vessel from cloth and stuffing. I have no use or desire for mortal food in the best of times. In this form, I lack even the anatomy to process it."

"Well, that'll be easy," Billy said. "You're coming to school today. It's show and tell. But you have to pretend to just be a toy, okay? Probably it's against the rules to bring demons. It's a Catholic school."

"As you command." He peered about. "Aren't there usually parents or servants to take care of children?"

"Dad is at work. I take the bus. He picks me up at the bus stop after, though. You can't let him know you're a demon either. He's the one who *put me* in Catholic school."

Vord clacked the claws of his talons against the table and crossed his arms. Rebellion against a strict religious upbringing. That could be useful.

"And your mother?"

"I only see her every other weekend. You can't tell her you're a—"

"I shall take it as a given that my demonic origins should be kept secret."

Billy made short work of his cereal and placed the bowl in the sink.

"So what is required of me for this 'show and tell'?"

"Just hold real still, like a regular plush. You're super cool looking, so everyone should love the showing part, and then for the telling I can just talk about how you were this great gift from my Papaw. Could you help clear the table? The bus will be here soon."

Vord sighed. "As you wish, Master."

He fluttered his wings and snatched up the cereal box, buzzing madly until he was able to lift it from the table and deliver it to the appropriate shelf.

"Thanks!" Billy snatched Vord by the tail and stuffed him into a satchel. "This is going to be so cool. Everyone just shows videos and memes and stuff during show and tell."

#

As infuriating as it was to be stuffed into a bag next to a banana and something called Lunchables, it at least gave him the opportunity to silently observe and plot. The amount of technological progress since his last trip was impressive. He'd had little to do with children in his prior visits, but it struck him as odd that they were routinely gathered together onto vehicles where they outnumbered the adults dozens to one. Were things to be done similarly where he came from, the adult in charge wouldn't survive more than three such trips.

Most children were two to a seat, but Billy was alone. That he had a mildly hopeful look as each new person approached and a highly disappointed look as each one passed suggested Billy would have preferred company if he could get it. Coupled with the largely solitary home life, it was beginning to trace out a pattern.

"I think I understand why he would summon a demon for companionship," Vord murmured to himself. "But I wonder why he needed to. He is no more detestable than any of these other children."

For a few hours, he peered out of the pouch of the satchel and watched as the children were educated with surprisingly complex mathematical, scientific, and linguistic concepts. They were also given a dose of unsurprisingly inaccurate history. It seemed human society had continued its habit of redefining past events to suit their whims every few decades.

Finally, the event for which Vord had been toted along came. The children mostly mashed their filthy fingers against what the demon would have identified as a typewriter sitting in front of a broken television, but had apparently now come to be called a computer. They summoned various inane recordings and talked about why they liked them. The reasons were seldom convincing, and appeared to hinge upon randomness more than anything else. Then it was Billy's turn.

Vord gritted his soft teeth and waited to be pulled from the bag.

He released his control over his limbs. They popped to a neutral position as he prepared for quite possibly the most humiliating moment of his immortal existence.

"This is my new plushie! His name is Vord and he's a…" Billy paused and looked at the demon critically for the first time. "Sort of a goat… lion… bird… bat."

"You still play with *dolls?*" scoffed a boy from the front row.

Vord fixed his eyes on the boy, not that it would be evident that the black, glassy orbs were even capable of focusing to an outside observer.

"Daniel, behave," the teacher instructed, with predictable results.

"It's not even a Pokémon. It just a dumb knockoff. What a nerd."

"Daniel, that's enough!" the teacher said with the sort of authority that probably should have been applied after the first comment.

There was further reprimand, but Vord couldn't bring himself to pay attention to it. He was too busy seething with anger. It wasn't that the boy had insulted his appearance. That much was a point of agreement. The fury he felt was, for some reason, entirely stoked by the hurtful words aimed at Billy.

He remained stationary, as ordered, but the voice and face of the boy was seared into his memory. Billy hugged Vord tightly.

"And. And… He's… I guess that's it," Billy said, heroically holding back tears. "I'm done. Can I use the bathroom now?"

"Go ahead, Billy."

The boy squeezed Vord tighter and scurried off. The demon could already feel the boy shuddering his way through the early tremors of a sobbing fit. He reached the solitude of a bathroom stall and released Vord so that he could more effectively devote himself to the full-body process that weeping tended to be for children.

Vord fluttered his wings swiftly enough to keep himself from touching the floor and absorbing something unspeakable from the tiles. Billy sobbed openly for a minute or two, then slowly started to recover. When the episode had reduced to a series of gasping, involuntary sniffles, Vord fluttered up to him.

"Are you through. Can you speak now?"

Billy wiped his nose and nodded.

"Does that boy do this often?" Vord asked.

"All the time," Billy said.

Vord flitted up to the boy's face. "How many *pieces* do you want him in?"

"Wha… NO! No, you can't hurt him."

"You haven't made it *easy* for me, but I assure you, have all manner of methods available to me to extract the precise amount of suffering you desire."

"I don't want you hurt him."

"I can *guarantee* you he will never be cruel to you again."

"Dad says if you hurt the people who hurt you, that's just two people getting hurt instead of one," Billy said.

"I see." He buzzed back and forth. "I don't suppose your mother had an opposing view."

"No. She feels the same way."

Vord tightened his claws into fists. "A great deal of work has been put into poisoning the minds of humanity with hatred and pettiness, and I am sorely disappointed that you somehow ended up with two parents who have escaped our machinations."

"What?"

"Nothing. What do you want me to do?"

"Just don't hurt anybody."

Vord trembled. It felt like he was a tea kettle too stopped up to release its steam. The pressure continued to build and this blasted opposite-of-a-brat refused to allow him to release it.

"Define 'hurt.'"

"Just don't hit him or kill him or anything."

A horrifying grin curled Vord's cute little muzzle.

"As you wish, Master."

#

Billy stuffed Vord back into the pouch and returned to his seat. The stuffed animal waited until all attention had been turned to the next "show" of the endless parade of inanity. When they were suitably distracted, Vord called upon his demonic power for the first time since he'd been summoned. Without a hulking, physics-defying form to animate, he had a considerable surplus of power available to him. It was a simple matter to render himself invisible. He crawled from the pouch and tapped lightly along the floor until he reached Daniel's desk.

With slow motions to avoid detection, he climbed up the back and peered at the boy's head. The thoughts of mortals were horribly complex and difficult to sort out. There were some demons capable of reading minds, but he'd never developed the knack. Fears, however. They were never far from the surface, and crystal clear to even the most untrained intuition. Daniel had no shortage of them. Lurking beneath the abrasive exterior of every bully was a frightened, anxious ball of misery. Daniel had a smorgasbord of poorly hidden terror.

There were many, many ways he could reduce this boy to a quivering mass of fear and regret. But Billy was a sharp boy. Were the vengeance *too* obvious, he would notice. Anything that fell short of injury or death was allowable by the current criteria, but were he to do something that Billy would realize was his doing, the leash would surely pull tighter.

Vord made a few choice selections from the churning fears, then huddled in the little shelf beneath the boy's seat and wove at the air with his invisible claws. Threads of gossamer will streaked from his digits, as though he was scratching the very fabric of existence. The pattern he crafted in the air resembled some sort of dark mockery of a dreamcatcher. When it was crafted, incorporating as many of the pieces of nightmare fuel as he could assemble, he climbed back up and draped it like a cobweb over the boy's head. It faded down, sinking into his psyche. Satisfied, Vord made his way back to the pouch of Billy's bag and allowed the veil of invisibility to drop. When next the boy slept, he was in for a tremendous comeuppance.

For a few seconds, he basked in the warmth of his action. All too soon, his meticulous mind wiped its hands of the recent accomplishment and turned to the task of unraveling his motivation for it.

"Why… why *did* I do that? The boy deserved it, but since when does that matter? I could have simply sat here and far more effectively followed the orders I was given. Is it… Is it that I was summoned specifically to be a friend? Surely the invocation would have to be altered to make a change *that* fundamental…"

He grappled with the riddle, carefully ignoring the handful of possibilities that centered on softheartedness. True or not, embracing even the *notion* of such a thing would be ruinous for his reputation when he inevitably returned to the Darklands. Eventually he set the riddle aside and focused on the far more familiar pastime of stewing in fury over having to endure this horrid existence. Anger was a far more comfortable state of mind than uncertainty for a demon.

Slowly, beneath the pleasant layer of simmering fury, a thought subtle enough to slip past his vigilant watch for positive thoughts smoldered. When school was through, and they were back home, perhaps the boy would decree that they would return to the video game.

That would be fun.

Joseph R. Lallo

The Tale of
Amberbelly

The Tale of Amberbelly

A few years ago, I watched a video on the internet that made me laugh. A year or so later, I was telling Fable, one of my illustrators, the anecdote from the video. Fable suggested I write a story from the opposite point of view from the anecdote. And so I did.

Joseph R. Lallo

"Tell us again! Tell us again, Grampa!" cried eager voices.

He was tired. His muscles were stiff. He'd eaten his fill and what he wanted, more than anything else, was to sleep. But it was so hard to say not to those excited little faces. Faces so like his own back when the tale they were asking for began. He hobbled forward.

"Very well. Just once more. Gather 'round. Gather 'round," he said.

They huddled close around him in the warmth and darkness of the shelter. He shut his eyes to bring the events once more to his mind.

#

It was here. Quite near here, at least. Just outside. I was young. Hungry. It was winter. I'd stored more than enough food to last me, but weather isn't always so obliging. The snow was thick, and getting thicker. It was that terrible mix of snow and rain. The sort that sticks the hair, weighs it down. Freezes into a thick crust on the stuff still on the ground. Can't get through it. I thought I was done for. But then I saw them. It was the first I'd seen of them. The first any of us had seen of them. The silos.

Imagine how it must have seemed. My belly was empty. My feet were freezing. And then salvation was dangling above my head, glorious and brimming with more grain than I'd ever seen. I didn't know why they were in the sky. I didn't know why they were clear. Perhaps to taunt me with their hearty contents. But it didn't matter. It was food, and I meant to have it.

You would have laughed to see me in those first attempts. I tried everything that we tell you *not* to try now. I tried to climb up the pole. It was far too thin, far too slippery, and far too cold. But that didn't stop me. I would haul myself up. Sometimes halfway. Sometimes nearly to the top, but always I would slip and down I'd go, back to the snow and ice. I tried for too long. Tried until I was numb. But I just couldn't make it.

Not from below, anyway.

I feel certain now that the food was hung there, hung in a place where someone would need to *fly* to earn it, for a reason. It was placed there as a test. As a reward for someone with the cunning, the boldness, or perhaps just the desperation to prove himself.

If only those who could fly could have this food, then I would fly.

I climbed the tree. Higher and higher. Whoever had placed those silos was clever. They'd placed them far from the tree. I'm sure they believed they'd placed them far enough that no one could reach them even from its thinnest branches. But up I climbed higher than the silos. And then out onto the branches until I was afraid they wouldn't hold my weight. It was still a long way to the silo. Worse. It was about this time the little winged devils came to start eating from the silo. They always got the best food. And just as the silo was built to confound me, they were built to cater to them. Quite literally. Pleasant little perches mounted below little holes, perfect for them to land, have a feed, and leave while I sat starving.

But not today.

I tensed myself, planted my feet, and hurled myself. I spread my limbs, kept my eyes on the silo. Those greedy winged beasts saw me coming. They hooted and hollered, scattering. The silo rocked and swung. I reached out, flailing, and just barely managed to catch the edge of the silo. My grip wasn't strong enough. I slipped and flipped end over end to crunch through the crusty snow. But the attempt wasn't a fruitless one. A precious little cascade of grain rained down over me. I scrambled to my feet and gathered it up. It wasn't much, but it was more than I'd eaten all day. Once I felt that precious food slide into my belly, it gave me the strength and motivation to continue.

Hours passed. I tried it in all different ways. Higher branches. Lower, thicker branches. I tried running first, swinging first. Again and again and again I bashed into the silo, got a fresh sprinkle of grain, and tried again. Maybe if I was someone else, I would have given up. But it wasn't just about survival now. It was about pride. I wouldn't let this one little trial stop me.

By now, you all know what I should have done, how I should have done it. But this was long ago. This was the day I learned it. There was no magic tactic. No one thing that bridged the gap between how far I *could* jump and how far I *needed* to jump. It was a combination of balance, of timing, and of strength. But that final leap brought me to the edge of the silo. I grabbed tight, hauled myself up, and reached inside.

Oh, how I feasted that day. Never had I had such a meal, dangling below the silo, stuffing my mouth with the finest grain. I ate until my belly was heavy with food. I ate until I feared I would *burst*. And then— like now, I might add—all I wanted to do was sleep. Maybe I'd spoiled myself with the luxury of such fine food, but I decided that huddling down in the cold and wet simply wouldn't do for me. Not anymore. I turned my eyes to the great structure.

I'd seen it there all my life. It and a dozen other things like it. Taller than the trees. Walls straighter and flatter than anything ought to be. But as I watched the snow pile on the roof, I knew that somewhere inside was warmth and safety. And if I could prove my worth in the trial of the silo, then surely that warmth and safety were within my grasp.

It took mere minutes. Scaling the wall was simple enough. And testing around the edge where the overhanging roof met the wall eventually revealed a weak spot that could be pulled aside. I squeezed through and basked in the warmth and darkness of this very room. The one that has kept our family safe for ages.

But the tale does not end there. Oh no. It seemed the Great Ones had more trials for me. I'd not yet proven my worth. I'd not yet earned my name.

For a few weeks, life was a paradise. The silos were inexhaustible. When I became hungry, I would slip out of my shelter, climb the tree, and leap to them for a meal. In time, I was able to reach them on my very first leap. And when the time came to sleep, back through the gap, back into the shelter. Glorious.

But one day, when I returned to the shelter, I found something else. Something terrible and yet fascinating. It was fashioned of the same smooth, cold stuff that formed the pole for the silo. But this time the form was so much more complex. A grid of the stuff, arranged into something of a box. There were pivots, latches, all manner of things I should have known to avoid. But I was blinded by what waited for me within.

A glob of food that smelled so heavenly, so decadent. It was fatty and nutty and sweet and oily. A mouthful of that stuff could keep me nourished for days. I was entranced by the scent. I couldn't pull myself away.

I thought I had moved with caution as I slipped inside. Closer and closer I inched. But alas, though I was clever, I was not more clever than the Great Ones. The floor moved beneath my feat. A heavy door swung shut behind me and I was locked inside. No amount of pulling, prying, or gnawing would budge the door even the slightest bit. I was trapped, a victim of my own greed.

As if they had been watching, a great, terrible light appeared from the ground in the corner of my shelter. I cowered as a form approached in the darkness. So massive, dozens of times my height. Alien in form, its body draped in odd colors and patterns. He grasped the top of what I now knew was a cage and lifted it, with me inside. I didn't know what would become of me. The visions of what followed are still a blur. I was carried through a place bright as day despite the late hour. There were flickering images. Colors I'd never seen anywhere else.

I was briefly taken to the outside, then I was brought to… one of *them*. Those things we dare not name, for fear that they may be summoned. Great, lumbering behemoths that trample us beneath their black feet. Things so large, that move so swiftly. I was placed *inside* of it. The thing roared to life. I could feel it moving. And then… redemption?

The Great One pulled me from within the horrid thing. He placed my cage upon the ground and, to my relief and astonishment, it raised the door. Ran for my freedom, for my *life*. And only when I was clear of the Great One, of the cage, and of the thing that we shall not name did I take a moment to learn what had become of me.

What surrounded me seemed like a paradise. There were great trees all around. Even with the snow on the ground, I could see places where the green grass peeked through. And there were so many like you or me there. Running around. Well fed. Content.

I could have been happy there. I *should* have been happy there. But my thoughts turned to the silo, to the shelter. In that place, I had everything I needed. That place was my home. I had *made* it my home. I refused to start over in this new place. I would have it back. As the unnamed behemoth roared away on the endless black expanse, I knew I had to follow.

The journey was arduous. There were many great structures. The all seemed so similar. But my nose was sensitive, my mind was cunning. I wouldn't be fooled by the pretenders. What had taken minutes in the belly of that beast took until morning. But finally I came upon it. Finally found the silos once more, still brimming with their treasures. I restored my strength and returned to the shelter. The cage was gone. I had passed another test.

The weeks to follow began what we've come to call "the great game." If I moved with caution. If I ate sparingly and kept from sight, I was permitted to remain. The silos would replenish, the shelter would remain mine alone. But if I made too much noise, if I ate too greedily, the cage would return. The glorious substance hidden within was always irresistible. Then, the slam of the door, a return to the nameless thing and freedom in some new place.

The second time, the place was more frightening, a place of loud noises, of many Great Ones. The third time, it was a place with different trees, different grass. And each time, the road home was perilous. But I returned in triumph each time. I lost track of how often it had happened. Twenty times? Thirty times? It didn't matter. I saw it for what it was. This place, this precious shelter with its endless food, it was not a place for the unworthy. I had to prove myself, again and again. And if that was the price, then I would pay it.

Time passed. The seasons changed. One final time, the cage appeared. I didn't even fight its call anymore. I understood my place, understood that the time had once again come to show I deserved my place within the great structure, and to pay tribute to the Great Ones for the bounty they provided. But this time… this time it was different. This time even before I was thrown into the belly of the monster, the Great One opened the door. With a speed and strength I couldn't imagine, it grasped me, held me up until my belly was exposed. I struggled, but there was no use. It was too strong, too large.

I blinked in the terrible light. Something rattled. And then, the great marking. A terrible, searing stench belched forth. Something with an unnatural cold blanketed my belly. I was thrown roughly into the cage, and the cage thrown inside the nameless thing. As it rumbled on yet another journey, I coughed and wheezed at the terrible stench and looked at what had become of me. My belly had been stained with an amber color, brighter than the peel of a lemon. I tried to scrape it away, but it clung to me.

I was dumped into the noisy place, the terrifying place that I sometimes found myself during such a trial. As terrifying as this place was, it was at least familiar now. I knew the way back. I dashed for all I was worth, bounding and jumping. Minutes of travel within the terrible thing had taken me there. It took mere minutes to return again. And when I did, I froze. The Great One was emerging from the unnamed monster. Its eyes settled upon me. I saw something in its face. Perhaps disbelief? No. It was respect. The Great One watched as I scaled the wall. Watched as I slipped back into my shelter.

And that was the final time the cage returned. I had done it. I had once and for all proved my worth. The yellow that painted my belly was not a punishment. It was a badge. An honor bestowed upon me, labeling me once and for all as the one who had proved himself. The one who had earned a place in this shelter.

I was Amberbelly.

###

"Johnny, Johnny, you gotta tell the story," Tony said.

"Come on, I'm sick of tellin' the story."

"You gotta, Debora ain't heard it yet."

He rubbed his head through his thinning hair. "All right, all right. Fine. But just one more time.

"So I just moved in. First time I ever had a house with a yard, you know? And I wanted to do all the suburb stuff. I bought some bird feeders, I kept my lawn nice, the works. And every morning I'd sit in the breakfast nook or whatever the wife calls it and watch the goofy squirrels bouncin' off the feeder. We hung 'em from one of those poles, right? The ones that go up and over? And the little guy's'd just slide down the pole or jump off the tree and go wangin' off the side. Funny stuff.

"Anyway, a couple weeks later I started hearin' stuff up in the attic. Turns out one of the squirrels got in. So I bought one of those traps, you know? I put a bunch of peanut butter in it because that's what my cousin said they'd go for and, bam, caught the little guy.

"I didn't want to kill 'em, you know? That's what Lou would do, but screw him. So I threw the thing in the car and drove 'em down to the park, let 'em go. A couple days later, boom. More scratchin' in the attic. So I set the trap up again, more peanut butter, caught another squirrel. Took this one down by the boardwalk. You know, don't want people givin' me a hard time for dumpin' all my squirrels near their houses. Mix it up, you know?

"So this keeps happin'. Sometimes a couple times a month, sometimes a couple times a week. I catch a squirrel, drop him of somewhere out of the way, and that's that. Now, about this time I'm thinkin', 'Jeez, if this keeps up I'm gonna run out of squirrels.' And I got to a cookout with, whatchacallit… Danny from up the way. And I start tellin' him what I been doin' and how I been catchin' all these squirrels and he just starts laughin'. 'You dummy,' he says. 'Squirrels ain't dumb. They know their way around. You drop them off someplace, they'll just come back. You probably been catchin' the same couple over and over.'

"Now me? I'm sure that ain't so. But Danny ain't an idiot, so I figured, make sure. I grabbed that can of that ugly yellow spray paint, from when we made the cornhole boards, and I grabbed the squirrel and sprayed his belly before I dropped him off again. The way I figure it, if I see a yellow-belly squirrel floatin' around the neighborhood, I know Danny's right.

"Well, wouldn't you know it? I'm not home five minutes and I spot the little guy. Same one I just caught. He's lookin' right at me. Now either someone else is paintin' squirrels, or this little guy beat me home."

His guests laughed.

"And tell her the rest!"

He shook his head. "Fine. So I figure, if I been drivin' this dumb squirrel all around town, basically givin' him a field trip or vacation or somethin', all it's doin' is annoyin' me and annoyin' him. So I thought, screw it. What's one squirrel. I just let the sucker live in the attic. The way I figure it, he'll keep the other guys out."

"And did he?"

"No! There's a whole family of them up there. But they ain't doin' no damage, so let 'em."

"You're a real weirdo, Johnny."

"Trust me, I know."

BOOK ONE
WEIRD NOTHING
Joseph Lallo / Adam J Hall
DANGER
AUTHOR
PERSONNEL
HUG
DEA
© JOSEPH LALLO & ADAM J HALL
WEIRDNOTHING.COM

Weird Nothing

Many years ago, an artist named Adam J. Hall enjoyed the *Book of Deacon* and did some fan art for me. I loved it, and ended up commissioning him for some promo art, some character design, and some stuff just for me. After a while, he asked if I was interested in collaborating on a web comic. He showed me a pair of characters he'd drawn recently, and I spent a weekend jotting down what sort of a story I'd tell about them. We honed it a little, and I wrote the story. For about two years, the webcomic was released periodically under the name *Weird Nothing.*

As tends to happen when an artist is particularly talented and motivated, Adam started having more of a work commitment than he could manage while still keeping the comic active. He turned the story back over to me and gave me his blessings to make something of it. As the January Patreon release date approached, I decided it might be time to give it the novella treatment.

I tried to keep the story and some of its more unique gags intact. Because it was originally supposed to be visual, there were a handful of events in which a visual action would be taking place simultaneously with dialogue. Since this doesn't work in text, some of them had to be lightly rewritten. I also like to keep my stories in third-person limited perspective, where any given scene gives insight only into the things a single character might know or see. However, in the comic, there were a few instances where characters would leave and the "camera" would linger on other characters for the purposes of a reaction shot. In order to include those, you might notice a strange perspective shift in some scenes. The final lingering side effect of its origins as a comic script are the non-dialogue passages. Because describing the scene or characters with any sort of flavor isn't terribly important when there will be an illustration, a fair amount of the action and set dressing description was very dry. I jazzed it up a bit, but you'll probably find the prose a little more straightforward in some places.

This was a fun story to write, and I'm happy the world at large will finally get to see it in full. If I had it to do over, I'd probably try to structure it to have more narrative reward more quickly, so that we'd get into the meat of the story after just a few weeks instead of a few months. But regardless, I hope you like it!

Volume 1

Ray clacked the buttons on his handheld and entered the final level of his game. He'd started the trip by downloading a fresh new metroidvania. Now he had only the final boss to go and they weren't there yet. It had been that kind of trip.

The SUV swooped along the mountain road at a ruthlessly conservative speed. Despite the "best in class storage space" that had inspired his father to purchase it, it was both loaded down and loaded up with the necessities that they couldn't part with long enough for the moving company to handle them. Matching luggage formed a well-engineered and securely strapped tower on the roof. Ray's dad, in all of his bespectacled, professorial glory, drummed at the wheel and listened to the droning voice of public radio as it fought to get through the mountains. Ray's mom had a paper map open and was pleasantly marking down their progress with a red Sharpie despite the fact they had a GPS. She claimed this 'made it feel like an adventure.' Ray was nine years old and even *he* thought that was childish.

He picked up the fast food cups that were populating the six cup holders (also best in class) that he could reach from his seat. Finally he found one with some soda left and gave it a slurp. Despite loving sugar water and grease for any meal he had any control over, Ray remained rail thin and so similar to his father he may as well have been a prototype. Knowing the face glancing at him in the rear-view mirror was what he could expect from adulthood didn't improve the boy's sulky mood.

"We're nearly there, son," said his father.

Ray didn't look up. The missile pickup hidden in the floor of the level demanded his attention.

"You've been pretty quiet, kiddo."

"I'm in mourning. Yesterday was my last day as a part of the civilized world. We're moving to the woods."

His father raised an eyebrow. "I think that's a little overdramatic."

"Are there more trees than people?"

"Well, it's famous for its forest, so—"

"Then it's the wilderness. Is there a late-night taco place that delivers? What if I want a chimichanga at one am?"

"Probably not, but—

"No place without midnight fast food counts as civilization. Period. I'm surprised my cellphone even works. Even if it *is only 3G*."

His father sighed. "This is a great opportunity for the whole family! Your mother and I both got great jobs at the college. And it's safer. Back in the city there were criminals walking the streets.

"Yeah. Now we've got bears. Big improvement, Dad."

"You'll have a chance to make new friends."

"If I wanted friends, I would have made them at my old school."

"Raymond, someday you're going to realize life is a lot easier when you have someone you can rely on. On that day, you'll be glad you listened to your old Dad, right kiddo? … Ray?"

A pair of earbuds was shielding Ray from any further parental wisdom.

"Aren't we a few years early for the moody teenager phase?"

"He was always a gifted boy, dear. Skipped two years of classes, remember."

"Apparently he skipped childhood, too."

#

The SUV crested over a hill, revealing a scenic vista below. Flanked by pine trees was an idyllic little town. Scattered two-story houses formed neat little rows, all roughly identical except for colors and the tiny touches the average homeowner adds to a house before giving up and sticking a lawn gnome next to the sprinkler head. Each was surrounded by a sprawling lawn and ringed with a white picket fence. At the center of the town was a cross street with small Mom and Pop stores, a theater, and assorted other small-town conveniences. The whole place had the *Edward Scissorhands* feel of a town built by a committee following a template labeled "wholesome neighborhood." Beyond it was a strip of forest and a single, towering, slate-blue mountain with a fenced-off military base nestled against it.

"Well, here's the town," Ray's dad reached back to nudge him. "Take those ear buds out, we're almost there. Wait until you see the house!"

"Let me guess, it looks a lot like that one. Or that one. Or that one," Ray said.

They pulled up to the driveway of a house that was distinguishable from the others primarily due to the "For Sale" sign with the word "Sold" plastered across the front.

"And look at this! The neighbors are here to greet us. Wait'll you meet them, they're a great bunch," his dad said.

The father got out to shake hands with a portly and jovial gentleman waiting to greet them. Ray stayed behind in the car with his game system.

"... And wait until you meet his son," his dad said.

Ray was rattled out of his game-induced stupor by what sounded like a raw pork chop slapping against the window. He looked up and was startled by the face of a chubby little boy smooshed against the window.

"Gah!" Ray yelped.

"Are you my new neighbor?" the boy mumbled gleefully.

Ray turned his head aside, looking askance at the over-enthusiastic stranger.

"I sure hope not," he said.

The boy opened the door and held out his hand.

"Pleased to meet ya, neighbor. I'm Lewis. Lewis Banks. What's your name?" he said.

Ray gave the offered hand the same look he would have given a moldy hunk of cheese thrust in his direction."

"Raymond Niven," he said.

"Hiya, Ray!"

"Raymond," he corrected.

"I'm gonna show you around town, okay, Ray?"

"Raymond. And I don't really want to. I've got to set up my computer, so—"

"Hey, Dad, can I show Ray around town?" Lewis shouted.

"Fine with me!" Mr. Banks turned to Ray's father. "How about you?"

"But I don't really want to. I've got to check my—" Ray objected.

"Sure," his dad said. "It'll keep you busy while we unload the stuff. School starts tomorrow. It'll be good to spend some time outside."

"But I really don't want to! My desk is—"

"Come on!" Lewis proclaimed. "All the cool stuff's this way."

Lewis marched down the street. Ray paused and looked around.

"... I *am* talking right now, right? People can hear me, right? ... Fine."

\#

The boys made their way through the main street of town. Lewis marched ahead of Ray with the air of a tour guide.

"So this is the town center," he said with a magisterial spread of his arms.

Ray gave the meager street a doubtful look. "How can you tell?"

"Well, look at it! All of the really great stuff is here. Over there's Miss Smith's candy store. That's Mr. Wilson's theater. There's the church."

"What kind of church?"

"The regular kind. Across the street is the O'Malley bookstore. The market is next to that. That belongs to Mr. Richards. Here's Mr. Middleton's record store."

Ray squinted through the window. "Your record store has actual *records* in it."

"Dad says he managed to not sell anything just long enough to be able to stick the word 'vintage' on the sign and 'bilk hipsters.' So what do you think of the town? Pretty neat, huh?"

"It's… wholesome. Like living in a big bowl of oatmeal. Just a big bland mushy blah."

"Oh, yeah?" He crossed his arms and glanced about in a minor panic, seeking something impressive. "Well, check this out!"

He rushed down an alley to a parking lot behind the record store. A safety railing blocked off a steep hill that led down into a belt of pine trees. Just visible on the other side was a dilapidated set of barracks and a large office-type building with the word *laboratory* just visible.

"Wow. What is that place?" Ray said, genuinely interested for the first time in the tour.

"Hah! I knew that'd get you." Lewis cocked his head triumphantly. "That's the abandoned army base and lab. Morningvale was built for fighting the Russians in World War III."

"And then it didn't happen. So this is a leftover from the fifties. One giant anachronism."

"So it's… like… a big spider with bad eyesight?"

Ray stood in dumbfounded silence for a moment, hoping for some sort of indication this was a joke.

"No. Anyway. I guess that's kinda cool. I bet it's full of scientific instruments and stuff. Can we go check it out?"

"Well, I don't know if we can *go* there. It's kind of—"

Ray smirked and nodded, fully expecting the excuse.

"It's, it's kind of," Lewis stammered. "Kind of my Grandpa's thing! He'd know how to get in there. Come on!"

#

After enough running to get both boys huffing and puffing in the thin mountain air, Ray and Lewis reached their houses. Lewis waved at his dad, who was helping Mr. Niven carry the last of the boxes from the back of the SUV.

"I'm taking Ray to meet Grampa. He wants to hear about the old army base," Lewis said.

"That's fine, son. He's on the back porch like always. Just don't get him too worked up," his father said.

"And don't be too long, kiddo. The pizzas will be here in ten minutes for lunch," Ray's dad added.

They swung around the side of the house and headed toward the back. As they approached, Lewis slowed Ray down.

"Oh, uh. Listen. A few things you should know about my Grampa..."

Ray gave him a wary look. "Okay…"

"First, everybody just calls him Colonel. He was a big shot at the base back when it was still running."

"I figured that much, since you said he'd know about it."

"He… kinda flips back thinking he's still in charge. Sometimes two or three times in the same sentence."

"Okay, that's a little—"

"Also, don't say anything communist… whatever that is."

"Uh…"

"Oh, and uh, don't mind the helmet, and the gun isn't loaded. Come on!"

"Helmet? Wait, what gun!"

Ray hurried to catch up with Lewis as he disappeared around the back of the house. There he found an old man in a rocking chair. He was easily in his eighties, and the definition of grizzled. He wore a faded dress uniform, laden with various medals and badges of service, though from the look of them, a handful were crudely made duplicates, likely swapped in so that the more valuable ornaments didn't get lost or damaged. The steel combat helmet he wore, however, was real. As was the sidearm conspicuously holstered at his belt. He had an old ammo crate with a lemonade resting on top beside him and had an expression like he was trying to decide if it was worth the trouble to get up from the chair to get some antacids.

"Hi, Colonel!" said Lewis.

"Private," the old man acknowledged.

"I brought my friend."

The Colonel leaned forward to squint at Ray.

"A bit scrawny for a new recruit," he assessed.

Lewis continued as though this was a perfectly acceptable greeting. "His name is Ray. He wants to know about your old army base."

"Ugh. Don't get me started on that place. Gone completely downhill. No discipline, that's the problem."

"Lewis tells me that there was a laboratory on the base," Ray said.

"The lab? Just a bunch of college boys, eggheads, and pencil pushers. Nothing a green recruit needs to know about."

"What did they work on?" Ray asked.

"Classified projects. Strategic, Tactical, and Advanced Technology. Called themselves the Cobalt Ridge STAT Lab. Waste of time if you ask me."

Lewis rolled his eyes and whispered to Ray. "Here we go…"

"We came out of dubya dubya two with everything we needed to win any war we wanted."

Lewis joined in with a sing-song cadence.

"The best men, the best guns, and the bomb," they said in harmony.

The Colonel continued: "The rest is just smoke and mirrors. No wonder they had me lock it all down way back when."

Ray perked up. "So you were one of the ones who helped shut it down?"

"Not a whole lot of folks with the clearance to do it."

"Do you still have the keys?"

The Colonel twisted his head and half-snarled. "You ask an awful lot of questions for a new recruit. Has this man been thoroughly checked, Private? Are we sure he's not a commie?"

"Sure, Colonel. We checked him out," Lewis said.

"Prove it. Who won the '62 World Series?" the Colonel snapped.

"How should I know?" Ray replied.

"Hah! I knew you were a commie! Get this red out of here before he learns any state secrets!" he barked.

Lewis fired off a crisp salute.

"Yes, sir, Colonel!" He leaned close to Ray. "Come on, we'll try again tomorrow. He won't remember you."

Back around the side of the house, Lewis dusted off his hands.

"Well, that's that, I guess."

"Your Grampa is crazy," Ray said.

"He's not *crazy* crazy. A little bit of the cheese slid off his cracker is all."

"You think he really still has the keys?"

"Oh, sure. He never gets rid of anything."

Ray pulled out his smartphone.

"Then let me borrow your hat, I have an idea."

After a quick bit of research, Ray donned the cap, pocketed his glassed, and trotted to the back of the house.

"New drill sergeant reporting for duty, Colonel!" Ray said with regimental enthusiasm.

"It is about time they brought in a new drill sergeant. Been ages since I saw anyone running any drills."

"I just need the keys so I can, um… inspect their footlockers for… donuts, then insult people if I find any."

The Colonel set aside his lemonade and popped the top of the ammo box.

"Of course. Get to it, soldier."

He revealed the keys and motioned to hand them over, but before Ray could grab them he paused.

"Wait… you aren't a commie are—"

"The Yankees won the 1962 World Series in seven games against the San Francisco Giants. On a score from third by Bill Skowron," he rattled off.

The Colonel tossed him the keys, a tear in his eye.

"There may be hope for this fighting force yet. Make Uncle Sam proud, son."

Ray saluted and walked back around the corner of the house, handing over Lewis's hat and twirling the keys on one finger.

"It's a good thing they didn't have Wikipedia during the Cold War or democracy would have been doomed," he mused.

Ray's father shouted from the front porch. "Ray! Pizza's here! Come get something to eat and you can play with your friend later."

"Great timing, Dad," he muttered. "Lewis, do you know the best way to that lab?"

"Of course!"

"Okay, well, here are the keys. After lunch I'll be back and we'll go check it out."

"Uh... I'm not sure I'll be able to get permission from my dad to actually *go* there."

"Then don't tell him we're going there. Just say we're hiking or something."

"Oh. Like a *secret* adventure. Sure!"

Ray walked away. Lewis lingered behind. He was able to keep his cool for a moment. When he was sure Lewis couldn't see, his face twisted with barely contained glee.

"Dad! I've got a play date! Quick, I need my cool T-shirt!"

#

After what apparently passed for a pizza in this part of the country, Ray walked out of his house.

"Bye-bye, honey! Have fun!" his mom called from inside.

"Bye, Mom and Dad. I'll be back in a few hours!" he called over his shoulder.

When he turned to see where he was going, he nearly ran into Lewis. The other nine-year-old was literally bouncing in place, an almost demented level of excitement on his face. He dressed as though he was going to go on an expedition. He had a fisherman's vest, oversized enough to be his father's. It was composed almost entirely of pockets and pouches, each stuffed to capacity. A tool belt, also heavily loaded with doodads, was more likely to pull down his pants than hold them up. He had a large butterfly net propped against one shoulder like a rifle, and a comically oversized ancient flashbulb camera hung around his neck. Evidently the assorted cargo garments weren't nearly enough to carry all his gear, because he had an overstuffed pack on his back as well. The vest was open and the camera was conspicuously pushed aside to proudly display his t-shirt, which featured a dog wearing sunglasses.

"You ready to go? I'm ready to go! You ready to go!?" Lewis gushed.

"Yeah, okay, fine. Calm down," Ray said.

"Great! ... Where's your bike?"

"I don't have one."

"What do you mean you don't have a bike? How did you get around in your old town?"

"In my old *city,* everything I wanted to do was within five blocks of my house. I walked everywhere."

"Oh. Well you want to ride on my handlebars? The road there is five miles."

"That didn't look like five miles from that parking lot."

"From there? I mean, as the crow flies it's probably only a mile and a half, but that's straight through the forest."

"As the crow flies? Are you a hundred years old? Besides, you're all country folk out here. You probably ran around in the woods barefoot, right? You know a shortcut, don't you?"

"I didn't get my wilderness survival badge for nothing!"

He hurried off toward the trees.

"Wait. That's a real thing? You actually have merit badges?" Ray said, trotting after him.

#

Ray and Lewis had been walking through the forest for a few minutes. Each of Lewis's steps was accompanied by a strange jingling noise. After enduring it this long, Ray finally spoke up.

"Okay, I give up. Why do your shoes sound like a Christmas sleigh?"

"Bear Bells."

"Was that an answer, or are you just saying random words?"

Lewis pointed to small silver bells on his shoes. "These. They keep away bears. Animals don't like loud, strange noises, so a couple of little bells on your shoe is all it takes."

"So… There really *are* bears here. Do the bells actually work?"

"Sure! Well, except for grizzlies. But there aren't any around here."

"How do you know?"

"By the poo. Brown bears have nuts and berries in their poo."

"What do grizzlies have in their poo?"

"Little bells."

"Oh, ha ha," Ray scoffed.

"What? That's what Col. Grampa says anyway. So, I'll bet you didn't have a nice big forest back in the big city."

"No, I sure didn't. And there were lots of other great things about it, too."

"Oh! Since we're coming this way, we can check my trap!"

He hurried along a line of trees, then crouched down and crept up to a dense cluster of bushes around a clearing.

Lewis held his camera ready and crawled through the bushes.

"Get down. I don't want to spook him if I caught him."

"I'm sure I'm going to regret asking, but who exactly are you trying to catch?"

"Shh!"

He sprung out of the bushes, madly snapping pictures. When the flurry of photojournalism was through, he lowered the camera. The clearing was empty except for a circle of orange warning flags around a length of rope leading up to a large hanging net. The net was covered in pots and pans that clattered softly in the breeze.

"Darn it! The bait's gone, but he got away. He got lucky again," Lewis said.

"Who?"

"Sasquatch. I'll just have to set down more bait and try again.

Lewis reached into one of his pouches and pulled out a packet of beef jerky.

"Okay. Let me get this straight. You're trying to catch Bigfoot," Ray said.

"His *name* is Sasquatch. The bait goes here. The rope releases the net. The pots and pans rattle. I come take a picture. Simple."

"And you're leaving jerky as bait."

"I know what you're thinking, but peanut butter cups would melt in the sun."

Ray sighed. "Ignoring the fact that no sane person would ever think anything like that, what difference would it make if they were melted or not?"

Lewis gave him an incredulous look. "Have you ever heard of a Sasquatch eating melted chocolate?"

"Well, no, but—"

"There you go!"

"By that logic, Bigfoot is just as likely to eat tuna sandwiches. I've never heard of him *not* eating them either."

"Hmm… good point. If jerky doesn't work this time, we'll try your suggestion."

Ray palmed his face as Lewis began carefully arranging the jerky in the center of the circle.

"So… If you *had* caught Bigfoot—"

"Sasquatch."

"Right. Anyway, if you *had* caught him, wouldn't we have heard the pots and pans already?"

"He could have been holding still, waiting for us to leave. Sasquatch is sneaky."

"So you really believe in the Bigfo—in Sasquatch."

"Yep. Also the wolfman, ghosts, draculas. Not aliens, though. I'm not a weirdo."

"Wait, wait. Aliens make sense. There are billions of planets. Some have *got* to be inhabited. The rest of that stuff is magic, which is bogus."

"If magic isn't real, then how would aliens get here?"

"Science."

"Same thing. Science is just magic that went to college. Okay. The bait is set. Let's go."

#

Another half hour of walking brought them to the base. Lewis and Ray ducked under the chain across the road. Over it was a huge sign proclaiming the area *Cobalt Ridge Army Base*. It was entirely deserted, and practically a time capsule of the late eighties, when it was presumably shut down. There were a few barracks, a mess hall, some training grounds, and an administrative building. At the rear of the base was the laboratory.

It was eerie to be pacing through such a big, well-kept place, but have it completely empty. Exploring the place properly would take weeks, because it turned out every door they came to, be it barracks or administration, had a matching key on the ring that would let them inside.

Ray snagged an old pair of binoculars in the watch tower to keep as a souvenir. Lewis was a bit less discerning in his souvenir hunting. He was teetering under the weight of his goodies, which included an old metal plate and silverware, a "Cobalt Ridge Recreational Area" sign, and an old pair of boots. He also snapped pictures with his old camera at the slightest provocation.

"This is great! On the field trips they only take us inside the mess hall," Lewis said.

Ray glanced at the sagging sun. "We're probably going to have to head back soon, so let's head to the lab, okay?

"Sure thing, buddy!"

They hurried to the rear of the base. What looks like an office building was waiting for them. It started roughly where the edge of the bluish slate stone of the mountain ended, such that a fair amount of the building had been dug straight into the mountain itself. Lewis searched through the keys.

"This was a great idea. Coming out here. Exploring. Like pals do."

"Let's not go crazy with this 'pal' stuff, okay. You're my neighbor who has keys to a cool lab.”

Lewis found the key and started fiddling with the door.

“And you’re my neighbor who goes on adventures with me. You might not have noticed, since I’ve been playing it cool…”

“This is playing it cool?” Ray muttered.

“… But I don’t have a lot of friends. People think I’m a weirdo.”

“With the Sasquatch stuff, I can’t imagine why.”

“I know, right?”

“Well, I wouldn’t worry about it. I don’t really have any friends either. But it was by choice.”

“You didn’t *want* friends?”

“I prefer to be alone. Most people are idiots.”

Lewis gave him a look. “Are you sure not having friends was *your* idea?”

“I really don’t see what the big deal is about having friends.”

“Well, for one thing, without a friend, you wouldn’t have been able to see this.”

He opened the door. It reveals a dim, unimpressive reception area.

“Uh… I kinda thought there’d be a lot of cool stuff right there.”

“Uh-huh.” Ray flipped the light switch, to no effect. “Figures there’s no power. You got any flashlights? Let’s check this place out.”

Lewis produced two old-school bulb and D-battery monsters and they commenced the exploration. After a lackluster lobby, Ray began to show the same enthusiasm that Lewis had shown in the rest of the base. They found room after room of big, fancy machines and instruments. Microscopes, test tubes, and Bunsen burners… Everything an aspiring mad scientist would need short of that thing that sent the bolt of lightning racing up two wires for no reason. Lewis was less enthusiastic, looking increasingly anxious about the spooky atmosphere as they probed deeper. It didn’t stop him from continuing to take souvenirs, though.

Their exploration took them down several floors, into a basement level that seemed to be the bottom floor of the building. It was well below ground. Lewis managed to pull a radiation warning sign off a door and slide it into his pack as Ray walked up.

“That’s gonna look so cool on my bedroom door,” he said, rubbing his hands together.

“I think that’s a scanning electron microscope over there. I’ll bet it’s one of the first ones!”

"Yeah, that's great and all, but it's going to start getting dark soon. We should start heading back," Lewis said.

Ray gazed at the door that Lewis had just harvested the sign from.

"In a minute. I just want to see what's behind this door." He squinted at the faded sign. "Does that say Sub Lab?"

Lewis flipped through his keys.

"I don't see one for that. Actually, I don't even see a keyhole on the door."

"There's a keypad here. No power though, so that wouldn't work," Ray said.

"Well, I guess that's that! This place is giving me the creeps anyway."

A squeaking noise drew their attention to a ventilation grate just beside the door. A rat squeezed through a hole chewed between the grate and the concrete of the wall.

Ray stroked his chin, then tugged at the grate. A few seconds of effort sent a cascade of concrete crumbling from the weakened wall. One more firm tug and the grate slid free. He ducked down and shined the flashlight through.

"It leads to a staircase. I guess a few decades and a few rats are all it takes to defeat Uncle Sam's best security. Come on."

Ray slipped through the grating and, after a moment of hesitation, Lewis squeezed through after him. The stairs led down a long way, eventually ending at a door marked *Experimental Wing: Project Back Alley*.

"This place must be dug straight into the center of the ridge. It's like Cheyenne Mountain," Ray said.

"Where?" Lewis asked.

"The place where NORAD is."

"Oh... What's that?"

"That big government complex where they launch all of the missiles from in the movies."

Lewis stared blankly.

Ray rubbed his face in defeat. "They track Santa."

"Oh, *that* NORAD!"

They pushed through the door and found themselves in a massive room with high ceilings. It was filled with decidedly more mad science-y gadgets. Test tubes, electrodes, etc. They all looked a lot older than the stuff in the rest of the lab. Closer to the sixties than the eighties. Ray scampered around the place, marveling at the slice of scientific history. Lewis was apprehensive.

"We should leave. This place looks like where they made

Frankenstein," Lewis said.

"Frankenstein wasn't the monster, he was the scientist. And this is just a government lab. Think of it as a post office with test tubes."

"Yeah, but I don't... Whoa..."

Lewis was drawn to a device in the center of the room. It was about the size and shape of a hot water heater, roughly cylindrical and covered with knobs, tubes, dials, buttons, and switches. It was on a wheeled cart and not hooked up to anything.

Lewis said, "So many buttons... You think it's safe to push them?"

Ray didn't bother looking up, too fascinated by the other bits of apparatus in the room.

"The power is shut off, and it looks like no one has been here for decades. It's just a hunk of metal now. Go nuts."

Lewis hurled himself at the device, twisting knobs, pressing buttons, and making sci-fi noises.

"Pyoo, pyoo. The aliens are too strong. We're outnumbered." Flipped up a flap to reveal a big red button. "We must deploy the *secret weapon!*"

Lewis slapped the button. There was an immediate *THUNK* noise, then an ominous hum. Bulbs and tubes all over the device started to take on a dull glow that steadily increased.

"Huh... Glowing and humming. Ray?"

Ray looked. Lewis pointed.

"Glowing and humming," he repeated.

"Oh. Maybe the power is on down here after all."

He flipped a nearby light switch. Nothing happened.

"Nope."

"Maybe it runs on batteries?" Lewis suggested.

"Nah. The batteries they had back then would be dead by now. Whatever. Just shut it off."

Lewis slapped the red button again. The device continued to glow.

"It didn't do anything. What kind of machine has an on button but no off button?"

Ray walked over to the machine and shined the flashlight at it, looking it over. Suddenly he froze, eyes wide as saucers.

"You want to know what has an on button but no off button?"

He pointed to what the flashlight had revealed, a radiation danger sign on the device.

"How 'bout a *bomb!*"

"What! No! You said I could hit any buttons I wanted!"

"I didn't expect you to find a nuclear weapon down here! They should warn you about that sort of thing on the entrance!"

Lewis reached back to push the stolen warning sign a little deeper into his pack. "Yeah..."

"What buttons did you push?" Ray asked anxiously.

"The big red one and a bunch of others! Oh-jeez-oh-jeez-oh-jeez, I can't die now! I just made my first friend!"

Ray dove at the device, hitting every button he could reach.

"What are you doing? You might make it worse!" Lewis said.

"A nuke is about to explode in our faces, Lewis. How exactly are we going to make that worse?"

"Good point!"

The boys began randomly assaulting the device as the glow and hum grew steadily stronger. Finally, both boys grabbed onto a tube on one side of the device and pulled frantically at it. The hum turned first to a thump and then to a clap as waves of energy danced across the surface of the device. They tugged harder at the tube. A sudden burst of light blasted from the device, striking the boys and sending them hurtling back, pulling the tube free with them. They blearily got to their feet to find the device had gone dark and silent once more.

"We did it! We're alive!" Ray said.

Lewis dusted himself off and wiped his head in relief.

"I've always been good at breaking stuff. Say, you don't think that mutated us, do you?"

"Radiation doesn't mutate you. It makes your hair and teeth fall out and you die."

Lewis's eyes widened. "Is that supposed to make me feel better?"

"No, you should at least freak out about the right thing."

Lewis pawed at his chest and belly. "I don't *feel* like I'm gonna die. I just don't want another arm. It took forever to find a cool shirt that fit me."

Ray tipped his head. "You know, I envy you. You're not bright enough to understand how dangerous this really was."

"Thanks!" he said brightly.

Ray adjusted his glasses and looked over the room.

"Okay. Here's what we do now. We go home, we say we spent the day hiking, and we never speak of this day again."

Lewis led the way up the stairs.

"Sure thing, pal. So, uh... Is it too early to talk about what we're going to do next weekend?"

#

Ray stopped Lewis as they passed the Bigfoot trap, which he knew was only a short distance from their houses.

"Let's exchange phone numbers," Ray said. "*Only* call me if you notice side effects of that thing that *ABSOLUTELY DIDN'T HAPPEN* today."

Lewis scratched his belly. "What kind of side effects?"

"Clumps of hair falling out, stuff like that. That way we'll have a fighting chance of getting to the doctor if we have to."

"Oh. Sure thing!"

He pulled a pad from one of the vest pockets and scribbled a number. He tore the page and Ray scrawled his own number on the next one. With the number in hand, Lewis practically pranced away. Ray shook his head as the little boy went.

#

In each of the houses, dinner was on the table. In the Banks household, Lewis sat down and his dad put a steaming plate of meat and potatoes in front of him.

"So, what did you do today?" he asked.

"We hiked and checked my Sasquatch trap and took pictures and explored and he's my best friend and we're gonna do stuff next weekend and…" he rambled, barely willing to take a breath.

In the Niven house, dinner was garden salad and salmon. Ray's dad drizzled some vinaigrette on his greens. His mom took a sip of wine.

"So!" his mom said. "So, what did you do today?"

Ray, rigid with anxiety, twitched. "Nothing…"

#

Later that night, Lewis leaned forward to check his forehead in the mirror.

"I guess a third eye wouldn't be *too* bad. I'd need new sunglasses."

A smash and clatter caused him to jump. He ran to the window.

"My Sasquatch trap! Sasquatch Sasquatch Sasquatch!"

He grabbed his camera and rushed outside, sweeping past his father on the way.

"Bye, Dad, be back in a minute! I finally caught Sasquatch!"

"Okay, but be careful. And hurry back. It's almost bedtime and you have school tomorrow," his dad said with the practiced air of a

218

nightly ritual.

Lewis ran the short distance into the woods, getting steadily more excited as he approached the site of the trap. He could hear the pots and pans still rattling.

"I'll show all of those people who said I was crazy to believe in Sasquatch!"

He jumped out of the woods, camera at the ready.

"Say cheese, Sas—" His eyes widened and his face dropped. "Oh, poop..."

Rather than Bigfoot, his net had fallen on a bear, which was slightly tangled, but mostly interested in finishing the last bit of jerky.

"Okay... This isn't a problem. He's tangled up in a net."

The bear stood and effortlessly shed the net.

"Poop! Okay. **Remember your scout training.** "

He envisioned the scout guidebook. It was fresh in his mind, the words clear on the page. *Back away and make soothing noises.*

"Good bear. Nice bear. You don't want to eat the little husky kid."

The bear started to walk toward him.

"Pooooop!"

He envisioned the book again. *The bear is approaching: Make yourself appear as large as possible, and shout at the bear.*

He waved his arms.

"GO AWAY! I AM A MIGHTY HUNTER!"

There was a crunch of grass behind Lewis. The bear's eyes suddenly went wide. It turned and ran away in fear, dragging the net behind it.

"Ha! Scout training saves the day again! Wait'll I tell Dad what I—"

He turned and froze in place. Something was in front of him. His brain wasn't quite up to the task of identifying it, beyond noting that it was big, gray, pointy, and not a bear. Without raising the camera, he snapped a picture. This turned out to be a miscalculation, as it robbed him of his night vision. Now the monster was little more than a grayish blob moving slowly toward him as purple spots blotted it out.

"What would the book say about *this?*" he whimpered.

He envisioned the book once more, conjuring to mind a page labeled *What to do when you find a big scary monster.* Unfortunately, his brain wasn't up to populating the fictional page with anything useful, either.

He took a step back. The thing took a step forward.

"Okay, what would Col. Grampa say?

That question, his memory had an answer for, as it was practically a catchphrase for the old man. *When in doubt, run like hell.*

Lewis desperately sprinted from the clearing, bellowing in fear. He ran through the short strip of forest, through his backyard, and back into the house, screaming all the way. The beast was lumbering behind him, thumping ever closer. Lewis slammed the back door of the house and braced against it. The steps thumped closer, then stopped. He braced for impact.

Nothing happened.

Carefully he opened the door. Very large, very obvious footprints ended just a few steps away from the house. His father stepped up behind him, startling him.

"Lewis? What was that all about? You look like you've seen a ghost," he said.

Lewis glanced back at the prints again.

"Uh... I don't think it was a *ghost*." He rubbed his face. "I need to use the phone."

#

Ray's smartphone was on his dresser, plugged into the charger. His room was still piled with boxes. Waiting to be unpacked. As he brushed his teeth in the bathroom across the hall, the phone started to vibrate. A shadowy figure, no larger than an action figure, scampered up onto the dresser. It hefted the rattling phone, tugged it free of the cord, and scampered away.

#

Ray stood at the edge of the road with his backpack on, waiting for the bus. Lewis wandered up. He looked disturbed, and clearly hadn't slept.

"Hi, Ray," Lewis said woodenly.

"Hi."

"I, uh, I tried to call you last night."

"Did you? My phone ended up on top of the refrigerator somehow, with a bunch of candy wrappers around it and a dead battery."

"Oh. Well, you know that thing we did yesterday?"

"No.

"The thing at the lab."

Ray clenched his teeth.

"No, Lewis, I don't know about that secret thing that we said we'd never talk about."

"Oh! Uh, me either... But if we *did* do a thing we agreed only to talk about it if we noticed side effects, would seeing monsters count?"

"Lewis, you already insist you can catch Bigfoot with jerky."

"Sasquatch! And it turns out jerky is better for catching bears."

"Whatever. Seeing big scary monsters isn't a symptom of radiation poisoning, it is a symptom of being Lewis."

"This is different! This was something I've never even heard of. And it was *evil!*"

"If you've never even heard of it, how could you tell it was evil?"

"It was pointy."

Ray looked him in the eye. "It was *pointy*."

"Yep! Evil things are pointy. Dracula has fangs. Wolf Man has claws. Even the evil parts of nice things are pointy. Puppy teeth, kitten claws…"

Ray pushed his glasses up and pinched the bridge of his nose.

"Look, you're just imagining things. Otherwise *I* would be seeing things, too."

The bus pulled up.

"No more talking about the thing that totally didn't happen, got it?"

Lewis slouched. "Okay..."

#

A teacher stood outside her classroom. She was tall, portly, and had angular glasses and smoker's teeth. Most of the children were already seated inside. Ray walked up, looking over a sheet of paper with his classroom assignment.

"Um… Mrs. Twist?" he said.

"Yes? Oh, are you Raymond Niven?"

"Yeah. This says I'm supposed to be in your class, but there must be a mistake because I skipped ahead."

"They told me all about it. We don't do that here. Kids should be with others of their own age."

"But I scored in the 99th percentile. I know this stuff better than *you* do."

"You could stand to learn a few things about first impressions, for starters," Mrs. Twist murmured.

"What?"

"I'll have a word with the superintendent after class. Until then, you'll just have to spend some time in third grade."

They entered the classroom. Math problems covered the entire chalk board behind them

"Good morning, class. I'll be your third-grade teacher, Mrs. Twist."

"Good morning, Mrs. Twist..." Droned the class in an unenthusiastic chorus.

"This is Raymond Niven. He just moved to town, so give him a warm welcome."

"Good morning, Ray..."

"Uh, Raymond, actually."

"Go have a seat, Ray," said Mrs. Twist.

Ray muttered angrily under his breath along the way. "Why does *everyone* have to call me *Ray?*"

The teacher took a seat at her desk.

"There are fifty math problems on the board. Start copying and completing them on a clean sheet of paper. Raise your hand if you need help," she said.

The students got to work. Ray put his head down and industriously scribbled away at problems he would have found boring when he was seven years old. Something fluttered by his ear. He waved at it irritably and continued writing. When it flitted by again, he snapped his head toward it, expecting a moth.

It was not a moth.

There before his eyes was a small, flying, clearly mythical creature. He would have called it a fairy if his mind would allow him to address that it was really there. He glanced around. One or two of the other kids looked in his direction, but none appeared to notice anything wrong. He looked to Lewis in the seat behind him and to the left. The little boy's eyes were wide open, locked on the fairy.

Ray snapped his eyes back to the notebook and muttered to himself.

"It isn't real, it isn't real. Just ignore it..."

The creature flitted down into his field of view and grabbed the eraser end of his pencil. With remarkable strength, it started tugging. He pulled it back down. It immediately yanked again, this time pulling it out of his hand. He reached up and grabbed it, but the creature was able to hold on tight enough and pull hard enough to keep him from pulling it back. He struggled with the pencil at arm's length for a while.

"Raymond?" said Mrs. Twist.

He continued to fight.

"Raymond?" she said more insistently.

Ray turned to her and realized that she, and the rest of the class, were watching what appeared to be a child frantically waving his pencil in the air. The girl sitting in the seat to his right, seemed to be taking a greater interest than the others.

"Did you need something?" asked Mrs. Twist.

Ray looked back and forth between the teacher and the fairy. After a paralyzing moment of indecision, the fairy shimmered and vanished, leaving him holding the pencil up.

"Uh… I need to use the bathroom?" he said.

"Okay. Who would like to show Raymond where the bathroom is?"

Lewis's hand shot up.

"I will!" he crowed.

Without waiting to be acknowledged, Lewis grabbed Ray walked out of the room as Nancy watched with a bemused look. When they were gone, Nancy leaned over to the girl next to her.

"Did you notice anything funny going on just then?" she asked.

"You mean besides the new kid acting like a spaz?"

"No, I mean it looked like his pencil flew out of his hand… Never mind. It was probably nothing."

#

"So, you believe me *now?*" Lewis whispered, glancing back at the classroom.

"It isn't really happening. It's probably psychosomatic."

"Psycho-some-attic. How is it part of the top floor of a crazy person's house?"

"No, I mean it was just my imagination. Because of stress or something. No one *else* saw it."

"A little pixie thing tried to steal your pencil. Did you imagine it so hard *I* saw it? Because that would be really neat."

"Look, I don't know what's going on, okay? But there's got to be a reasonable explanation."

"HA! Someone *always* says that when something supernatural is going on."

"Talk to your Grampa. Try to find out more about that thing we totally didn't activate. But don't let him realize we saw it."

"Like a secret spy mission? Neat! This is gonna be fun. I've been having a great time since you showed up, Ray!"

Ray twitched and turned to Lewis. "First, radiation exposure is not 'a great time,' and second, stop calling me *Ray*. It's *Raymond*."

"I know, but Ray is your nickname."

"No, because I don't *have* a nickname. I *hate* nicknames. Full names are a sign of respect. You don't hear people calling Albert Einstein 'Al' or Leonardo Da Vinci 'Leo'."

"Hey. At least you've got a *good* nickname."

"As opposed to?"

A random student passing by spotted the pair.

"Hey, Screwy Louie! Catch any leprechauns lately?" he snickered.

"Hi, Roger," Lewis said, trying to keep a smile on his face.

When the boy was gone, Ray nodded. "Okay, you've got a point. But still, we've got to find out what happened and how to fix it, and that means learning more about that lab. Now come on, let's get back to class."

"But the bathroom."

"I didn't need to go to the bathroom. I was being robbed by a fairy, remember?"

"Oh, yeah… Well, I kinda do, so let's go."

#

The school day had been long and, for Ray at least, terribly boring. Now they were headed home, seated beside each other on the bus and discussing their little situation.

"So you're going to talk to your grandfather, right? Without letting him know what exactly happened?" Ray said.

"You met Col. Grampa. Even if I *did* tell him, in a minute he'd be talking about how the SOS the mess hall had was too runny today."

"What's SOS?"

"Something Col. Grampa eats. Why is it so important we don't let anybody know about this? It seems like a real 'tell your parents' sort of thing."

"We snuck into a secret lab and got zapped with radiation by a bomb. They lock people up for that stuff."

"Well, sure, we can't tell people *that* part, but the why not the fairies and stuff?"

"Because they lock people up for that stuf,f too, but in rooms with padded walls and pudding on Tuesdays."

"That doesn't sound too bad. I love pudding!"

"I'm talking about a mental institution!"

"Oh… Still, pudding on Tuesdays."

#

Nancy rocked back and forth in her seat as the two weird boys from class continued to chat in hushed tones. Most of the rest of the bus wasn't paying any attention to them. But she couldn't understand why not. They were the most interesting thing going on right now. She was in the seat behind them, straining her ears. The bus pulled up to a stop and her seatmate got up to leave. Once she was alone, she didn't have to be quite so subtle about trying to hear their little conversation. Even practically leaning against the back of the seat, she could only catch a word here or there, but what she heard was very strange.

"… fairy … Sasquatch …" Lewis said.

"… laboratory … radiation …" Ray said.

"That must be one crazy movie they're talking about," Nancy mumbled.

Something caused Lewis and Ray's window to rattle. Nancy didn't see anything, but the boys recoiled.

Lewis pointed excitedly and exclaimed, "Monkey bird!"

A few kids looked.

"It's nothing, everyone, it's nothing! False alarm," Ray said in a frazzled tone.

Lewis leaned close to the window, seeming to inspect it. The bus stopped outside their houses.

"We're here! Let's go!" Ray added in a harsh whisper. "Stop staring at it."

The boys hurried off the bus. As the doors closed Nancy moved to their seat. The window was fogged up from breath. She wiped her finger on the window, but the fog didn't come off.

"Fogged up on the *outside?*" she said quietly.

#

Ray sat at his desk with his books splayed out around him. As he tried to do his homework, a tiny robot appeared on the desk. He froze, eyes on the little mechanism. It panicked and started running amok. With the sigh and look of a person who has had far too much experience with this sort of thing already, he dumped out his wastepaper basket, slammed it down over the robot, and weighted the top with a textbook. His phone rang. It was Lewis.

Ray answered. "I need good news, Lewis."

"Mission accomplished. Col. Grampa had this big binder with research stuff. By the way, what's 'Redacted' mean?"

"It means it was removed because it was a secret."

"Oh. Well, there's a lot of that."

"It figures. Well, bring it over here. We'll see if there is anything useful."

"I can't. Dad's rule is I can't go outside on a school night until my homework's done."

The robot began ramming into the side of the basket, edging it closer to the edge of the desk.

Ray scooted it closer to the center of the desk.

"Then tell him you're coming over here to do homework together. We've got to get this figured out. I'm having robot problems."

"Aw, you got robots, too? All I've seen so far was that big scary monster, the fairy, and that stupid monkey bird. You keep getting the cool stuff."

The robot managed to push the basket off the desk. It fell to the floor and resumed its tiny panic attack.

"Just get over here!" Ray snapped.

"Okay, okay! Uh… Can I actually bring my homework? It's long division."

The robot knocked over the hamper produced a triumphant bleep, and vanished.

"Yes, fine, whatever. Just hurry."

#

After Lewis arrived, the pair sat at his desk. Ray pored over the contents of the binder. Lewis struggled with his math.

"This is ridiculous. It's nothing but a bunch of blacked-out lines," Ray grumbled.

"Yeah. Kinda makes you wonder why they have reports at all. Hey. How many times does six go into two hundred and forty-three?"

"Forty, remainder three. Hmm. There's a researcher named Dr. Van Vleck, head of a research team. Even the names of his projects are redacted."

"Oh, yeah. Dr. V worked at the lab alright."

"Dr. V? You know about this guy?"

"Dad's the only barber in town. We know everybody. He lives in a big cabin on the far side of Cobalt Ridge."

"Lives? You mean he's still alive?"

"Yeah! He's like a million years old though. And a real grouch."

Ray shut his eyes and shuddered. "You knew the address of a top researcher at the lab where we had our accident, and you waited until *now* to tell me?"

"Yep! Where do I put the remainder again?"

"Just write it on the right. I'm going to get this guy's number and…"

"You can't. It's unlisted."

Ray shook his head. "Do you know how to get to this guy's house then?"

"Yeah. It's kind of a long way, though. We'd need to use my bike. And it's kind of late. Dad would get worried."

"Just sneak over and get your bike. I'll tell my parents I'm going to your house, your dad already thinks you'll be here. No problem."

"I don't know… I don't like sneaking around and disobeying Dad like that. Are you sure we need to do this?"

Motion drew their attention. A small multicolored lizard with entirely too many eyes walked up the wall, opened its mouth to reveal venom-dripping fangs, and then promptly vanished. Ray looked at Lewis.

"I'll get my bike."

#

One sneaky trip to grab a bike later, they were pedaling along a bike path through the forest. Ray sat precariously on the handlebars. Lewis wasn't handling the task of peddling his bike for both of them while leaning aside to see where he was going particularly well. Fortunately, Lewis had helmets for both of them. Unfortunately for Ray, his was a bright pink one with unicorn stickers on it.

"You really… need to get… your own bike," Lewis panted.

"Or at least my own helmet. Where did you get this thing?"

"It belongs to my cousin," he huffed, "who visits now and then."

A bump nearly dislodged Ray.

"Are you sure this is the best way? Wouldn't a real road be better?"

"The road circles around the forest. Cutting past the base skips like fifteen miles! We're about halfway there. Wanna swap?"

"I don't know how to ride a bike."

"Well, you better learn if we're going to have any more adventures." He panted a few more times. "So, why do you think things are magically appearing?"

"I'm still not convinced they are. No one else can see them but us. Maybe it's in our heads."

"The Big Scary Thing left footprints."

"Did anyone else see them?"

"No one really looked."

"Here's what I think happened. The radiation hit us and it super-excited the neurons in our brain, see?"

"Neurons?"

"And the neurons synchronized. So now you and I have a telepathic link."

"Telepathic?"

"One of us, probably you, is having vivid hallucinations and it is affecting both of us. So it is sort of a symbiotic radioactive psychosis."

"… And you think that's *more* likely than magic?"

"Just keep pedaling. I can see the base over there. And…" His eyes opened wide. "Lewis? The, uh, the 'Big Scary Thing.; How big was it?"

"I don't know. Bigger than a bear. Not as big as an elephant. Why?"

"I need you to listen very carefully. Don't look toward the camp, and don't slow down."

"Why? It's here, isn't it? I was right, wasn't I? Totally evil! Where is it? Let me see!"

Lewis lurched aside to try to get a look at the creature, which was in a clearing closer to the camp. The sudden shift in weight threw the bike out of control, sending them tumbling into the bushes.

Ray shook his head, dazed from the fall.

"What did I *just* say? Come on! We've got to get going again before…"

The ground thumped with the footsteps of the creature. It was just a few steps away, and already towering over them. Both boys looked up, paralyzed by fear.

With the better light, it was easier to see the monster in all of its fearsome glory. That was *not* a good thing. The monster looked to have been assembled from stone. The body, vaguely ant-like but far more broad, stood atop six stout legs. A vaguely humanoid torso, also stony in appearance, sprouted two additional stony arms. The face had a jagged beak in place of a mouth and a cluster of green crystals which might have served as eyes scattered over the top of its head. Its fingers ended in needle sharp points, and all of its joints had a sharp, "broken stone" look to them.

"So very pointy…" Lewis said.

A voice boomed from behind them.

"Lle mah-ye towloo! Qualahn!"

A crackling sound filled the air. It managed to draw Lewis's attention away from the lurking doom. There was a woman, though the word seemed terribly simple for the creature before him. She was practically a goddess. Her hand was raised over her head, crackling with radiant green energy. The trees, bushes, and grass twisted and curled all around her, blossoming and sending out new shoots of growth. There was a look of noble defiance in her eyes.

"Shah tahmas shoo!" she proclaimed.

The woman swept her hand forward. The energy took a fluid, darting path through the air, seeking out the monster as though alive. The ground beneath the bolt of energy erupted with new growth, sending a shockwave along the earth beneath the attack. When it flew overhead it stoked the growth of the bush suddenly and powerfully enough to entangle the bike. A tree sprouted from the ground beneath the boys. Before they knew it, they were clinging to branches twenty feet from the ground. The energy struck the monster and coalesced into stout vines of ivy that quickly entangled the beast. She stalked toward the creature, stirring the air with her hand once more.

Lewis held tight to a branch, dangling in the air from the tree that had hoisted them up.

"She's beautiful…" he murmured.

The rocky monster tore free from the vines and burst aside as the woman unleashed a second blast of energy. It struck the ground, causing another explosive surge of growth. Vines churned up and split the earth, upsetting the roots of the tree that held the boys. It lurched to the side, bashing Lewis in the head and dazing him. The tree teetered, threatening to fall. The boys dangled lower. If the tree shifted any farther, it would either crush the boys or tumble them into the crossfire of the supernatural clash. Ray slipped free from his branch. He barely managed to grab another one. Lewis splayed out on the crook of a branch, delirious. Below them, the rock monster stalked into view, looking up at the dangling children like a shark waiting for the ship to finally sink.

Lewis's eyes fluttered. He started to lose his grip.

"Lewis! Lewis!! *Snap out of it!*" Ray shouted.

Suddenly there was a loud snap, and the tree began to topple toward the creature…

Volume 2

In a hazy scene, atop a crumbling castle, Lewis raised his sword. His armor was glorious, gleaming and gold with a crested and plumed helmet. The monster stood before him, tall as the castle itself and made from the same gray stone. It was hulking, vicious. Belching flame, and so terribly, terribly pointy.

He leveled the sword at the abomination.

"Back, beast, or taste my steel!"

The beast bellowed a terrifying roar and spoke in a voice like hissing steam. "You cannot defeat me, Sir Lewis of Banks! I will grind your bones to make my bread!"

"I think not, you contemptible creature. For I am virtuous and pure!"

He hacked at the creature.

"I know you are the fiend who summoned these evil creatures who invade my kingdom!"

He sliced again, forcing the creature back. A voice from thin air called for him.

"Lewis!"

Lewis continued the battle. "When I vanquish you, the curse will be lifted, and the monsters will vanish!"

The voice called louder. "Lewis!"

Lewis glanced angrily aside, answering in a decidedly less heroic voice. "In a minute, Ray, I'm busy vanquishing!"

"*Snap out of it!!!*" the voice bellowed.

Suddenly, the stones of the castle beneath Lewis's feet gave way and he plummeted. Reality swept in like an unwelcome alarm clock on a school morning. The tree was falling toward the rock creature below, but the terrible creature raised two powerful arms and caught the tree by a few lower branches. Ray barely kept his grip, dangling from a branch directly above the rock creature. Lewis wedged in place in the crook or a branch and started to shake away the cobwebs clouding his mind.

"Huh?" he muttered. "Oh, wow, this first dream is still happening. The one where we got zapped by radiation and cool stuff kept showing up?"

"It isn't a dream, Lewis! We're about to die!" Ray shouted.

The rock creature looked up to them, but a bolt of green energy clashed against it, prompting a roar of pain. It lowered the tree to the ground and charged toward the magic lady. The boys, against all odds, ended up unharmed as the tree settled to the ground. They crawled free of the tangled mass of branches. Ray ran for the bike, Lewis stumbling after him.

"Come on, come on, we need to go!" Ray urged.

"But there's an epic battle between good and evil going on! Tell me this is not the coolest thing ever!"

"Yes, Lewis, it's very cool, but what exactly do we do if the forest lady loses?"

"Oh… Good point."

They both tugged madly at the bike while the battle raged on. Just as it pulled free, the monster began to fade away. The woman raised her hand triumphantly, then saw that she was beginning to fade as well. She turned to the boys.

"Tamastah Terriethriel!" she cried.

Lewis looked back as he got the bike moving. "Thanks, Magic Forest Lady!"

#

The boys laboriously climbed the mountain road. Rather than struggle with the bike, they were walking it up the slope.

"Do you think Magic Forest Lady knows how to turn people into frogs?" Lewis asked.

"I don't know," Ray said.

"Do you think she has an animal sidekick?"

"I don't know. Listen, can you at least pretend to treat that with the respect it deserves?"

"I am! It was the coolest thing ever."

"If those things weren't real, we're nuts. If they *were* real, we almost died!"

"That's the price of adventure! Here's Dr. V.'s place."

At the edge of the road they found a small log cabin. It seemed normal, except for a few little details. There were a few more power cables going to it than seemed necessary, and an oversized satellite dish was mounted to the top of a tower tall enough to poke it up above the treetops. A separate garage sat beside it. There were multiple signs warning against trespassing and solicitation. A mailbox said *Maxwell Van Vleck*.

"Max Van Vleck. That's the guy from the lab reports," Ray said.

"Told ya," Lewis said.

"How did you know exactly where he lives?"

"Trick-or-treating last year. He gave out full size chocolate bars. You don't forget a thing like that."

They walked up to the door and knocked.

"Whatever it is, I don't want any!" said a decrepit-sounding voice from within.

"Please, sir, it's very important," Lewis said.

"Don't want any!"

"But, sir! … Sir?" Ray shouted.

"You'll never get him to answer the door," said a little girl across the street.

Ray and Lewis turned. It was Nancy. She was standing on her porch, a garbage bag in her hand.

"Hey, look, it's Nancy from school. Hi, Nancy!" Lewis said.

Ray covered his face. "Remember how we were doing this secretly so our families wouldn't find out?"

Nancy dropped the garbage in an outdoor bin and walked over to them.

"You're the new kid, right? Ray or something?" she said.

"Raymond."

"Yeah. You two have been acting weird. Lewis always acts weird, so I guess he's acting normal, but you're acting as weird as him."

"I'm not acting weird," Ray countered.

Lewis nodded. "Yeah, we're just dealing with weird—"

Ray elbowed him. "Secret," he said amid subtle coughs.

"—Nothing. We're dealing with weird nothing."

"Weird nothing like your pencil shooting out of your hand and something fogging up the window from the outside?"

"Ha! I knew other people—ow!" Lewis yelped as Ray elbowed him again.

"Yes, weird nothing like that. Why won't the doctor open the door?"

"He never opens the door unless food is involved. If it wasn't for Girl Scout cookies I wouldn't even know what he looks like," Nancy said.

"Great. What do we do now? We really need to talk to him," Ray said.

"Yeah. For a science report," Lewis added.

"We don't have a science report due. We just have that social studies report where we have to interview somebody," Nancy said.

"Lewis paused for a moment. "This is a special *secret* science—ow!"

Ray stepped forward and stood between Lewis and Nancy, in hopes of perhaps keeping him from earning another elbow.

"Look, do you have any ideas how we can get him to answer the door?" Ray said.

"Hmm… Got five bucks?" she asked.

"Uh…" He dug through his pocket and pulled out a five. "Yeah."

"Give it to me. And wait here," she said.

She trotted back to her house a minute later she reappeared with a purple box of cookies.

"Here. He'll break the door down to get these," she said.

"Thanks… Why are you helping us?" Ray said.

Nancy shrugged.

"Whatever this is, it's the first interesting thing that's happened here in a while. I kinda wanna see where it goes. See ya."

She returned to her house. The boys turned back to the door and knock again.

Ray said, "Excuse me, sir?"

"Go away!" the doctor shouted.

"Purple Box Cookies!" Lewis proclaimed.

Footsteps thumped forward and the door flew open, revealing an elderly man. He was thin, dressed in a many layers of sweaters and cardigans. He peered at them through thick classes and frowned.

"Lewis Banks. The barber's boy. Are you a Girl Scout?" the doctor asked.

"No."

"Then why are you selling cookies?" He looked to Ray. "And who are you?"

"I'm his neighbor. I just moved in," Ray said.

"How nice for you. Welcome to Morningvale Hills. Sell me the cookies and go home. *Jeopardy!* is on."

"I just need to talk to you—" Ray began.

"Will it be about cookies?" Dr. V. asked.

"No, something we found in the sub-basement of the STAT Lab," he said.

Dr. V. eyed him suspiciously.

"The sub-lab is behind five locked doors, the last of which has no key. You aren't earning any points by fibbing, little boy."

"We kinda sorta got the keys from Col. Grampa," Lewis said.

"Rats chewed out the vent that led behind the last door," Ray explained. "We found something called 'Project Back Alley' inside the room beyond it."

Dr. V. shushed them frantically.

"Uh-uh-uh! Let's not say anymore where rival government research teams might be eavesdropping, shall we?"

He ushered them inside. The interior of the cabin looked like a time capsule from the sixties. All of the furniture and appliances were vintage and pristine. Most of the cabin was made up of a single room. One corner had a dusty and disused kitchen. Several bookcases loaded down with thick, very technical books were crammed wherever they could fit. In front of a roaring fire was an overstuffed easy chair. Beside it stood a small folding table with petri dish, a few beakers, some cruel looking dentist-style picks, and a pair of forceps being used as a plate, a mug, and silverware respectively. They contained some tea and a rather unappetizing microwaved entrée. There was a small black and white television with a circular screen and rabbit ear antennas on top sitting off to one side of the fire. Alligator clips were clamped onto the antenna and ran down between cracks in the floorboards. *Jeopardy!* was indeed on.

Dr. V. snatched the cookies and settled into the chair.

"Sit down," he instructed.

Ray looked around. The easy chair was the only seat in the place.

"Where do I sit?" Ray asked.

"The floor," Dr. V. said.

Lewis plopped down like a toddler at story time.

"I'll stand," Ray said.

Dr. V. waved his hand dismissively. "Fine. First some ground rules. No one says 'Project Back Alley' anymore. Certainly not outside and *certainly* not on the phone or the internet."

"Why?" Lewis asked.

"We hid it under one hundred feet of mountain. Does it sound like something we want the world to know about?"

"I guess not."

"Clever boy. Mention that project too many times in this town and you'll get a visit from the men in the dark sunglasses."

"Lifeguards?" Lewis guessed.

Ray and Dr. V. just looked at him.

"… I'll be quiet."

"We have a problem," Ray said to Dr. V. "We managed to activate this big… device in the sub-lab."

"There are a number of 'big devices' in the experimental wing."

"It looked like a hot water heater and the cockpit of a bomber had a baby," Lewis said.

"Mmm." Dr. V. sipped his tea. "I'm familiar with it. Don't worry about it, it doesn't work. Never did."

"Well it did *something*, Dr. Van Vleck. There was a lot of humming, and a lot of glowing."

"It probably still has a current flowing in its Seebeck Generator. It'll put on a show, but nothing more."

"Tell him about Big Scary Thing. And Magical Forest Lady," Lewis said.

Ray clenched his teeth. "I'm getting to that. You see, we've been seeing things—"

"And feeling things, and getting chased by things, and having things steal our pencils and stuff. There's one right now!"

Ray turned to see the pencil-stealing fairy fluttering around the room, inspecting the contents of a bookshelf.

"Yes. Lewis and I are seeing a small, winged person right now," Ray said, attempting to sound as sane as possible despite the content of the sentence."

"It's a fairy, duh," Lewis said.

Dr. V. frowned. "I'm sure you are… Have you boys ever been treated for any behavioral disorders?"

"No," Ray said. "Look, maybe your machine gave us brain damage or something."

"Or *maybe* the fairy is really there and he just can't see it," Lewis theorized.

"I guess there's an easy way to find out," Ray said.

He snatched the hat off of Lewis's head and threw it over the fairy. The fairy instantly darted madly about the room, dragging the hat with it.

Dr. V. set down his tea and folded his hands as he watched what appeared to him to be an empty hat dart around his house.

"This is… highly irregular. Dare I say… it is impossible."

"Why is it that all of the smart people keep saying that?" Lewis asked.

"Whatever that machine was, we turned it on, and it blasted us with energy or something and then this stuff started happening," Ray said.

Dr. V. shook his head. "No, no. Impossible. The project never functioned. There's no reason it would work *now* but not *then*. Unless… Follow me, and don't touch anything."

Dr. V. stood stiffly and walked over to a rug. With some difficulty, and while frequently looking to the still darting hat, he stooped down and pulled the rug aside. It revealed a hatch, which he then laboriously opened to further reveal a set of stairs leading to a darkened basement.

"I don't know. I'm pretty sure they said something in school about not following an old man into a dark basement," Lewis said.

"We've just conclusively proven that supernatural creatures are physically manifesting around us. I believe we are beyond what school can teach us," Ray said.

"I guess so, but be on the lookout for anything unusual," Lewis said.

Ray watched as the hatted fairy bonked into the open hatch and plummeted into the basement.

"Uh-huh," Ray said.

Dr. V. clicked on a light. The basement was considerably more in keeping with what one might expect from someone in Dr. Van Vleck's line of work. It was filled with scientific equipment both new and old. Oscilloscopes, polygraphs, etc. A large chalkboard was set up along one wall.

"I believe it was forty-two years, twenty-eight years, and fourteen years," Dr. V. muttered.

"What are you talking about?" Ray asked.

"The half-life of the three isotopes in the QFT device you activated." He flipped open a binder and scribbled some notes on the chalkboard. "Yes… It's just possible… You boys may represent the most significant advancement in quantum theory since the Higgs Boson. If I'm right, the scientific community has retroactively been playing catch up with *me*."

Lewis tried to snatch his hat off the fairy. "So you know what's going on?"

"Of course I do. I designed the device. Sit yourselves down. You're about to get an education."

He wiped away the contents of the blackboard and began to illustrate his points. First, he drew a mushroom cloud.

"With the first atomic detonation, the world entered the nuclear age. One weapon could destroy a city. War was both unavoidable and unthinkable."

He drew the hammer and sickle.

"No one dared fire the first shot, for fear of triggering Armageddon. We called this the Cold War."

He drew a simple man in a hat and trench coat.

"We needed spies, good ones. Spies that were impossible to see, and thus could prevent a third world war. I proposed a solution, the project we've agreed not to name."

He drew two stick figures, one as a dotted line.

"We created the Quantum Frequency Tuner to render matter invisible by knocking its quantum signature out of sync with this reality."

Lewis gave up on his hat for a moment. "Wow… So why aren't we invisible?"

Dr. V. turned away from the chalk board.

"The QFT utilized the interference pattern of three rare isotopes in precise proportions. When the project was abandoned, radioactive decay steadily unbalanced the ratio."

"O-o-o-oh…" Lewis leaned over to Ray. "Does this make sense yet?"

"I don't think he's done," Ray said.

"You were exposed to an entirely different interference pattern. Rather than sliding you into the quantum background, it destabilized your quantum makeup."

He turned back to the chalkboard and drew two cats, one with Xs for eyes.

"The many worlds theory, which you now empirically support, posits that there exist innumerable parallel universes. Different histories, different life forms, even different physical laws."

He drew an open door with two stick figures standing in it. One side he wrote "Us" and on the other "Everything Else."

"*Your* quantum signatures are clashing with *ours,* partially aligning you with *theirs.* Imagine standing in a doorway between worlds, allowing other things to slip through."

He turned back to them and gestured at the flitting hat.

"Creatures align with *you.* You align with *us. You* are aligned closely enough to see *them,* but *we* are too far out of alignment."

"Does it make sense now?" Lewis whispered.

"I think he's saying that the things we're seeing are really here but no one else can see them."

"So I was right?"

Ray rolled his eyes. "Yes."

"Hah! In your face, smart people!"

He looked at the hat, which smacked into another wall and fell to the ground again. It landed upside down and revealed a very dizzy fairy.

"So do we know why the fairy is sticking around so long? They usually go poof pretty fast," Lewis said.

"Did you wear that hat when you activated the device?" Dr. V asked.

"Yep," he said.

"Then it is likely that making contact with something that experienced the anomaly has a stabilizing effect on trespassers in our dimension."

The fairy fluttered up out of the hat and promptly faded away.

"Neat!" Lewis said.

"As interesting as all this is, I think the big question here is, can you undo the effect?" Ray said.

"Of course!" Dr. V. said. "The device was *designed* to manipulate quantum frequency. I'll just need a few days to work out the proper settings to stabilize you."

"What do we do until then? If these things are real, then we're risking our lives whenever they show up," Ray said.

"There's not much you can do. The one precaution I would suggest is staying away from the epicenter of the anomaly," Dr. V. said.

"The apple-center of the anemone? There are seeds and wobbly sea creatures involved now?" Lewis said.

"He means we should stay away from where this happened," Ray said.

"Indeed. You're a bright boy. The device has a fairly small area of effect, but even at rest its emissions can amplify your instability. As a matter of fact..."

He began digging around in some equipment tucked in one corner of the room.

"That explains why Magic Lady and Big Scary Thing both showed up when we got close to the base," Lewis said.

"And it means we'll need to take the long way home if we don't want another visit from those things," Ray said.

"Ah-ha!" Dr. V exclaimed.

He blew some dust off of a cobbled-together collection of instruments that looked like it was built in the 1950s. It prominently featured a radar-style screen and a seismograph style roll of paper with a squiggly line on it. A flip of a switch turned it on, revealing a small green blip on the screen.

"The old emissions detector," he said. "Any anomalous activity will be recorded here. Now, you boys get going. I've got work to do."

Lewis picked up his hat and put it on his head. "Could you give us a ride? Our folks think we're at each other's houses. If we take the long way, we'll be super late."

"Fine. But remember. Nothing said here leaves this building," Dr. V said.

"Why?" Lewis asked.

"Because you two are essentially lab rats right now, and you know what happens to lab rats in the big laboratories, don't you?"

"They get superpowers?" Lewis said hopefully.

"No, they get a short period of observation followed by a dissection."

"Well, that's no fun."

"Not for the rat, anyway," Dr. V. said. "Which reminds me. In the interests of science, please monitor your mental and physical condition over the next few days.

"How?" asked Lewis.

"Nothing invasive. Heart rate, blood sugar, electrolyte balance, things of that nature."

"I'll... see what I can do," Ray said.

"I'll contact Lewis when I determine how to reverse the effects. Don't miss the call. Anomalous effects like these are best corrected quickly."

"I'll tell my dad to wake me up if you call after bedtime. ... Oh, wait..." Lewis said, realization dawning. "I thought I had to keep this a secret."

"It's probably better if I just give you my cell phone number," Ray said.

"Fine, but be sure to answer. I'll want to apply the cure immediately. No dilly-dally. Now come on. And no sticky fingers on the seats."

"Hey, what about the money for the cookies," Ray said.

"I'm considering the cookies a consultation fee. That's a bargain.

I bill out at $500 an hour in the private sector.”

#

A few days had passed. All things considered, it had been rather uneventful. That said, there were quite a few things to consider.

The boys were on the school bus, on their way home.

“Did you see anything wacky?” Lewis whispered.

“That colorful lizard thing walked across the window from the outside,” Ray said.

“I guess I missed it. During gym class I think I saw that robot you said was buzzing around on your desk the other day.”

“Okay. Only one or two things per day. The doctor might actually fix us up before anything exciting happens.”

“Yeah… Still, I’m sure we’ll have another adventure soon.” Lewis glanced out the window. “Hey, look! Dad’s here to meet me at the bus. And your folks are here, too!”

Ray furrowed his brow. “They don’t look happy.”

“Neat, he’s got my pictures!” Lewis said.

“Wait... The pictures you took at the army base? *You gave them to your dad!?*”

“Well, yeah. I had to get them developed, didn’t I?”

“And you didn’t think maybe he might be mad when he sees we went to the base without telling him?”

“Oh, yeah...”

Ray smacked himself in the forehead.

“Well, I don’t usually misbehave. I’m not good at it yet,” Lewis said.

They stepped off the bus.

“Lewis Terrance Banks! What exactly did you think you were doing?” shouted Mr. Banks.

“Raymond, I am ashamed of you. We move into this beautiful new town and this is the impression you make?” growled Mr. Niven.

“It wasn’t his fault, Mr. Niven, sir. I offered to take him to see the base,” Lewis said.

“Yep. It’s all his fault,” Ray said eagerly.

“Raymond, don’t lie to me. Once I found out you boys went to a *laboratory,* I knew you had something to do with it,” his dad said.

“To your room. You are grounded, mister. One week,” Mr. Banks said.

“Aw, Dad…” said Lewis.

“You, too, Raymond. Grounded for a week,” said Mr. Niven.

241

"Sounds good to me!" Ray said.

"And no internet," said Mrs. Niven.

"Aw, Mom…"

His dad whispered to his mother. "That's a little harsh, Martha."

She crossed her arms. "You've got to be tough but fair."

His dad turned to him. "Say goodbye to your friend, Lewis. You'll only be seeing him during school until I feel you've learned your lesson."

Lewis lowered his head. "Bye, Ray."

Ray grumbled irritably. "Bye, Lewis."

#

A few minutes later, Lewis and his father were in the dining room. The photos were scattered around the table. They were various poorly taken images of Ray holding up old military paraphernalia and badly framed timer shots of the two of them. Lewis was looking at the scattered shots representing his attempts to capture Big Scary Thing on film. The best of them is a blurry gray blob on top of a blurry green background.

"Why do the legendary creatures always come out blurry?" Lewis muttered.

"What were you thinking?" his dad said. "Going to that camp without adult supervision? What if you'd found a loaded gun?"

"I wouldn't play with a gun. Only Col. Grampa is allowed to do that."

"And what about this?" He held up a photo of Ray inspecting an old pair of boots. "Are these the boots I found in your room?"

"Yes, sir," he said shamefully.

"I thought you found them in the basement or something! Why would you take these?"

"They were a souvenir! I took lots of souvenirs of my first adventure with Ray."

His father palmed his face. "Lewis, when it's private property, 'taking souvenirs' is called stealing. Go get the souvenirs. We're taking them all back to the base right now."

"We can't go back to the base!"

"And why not?"

"Um… I can't tell you. You won't believe me."

"Lewis, I'm your father. If you tell me the truth, I'll believe you."

"You promise?"

"Of course."

"Well, when we went there the first time, we found this quantum thing and hit a big button and it zapped us with science beams—"

Mr. Banks's expression became stern. "Lewis…"

"—which made monsters and stuff start showing up. Only we can see them, because of quantum, which has something to do with dead cats—"

"Lewis!"

"—but he said we can't go back because the apple-center of the anemone, whatever that is, will make bigger things will show up and—"

"*Lewis!*"

"Yeah, dad?"

"Get the souvenirs, we're going."

"But you said—"

"I said if you told me the *truth*, not if you made up one of your stories."

"But, Da-a-a-ad!"

#

Meanwhile, in the Niven household, Ray was on his way up the stairs. They still hadn't finished unpacking, so numerous boxes labeled with the names of rooms were piled along the floor. His parents were at the foot of the stairs. His mom was unplugging the wireless router.

"Now, you sit up there without the internet and think about what you did," she said.

When Ray slammed his door, the parents retired to the living room. The couch sat with its back toward the entry hall, where the foot of the stairs and the shelf with the wireless router stood.

"Okay, so how do we feel about this?" Mr. Niven said.

"What do you mean? We're only in town a few days and he's already making trouble," Mrs. Niven said.

"Yeah, but he's making trouble with a *friend!* And he was making trouble outdoors."

"That's true… it's definitely a step toward being more social and outgoing… we might have broken even on this one."

"We should invite the Bankses over for dinner. Lewis and his dad seem fine, but we should make sure they aren't a bad influence."

"And that Ray isn't a bad influence on Lewis."

Mr. Niven smiled.

"What are you so happy about?" she said.

"I'm just glad to have a non-internet related parenting problem. Hey, maybe soon we'll be able to bandage our first skinned knee?"

"Can you believe bodily trauma used to be the biggest worry? That's probably why they invented grounding. A kid can't get hurt in his room."

#

Upstairs, Ray's room hadn't changed much since they first moved it. Most of his stuff was still in boxes. The only fully deployed part of the room was the desk and the impressive PC rig Ray had gotten for his birthday. Two large screens, big speakers, a huge tower with various multicolored lights. Everything a growing nerd needed to feel whole. His parents, despite their punishment bordering on cruel in human, had overlooked one small thing when they'd unplugged the Wi-Fi. They didn't keep an eye on the router. It had taken some patience, but he'd managed to sneak down and plug it back in and was browsing a webpage. The sun was beginning to set, casting a long stripe of sunlight across the floor through his window. He glanced out the window. Lewis's house and what was presumably the matching window of Lewis's room, were staring at him.

And so was something else.

He sat rigidly in his chair as something buzzed up past his window.

"What now…" he moaned.

He slipped from the chair and walked cautiously to the window. Just as he reached it, a mechanical drone of some kind dropped into view. It was extremely futuristic, and once it deployed a cluster of weapons, it also was inarguably hostile. One of the high-tech guns shined a red beam at him. In a panic, he pulled a clipboard out of one of the packed boxes and held it up defensively. The continuous beam hit it and began to sizzle. A louder and more hostile whine signaled the charging of one of the larger weapons.

Ray was too terrified to do anything more than keep the clipboard held defensively and move backward. He reached the wall and clumsily reached for the doorknob with one hand while holding his impromptu shield with the other. The threatening whine seemed to have reached its maximum, and whole room filled with an ominous red glow. Then, just as suddenly as it appeared, the drone vanished.

He let out a shaky sigh of relief and eyed the smoldering clipboard.

"No more waiting for Dr. V. We need to do something about this right now…"

\#

Mr. Banks and Lewis pulled up to the Cobalt Ridge Base. The overgrown plants and torn-up ground from the prior clash between Big Scary Thing and Magic Lady were still apparent. He eyed the devastation.

"They really need to get a groundskeeper out here before the next field trip. Okay, Lewis. Where did you get all of this stuff?" said Mr. Banks

Lewis looked around nervously. "Mostly in that big building there. Except for the fancy science stuff. That came from the lab in the back."

"What's got you so nervous?"

"I already told you, but you didn't believe me."

Mr. Banks sighed and started leading the way to the lab. "Lewis, a great imagination is a wonderful thing, but you need to start learning about the difference between reality and fantasy."

The pencil-stealing fairy appeared and started fluttering around Mr. Banks's head.

"Some things just aren't real."

A unicorn trotted past behind him, then returned to stare curiously at the fairy.

"There's no such thing as werewolves, for instance, and fairy stories about goblins and bogeymen are just that, stories."

What looked like a snake with butterfly wings swirled up and snapped at the fairy. A bunny with rainbow fur and a pogo stick swatted at it with a net.

"The world has got enough wonderful stuff in it without having to make up things to hide in the shadows or prance in enchanted glades."

A beast that could best be described as two gorillas stuck together back-to-back cartwheeled up and tried grabbing the unicorn.

"Those things are fun to tell stories about, but you mustn't believe in them just because you want them to be real. And most importantly, you shouldn't be afraid of those things, because figments of your imagination can't hurt you. Understand?"

All of the mythic creatures turned suddenly to watch the sky. A shadow slid over the ground.

Lewis swallowed hard. "Uh-huh… we should go soon."

"All we have to do is drop this stuff in the lab and we can go."

He tried the knob.

"Locked. Where are the keys?"

Lewis tried to split his attention between the sky and the crowd of oddities that were milling about behind them. "Back at home, I guess."

Suddenly the gathering of magic beasts scattered like a spooked flock of birds. Lewis ducked and covered while his father obliviously walked onward.

"Well, I don't want to leave this equipment out to the elements. It was paid for by taxpayer's dollars, after all. I guess we can always…"

"We can always what, Dad?" He warily peeked his head up. "Dad?"

Mr. Banks had stopped in his tracks as though someone had simply pressed pause while he was walking. The Magic Lady was standing before him, her hand touching his cheek. She glanced down at Lewis, then pinched the air before Mr. Banks's eyes and seemed to draw a shimmering thread from his head. She took her hand from cheek and pinched the end of the glowing thread peeling a second one from it. When she released the first thread, it coiled back where it came from. A deft motion of her hand coiled the other in her palm. She gripped an amulet around neck with that hand. When she took her hand away again, the thread coiled around and faded into the amulet. She looked to Lewis.

"Hello, young Lewis," she said.

"Y-you can speak English? What did you do to my dad?"

"I borrowed his language and set him aside for a moment, such that I might speak to you."

"Why me? Why not him?"

"Adults ask much and believe little. Children are delightfully trusting. Besides, *you* have the aura of magic, not he. From whence came such an enchantment?"

"You mean how did people and things like you start showing up? I got zapped by this quantum machine thing."

"A machine? A spell powerful enough to open a window between your realm and a dozen others was conjured by a simple mechanism?"

"I guess. All I know is it's been causing all sorts of problems. We're trying to figure out how to fix it."

"Mmm. Take me to this mechanism. If I can determine the means of the spell's conjuration, I may be able to undo its curse."

"I can't. It's on the other side of that door, and the key is at home."

"A door? No mere door can long delay Terriethriel of Melomore."

She stirred the air with her hand, summoning crackling light, but as she did she began to fade. Quickly she grasped her amulet and concentrated, resuming solidity.

"It seems my link to this realm is a tenuous one. Any significant mystic incantation threatens to return me to my own world."

"You used loads of magic to protect us from the Big Scary Thing, but Ray was here then. Maybe you stick around better when he's here?"

"Protected you? Ah, from the foul one. Yes, that dark beast is a creature from my world. A mortal enemy of the righteous and pure."

"You don't have to tell *me* twice. So very pointy…"

"Listen, young Lewis. Fetch your friend and the key. I will depart to gather strength. When next you draw the window open, I shall return."

"I'll try."

"You will do more than try, young Lewis. You will succeed," she said forcefully. "I *declare* that you shall succeed, such that I might unlock the secrets of this curse that plagues you so."

Lewis saluted. "Will do, Miss Terry-Ethel-Ethel of Mallowmar."

She gave him a measuring look. "Yes… don't keep me waiting."

She tapped her amulet and promptly vanished. The moment she did, Mr. Banks awakened.

"—let the groundskeepers know when they come to fix the landscaping."

"Dad, maybe we should come back with the key and—"

"Oh no, son. You've spent too much time here already. Now come on. Let's get home and get supper started."

#

The next day at school, Ray looked half dead. He clearly hadn't slept, and during recess he reacted to the slightest sound as though a gun was being held to his head. In the cafeteria, Ray and Lewis sat alone at a round table in the corner of the lunchroom. Ray had a tray with various "wholesome" school meal items like Salisbury steak and creamed corn. Gravy and cream existed, it seemed, to differentiate "wholesome" from "healthy."

"You don't look so good, Ray," Lewis said through a mouthful of steak.

"I'm *not good*, Lewis. Some machine almost burned a hole through me. If Dr. Van Vleck doesn't hurry, we're going to end up dead."

"Well, I might have some good news then."

"Wait..." He glanced around. "Why are all of the other kids staring at us and talking low?"

"Well you're acting kind of weird. You don't want to know what people are calling you."

"What is it?"

"Cray-cray Ray."

"Cray-cray Ray!? That's not even clever! And it's Raymond, not Ray! Just use my whole name! Is that too much to ask!?"

He stopped ranting to find the entire lunchroom was looking at him.

"Well, this is just great," Ray sulked.

"Hey, you're lucky. You didn't want any friends anyway."

"There's a big difference between not *wanting friends* and not being able to *make friends*."

Lewis's head drooped. "Yeah... I know..."

"Oh. Right... Well, you said you had good news?"

Lewis snapped instantly out of it like an enthusiastic puppy.

"Oh, yeah. So Dad made me drop off all of my souvenirs, and that meant going back to the base."

"Like Dr. Van Vleck said not to, or else crazy stuff would show up."

"Yep. He was right, but one was Magic Lady. She pulled magic spaghetti out of Dad's head and said she could fix us."

Ray disregarded the spaghetti comment. "How?"

"We have to take her to the quantum thing. Then she'll use magic, I guess."

"There's no such thing as magic," Ray growled.

"There's probably no such thing as an octopus with feathers, but there's one trying to steal your dinner roll right now."

Ray snatched the roll out of the grasp of said creature. It vanished under the table.

"Good point. Do you know where the keys are?"

"Yeah. The same place Dad puts everything he doesn't want me to find. In the downstairs pantry in a box of canned tuna."

"Good, you get them, and tonight we'll go and see if this lady can help us."

"But we're grounded."

"I don't *care that we're* grounded. There's a charred hole in my math homework. That could have been my head! I'll take grounding over death."

"Aw, we're not going to get killed. We're boy adventurers. Boy adventurers don't get killed."

"This isn't an adventure story. This is reality!"

"Well sure, but it's a reality with feathered octopuses that steal dinner rolls."

"Okay… Well, how about this? When the time comes for the next adventure, boy adventurers are never grounded anymore."

"Hmm… Okay. Just one more time I'll disobey Dad. After this, though, it is only adventures with Dad's permission."

"Okay. I'll sneak out and meet you at the Sasquatch trap after bedtime. Bring the keys."

Nancy walked up to the table holding a tray.

"Bring the keys for what?" she said pleasantly.

"We're going to the lab so we can—" Ray kicked him under the table. "Ow! Quit doing that. "

"More Weird Nothing?" Nancy said.

"More Weird Nothing," Ray said.

Nancy glanced down as the unseen feather-pus dragged the roll away.

"What's up with your dinner roll?" she asked.

Ray snatched it.

"The table's crooked," Ray said.

Nancy looked at him flatly. "Uh-huh. Listen, we're supposed to interview someone for that social studies project…"

"We sure are. I'm going to interview Col. Grampa. He's awesome," Lewis said.

"I figured I'd interview Ray, since he's the new kid in town," she said.

"Darn it! I should have thought of that," Lewis said.

"Too late. I called dibs. Can I get your number, Ray?" she asked.

"Fine." He scribbled it on a napkin. "Here."

"Thanks. Have fun with your Weird Nothing," she said.

"We will! Nighttime adventure!"

Nancy walked away. Ray pushed his fingers up under his glasses to rub his eyes in frustration. The feather-pus took advantage of the distraction to snatch the roll and scuttle away.

#

That night, Ray limped in the darkness, lighting his way with an LED keychain and trying to find the sasquatch trap.

"Stupid YouTube. I don't care how easy those parkour guys make jumping out of a window look. Tuck and roll is *not that easy*," he grumbled.

"Is that you, Ray?" called an unseen Lewis.

"Who else would be wandering through the forest at this time of night? Why didn't you warn me how hard sneaking out would be?"

Lewis emerged from the bushes in his full "expedition" outfit, complete with two very large flashlights.

"You should have raked the leaves up to the house before bed and jumped into them."

"Yeah, thanks. I'll keep that in mind for next time."

Lewis handed him a flashlight.

"Here. Hold this. Let me get my bear bells on."

"Fine, but hurry up."

Lewis knelt to tie the bells onto his shoes.

"So! Any other stuff shoot at you today?"

"No, thank goodness."

"Me either. I think I saw that fairy again, but it could have been a dragonfly." He stood up. "Okay, this way, just like last time."

They began hiking toward the base, Ray's limp eased out as they went. For a few minutes they were silent and serious, dedicated to the task at hand. Inevitably, though, Lewis's mind started to wander.

"So what's the deal with tadpoles?" he asked.

Ray cocked his head. "What?"

"In science class today. I remember tadpoles, and I remember frogs."

"Tadpoles turn into frogs. It's called metamorphosis."

"But tadpoles are like little fish, and frogs hop on land."

"They're amphibians. They start in water and end up on land. Listen, can you please at least *pretend* that you're afraid?"

"Of what?"

"Getting eaten by a bear? Vaporized by a particle beam? Incinerated by a dragon? It isn't very often those are all distinct possibilities."

"Oh, we're safe for now. We're just on our way. The exciting stuff won't happen until we get to the lab. That's how adventures go."

"Just because adventure story-type things are happening, that doesn't mean things will turn out the same way. You never hear adventurers discussing tadpoles, right?"

"Duh, that's because we're between scenes right now. You can tell because nothing interesting is happening."

"That's circular reasoning! Nothing is happening because we're between scenes because nothing is happening?"

"So?"

"It's the same as saying something *is going to* happen because we aren't *expecting something*, and things always happen when you least expect!" Ray raved.

There was a massive crunch nearby. Ray's face fell. They slowly turned to find the Big Scary Thing towering over them.

"You know this is your fault, right?" Lewis said.

"Yeah, this one's on me."

"What do we do? Run and hide?"

"No. Stand perfectly still. Maybe they're like dinosaurs and they can't see you if you don't move."

They looked up at the thing, and held stone still. For a moment it seemed to be working. The moment didn't last long. Its head snapped down to look at them. Lewis and Ray didn't need to consult on what to do next. Millions of years of evolution had already made that decision. They ran screaming.

"Ray! You see those trees over there? The base is straight that way for like a half mile." Lewis stuffed the keys into Ray's hands. "Go and talk to Miss Mallowmar."

"What? What about you?"

Lewis gasped. "I'm a stubby, chubby kid. You can run farther. Find Magic Lady. I'll hide. She'll fix things. Monster disappears. Easy!"

"Okay, but don't die!"

"Good idea!"

They split up. For a few terrifying footsteps, the creature followed Ray. Lewis skidded to a stop and jumped up and down.

"Over here, you pointy monster!"

It ground to a halt, then turned to him. Ray disappeared among the trees. Lewis turned and ran in the other direction.

"Great! Now I just find a cave, or climb a tree or—oof!"

He'd made it all of three strides before the creature snagged his foot and he fell forward. It hoisted him into the air, holding him level with the sparkling cluster of gem-like eyes.

Lewis flailed about for a moment, but tried to gather his wits.

"It's okay, it's okay. Just think of what Col. Grampa would do again."

He envisions the old man. He envisioned what the brilliant

tactician's advice would be. Unfortunately, the topic of escaping the clutches of a rock monster had never come up in any of their many conversations. When he conjured the colonel's voice to mind, all he heard was, "You're on your own, private."

Lewis shut his eyes tight. "Poop."

\#

Ray was gasping for air as he approached the lab. He was *not* accustomed to doing this much running. Every step closer to the source of their woes conjured more weird creatures, just as had happened for Lewis. In Ray's case, the impossible things had a more sci-fi vibe. Ray ran through the base, ignoring, shoving aside, hopping over, or kicking the robots and aliens that were getting in his way, all the while yelling for his would-be savior.

"Magic Lady! Miss Mallowmar, or whatever! … What was I thinking, leaving him behind!? This is the stupidest idea I ever—What the!?"

He braced himself as a veritable stampede of crossed-over creatures rushed past him. When the racket died down, he opened one eye to find the statuesque Terriethriel standing before him in all her divine glory.

"Hello, young one. You are the friend of young Lewis, are you not? You too share the aura of his curse."

"Uh... yes. He said you could help us. Listen, you've got to follow me. That big spikey thing is chasing him, and—"

"The surest way to help your friend would be to lead me to the mechanism responsible for your curse."

"But it could be killing him right now!"

"If I weaken myself, I may lack the strength to undo the curse. Waste no time. Take me to the mechanism!"

"But he could die!"

"The foul one is among the least of the threats likely to seek you. Countless lives are at risk. I *must* bring order to chaos."

Ray glanced toward the forest, stricken with doubt and concern.

"Alright... but let's hurry."

"Indeed. Time is of the essence."

Ray unlocked the door to the lab and headed inside. Terriethriel followed, leaving a few of the larger creatures of myth to emerge from hiding once she was no longer nearby.

\#

Back in the forest, minutes had passed and Lewis was still hanging upside down in the grip of the Big Scary Thing. He was no longer frightened. Instead he looked bored, and woozy from being upside-down. The creature was making various unintelligible clacking noises at Lewis.

"Uh... not that I'm complaining... but were you planning on *doing anything?*"

"RK CRK CRKL RKL KKR CLK."

"I mean besides crackling and clackering. I thought there'd be more, I don't know, excitement."

The creature showed some degree of visible frustration. With a free limb, it grasped a stone the size of a loaf of bread and began pulverizing it with little difficulty, jabbing it with the claws of the three arms not presently keeping him aloft.

Lewis gawped at the sight. "Okay, you can go back to clacking!"

When the dust cleared, a remarkably detailed statuette of Lewis sat in the creature's hand. The creature placed it on the ground.

"Hey, wow! Is that supposed to be me?"

"RKKL."

It grasped another rock and produced a duplicate of Ray, then a third of Terriethreil.

"Ray and Miss What's-her-face! You're pretty good. Can you make a kitty?"

The creature shook him and pointed at the Lewis figure.

"Yeah, fine, okay. That's me."

It pointed to the Ray figure.

"And that's Ray, I get it."

It picked up the Terriethriel figure and used the base of it to smash both figures of the boys.

"That's not good... My friend's going to meet her right now. Are you saying *she* wants to kill us?"

"RKKL."

"Why are *you* here?"

The creature crushed the Terriethriel figure.

"You want to help me stop her?"

"RKKL."

"I don't know. How do I know you're not just using me?"

It selected another stone and carved a bear. It then slapped it away.

"Oh, yeah... Well, I guess we're a team. What's your name, anyway?"

"CLKRKLCRKLK."

"I'll call you Ricky. We've got to do something, but I think if you stop touching me you'll disappear. What do I do? *Think.*"

He tapped his forehead and scrunched up his face. His hat fell from his head and hit the ground. He looked at it.

"Say…"

#

Nancy sat at a desk in her room, doing homework. She finished one subject and slouched, eager for some sort of a distraction. Her eyes found their way to the napkin with Ray's number on it, paperclipped to a sheet on the desk.

"May as well get started on the social studies project. Nothing better to do."

She picked up the phone and dialed the number. After a few rings, Ray answered. The connection was terrible, half-swallowed by distortion.

"Hello?" Ray said.

"Ray, it's Nancy. You got a minute to get started on the—"

"This really isn't a good time," he said quickly.

"Busy with Weird Nothing?" she said with a smirk.

"I really can't—we've got a bad connection, I'll—"

There was the sound of an explosion and the phone cut off.

Nancy jolted upright in her seat.

"Hello?"

She looked at the phone. Suddenly this wasn't a distraction, it was a very important mystery. The inner Nancy Drew lurking within every little girl awakened.

"The other day they had to visit Dr. V.… and they said they were going to the lab… Hmm…"

#

Dr. V. leaned over his notes and tapped away at a rather ancient laptop. It was good to have some decent scientific work to do after so many years in semi-retirement. It was so pleasant that it wasn't until he heard a knock at the door that he realized his perpetual scowl had faded. He quickly reinstalled it on his face and raised his voice.

"Go away!" he shouted.

"I came to ask about those boys who were here the other day," called Nancy from his stoop.

"I'm busy!"

"I brought two boxes of cookies," she said.

"What color?"

"Green."

Dr. V heaved himself from his seat and answered the door.

"Have you girls decided to start selling year-round like I've been recommending?"

"No, but I keep a few boxes in the freezer for bribes. Listen, would Ray and Lewis be doing anything dangerous at a lab?"

"I don't know what you're talking about."

"They were chatting about something like that at lunch, and I called him and I thought I heard an explosion."

Dr. V.'s scowl deepened. "It was your imagination."

He slammed the door and walked down through the hatch into his basement. Most of the basement was dark. He clicked on a lamp. The screen of the detector device he'd turned on when the boys had visited was blinking madly. A heap of scribbled-upon paper mounded up beneath the device. He took the end of the sheet in his hand and started reeling it in, looking it over as he went.

"What on earth are those boys doing...?"

His expression turned from irritated to worried.

"Oh, dear... Oh, *dear, I told* those boys to stay *away* from the anomaly site."

He pulled out a flip-style cell phone and dialed a number. After a few rings, the system informed him the call could not be completed as dialed. He angrily marched upstairs.

"Kids these days. Can't follow directions. It's all fun and games until quantum tunneling nucleates a lower energy vacuum state."

He threw the door open to find Nancy still standing there.

"Is it still my imagination?"

"Excuse me, little girl. I need to go."

"To the lab?"

"It doesn't concern you."

He got into his car. Nancy knocked on the window.

"Can I come?"

"Why on earth would I let you come with me?"

Nancy shook the boxes of cookies. Dr. V. pondered for a moment. He sighed.

"Keep them. The things I do for science…"

Dr. V. drove away. Nancy crossed her arms.

"Fine, be that way. It's not like I don't know where the lab is."

#

Ray finally pushed open the door to the sub-lab. Terriethriel looked around with a bemused look on her face. The room was filled with a scattering of crossover creatures, all of which gave Terriethriel a wide berth as she walked. A crackling ball of energy drifted above her hand as a threat

"Such a curious world you've carved for yourselves."

"There! The device is there! Please hurry. And… don't blow anything else up."

Terriethriel approached the device. She eyed it with an almost hungry stare.

"Yes… Yes, this is the artifact. It has a different aspect of your own curse, like a voice in harmony with your own."

She turned, an accusing look on her face.

"It is weak, however. It never could have cleaved the very veil of reality in its current state. What have you done to it?"

"We had to break it to stop if from doing… whatever it was doing."

"Restore it. I must sample the poison in its pure form before I can devise its antidote."

"Uh… okay. But please be quick about it."

He walked up to the device, shielded his groin, and reinserted the tube they pulled free. Finally, he slapped the red button. The device shuddered and activated. Terriethriel's eyes lit up further.

"Yes… I am not familiar with the operation of the mechanism… but I know the effect it is bringing about… I can offer aid."

She grasped the amulet. The irregular thump of the machine became a steady hum. The glowing became a warmer color. She placed a hand on the side of the device lovingly.

"So long I have sought this missing piece, young one. Fate be praised that the key found me instead."

"Are you doing it? Are you fixing what it did to us?"

"Patience, child. Care must be taken. It is delicate work."

"It's just that my friend—"

"The foul one lacks my strength of will. By now he has slipped back from whence he came. If young Lewis is clever, he is safe."

"See, that's what I'm afraid of."

The glow brightened.

"Ah! There. We shall begin by ridding ourselves of these unwanted guests."

With the merest gesture, she banished the crossover creatures in a wave of light.

"Thank God! You fixed it!"

"No, child. I have mastered it. It is a thing of chaos, but under my influence it will behave. Now to do things properly."

She touched her fingers to the amulet. A patch of grassy, sunny ground began to spread out around the QFT. Ray backed away from the growing circle of meadow.

"Wh-what are you doing?"

"Bringing over a proper force. It shouldn't take many. Your people are laughably ill-equipped to resist the mystically adept."

"No. No, no, no, you were supposed to fix it, not make it worse!"

"I was not and am not beholden to a *child*."

She waved a hand. Vines began to sprout from the earth, weaving themselves into crude soldiers.

"Immense power and endless ambition are a blessing when there remains a prize to seize. But what becomes of the conqueror when the final battle is won? For me, the answer was clear. Seek out the other worlds. Those still wandering in the darkness, waiting for a firm hand to guide them. My hand. Alas. Crossing the veil was beyond my nearly limitless capacity. And then I felt the barrier weaken. You are to be applauded, child. You shall be remembered for opening the door to a golden age of sanity, order, and control."

As she pontificated, she tapped the soldiers one by one, waking them and conjuring up weapons for them.

Ray brandished his flashlight. "Not if I can help it!"

She thrust out her hand, hurling him against the wall and binding him there with vines.

"You can*not* help it, child. You are *nothing*. I would crush you now if not for that fascinating affliction of yours. It might prove useful."

There was a rumble from the doorway, a telltale clatter. Terriethriel narrowed her eyes.

"The foul one," she hissed.

She waved a hand. The door slammed shut. Glowing phantom chains coalesced and reinforced the door. An instant later it shook against its hinges.

The powerful mystic addressed her soldiers.

"Guard that door. Destroy any who would enter."

There were two more slams, then a long silence. Finally a third slam occurred, not against the door but the wall. Ricky came roaring through the hole. He wore Lewis's hat, and Lewis was on his back.

The young boy waved frantically. "Weeeeeee! Hi, Ray! Remember Ricky? It turns out he's a good guy!"

Lewis jumped from Ricky and rushed toward Ray. Ricky clashed with the assembled soldiers conjured by Terriethriel. He tore through them easily, but no sooner did he dispatch one than two of them formed in replacement. Lewis reached Ray, flicked open a Boy Scout knife, and started cutting the vines.

"The Magic Lady is evil. She wants to take over the world!" Ray shouted.

"Well, if one of them was good the other was gonna *have* to be bad, right?"

"She fixed the device and she's using it to bring over these henchmen. We've got to figure out how to stop her."

"Well, it's obvious, isn't it? We've got to bust the doodad again."

"What? I don't think that's a good idea. Breaking it didn't solve our problem last time, and she's done stuff to it since then, so—"

Lewis turned to Ricky, who was still clashing with the soldiers and swatting aside mystic attacks from Terriethriel.

"Ricky! She's using that thing! Bust it!"

"Wait! Let's think about this for a minute!"

The warning fell on deaf ears and Ricky charged toward the QFT, plowing aside soldiers.

Terriethriel clutched her amulet. "No, you fool!"

She blasted him with a vicious bolt of energy that threw him aside. A flailing swipe still struck the machine. It instantly started pulsing and throwing off arcs of energy. Where they struck the walls and ceiling, rifts opened, revealing slices of other worlds. They flashed open and closed, dumping hapless residents of their respective worlds. One was a knight in shining armor with a short magic sword. Another was a strange looking alien with a ray gun. An odd black and white critter with a flickering red bead on its neck dropped down and scampered away.

"Whu-oh..." Lewis said.

"It's radioactive, Lewis. You can't stop it just by hitting it!"

Terriethriel summoned a pulsing ball of energy.

"Rise, my minions. Protect me while I undo the damage done by these blundering simpletons."

Scores of soldiers began to burst up from the ground to fend off Ricky along with the confused and panicking newcomers through the rifts.

"Well, what do we do now?" Lewis said.

Ray dodged a stray blast of some kind. "I suggest we start by staying alive!"

Another blast caused them to scatter. The laboratory was in pure chaos, new rifts opening and closing constantly, dumping new creatures into the mix and ejecting others. The knight fell into another rift, leaving his sword behind. Ray snatched it up and started swinging. It effortlessly cleaved the two nearest soldiers, but he was terrified nonetheless. Elsewhere, the bizarre alien creature placed down the gun to investigate a piece of scientific equipment in the lab while hiding behind cover. Lewis snagged it.

"I need to borrow this!"

He began blasting, clearly enjoying himself. The boys worked their way through the crowd and bumped into each other back-to-back. They turned, saw the weapon the other was holding, and compared it to their own.

"Trade ya!" they said at the same time.

They swapped weapons and stood back-to-back, putting their weapons to use. For the first time, Ray seemed to be enjoying it too.

"So what do we do?" Lewis said.

"Well, we've tried breaking the device and that didn't go so well. There's only one more variable."

"Miss Mallowmar!"

"She's always clutching that thing around her neck. Maybe if we get it away from her."

"Sounds good to me!" Lewis pointed his sword. "To battle!"

Near the QFT, Terriethriel and Ricky faced off. She was holding him at bay with her magic, but only just.

"Your kind have long been thorns in my side, Foul One. I shall end you, and with this world as my stronghold, end you *all*."

Lewis bellowed from behind her. "Incoming! Yaaaaaa!"

Terriethriel managed to encase Ricky entirely in thick vines and stepped back in time to watch Lewis dive by them with the sword over his head. He flopped onto the ground harmlessly.

"Probably shouldn't yell next time," he groaned.

"It will be a mercy to this world when I blot your kind from it."

"I was just thinking the same thing," Ray said.

Terriethriel turned to find Ray with the gun leveled at her head.

"This is a ray gun. It turns bad guys into scorch marks. Call off your soldiers, fix all of this, and *get off my planet!*"

She reached for her amulet.

Ray pulled the trigger enough to make the barrel glow ominously. "Don't."

She held still, but her face showed no fear.

"You cannot solve this without me. You dare not pull the trigger."

"Hey, I'm just a stupid kid. Who knows what I'd do?"

"I could crush you with a thought."

"I could blast you with a twitch of my finger."

Terriethriel narrowed her eyes. Behind her, Lewis started to scale the QFT.

"You don't have the strength of will…" Terriethriel asserted.

"Maybe I do, maybe I don't. But I've got a best friend," Ray said.

Lewis leaped from the QFT and wrapped his arms around her neck, grabbing the amulet.

"I've got a friend and I'm vanquishing evil! BEST PLAY DATE EVER!"

Terriethriel screeched and clawed at his stubby little fingers, stumbling about, trying to regain her balance. With Lewis clutching the amulet she seemed to have lost a degree of control over the soldiers and several other spells. Ricky began to break free.

"Get *off of me yo*u miserable *urchin!*" Terriethriel shrieked.

She finally managed to grasp Lewis by his arms. She flipped him over her head, and hurled him at Ray. Both boys tumbled to the ground. Ricky finished breaking free and eyed up Terriethriel. She reached for her amulet. It was gone.

Lewis dizzily held the amulet up.

"Looking for this?"

"No… You cannot do this to me. I am Terriethriel of Melomore. I am—"

Any further boast was cut short as Ricky grasped her and hurled her at the QFT. The glow around it grew brighter. It began to blast ever more bolts of energy, each one opening another rift until most of the walls and ceiling were covered with gateways to other worlds. The visitors and soldiers began to drop through them. Ricky grabbed the boys and bounded through the hole through which they had entered. Once free of the lab and in the stairwell, it huddled down over them. There was a massive flash of light, then darkness and silence. Lewis tossed away the amulet and rummaged in his backpack to find an electric lantern. He switched it on. Cautiously, he leaned through the hole and held the lantern out. The lab looked like a war zone. Scorches, gouges, craters, and smoldering embers were everywhere. A few pieces of broken golem were scattered about. Not a single piece of lab equipment was intact, and there was no sign of the QFT or Terriethriel at all.

"Wow… Is that it? Is it over?" Lewis asked.

"I guess the fact the Big Scary Thing—" Ray began.

"Ricky," Lewis corrected.

"I guess since Ricky is still here, then our problem isn't solved."

"But no *other* wacky stuff is popping up, so it's not as bad as it was while the doodad was still here."

He walked up to the sword, which was intact and laying on the ground.

"Awesome! I get to keep a souvenir after all. How come it didn't fade away?"

"I guess because it fell through a portal." He looked around. "Some chunks of those soldier things didn't go away either. Maybe she was making them permanent."

"What on God's green earth did you two do to my lab?"

They turned to see Dr. V., an over-engineered light in his hand, eyeing up the carnage.

"Dr. V.! Look, we saved the day!" Lewis said.

"Is that what you call this?"

"Why are you here?" asked Ray.

"The little girl said you'd be coming here, and the detector confirmed it. Why are *you* here?"

"We thought Miss Mallowmar would help us, but she turned out to be evil. Ricky was here to save us, though," Lewis said.

Dr. V. pointed the light at Ricky. Only the hat cast a shadow. From Dr. V's point of view it was hanging in the air.

"Is there another fairy in your hat?" he asked.

"Not quite a fairy, no," Ray said.

Dr. V swept the light around the room again.

"Where is the QFT?" he asked.

"It kind of went away," Lewis said.

"Could you be more specific?"

"It went *very* away?"

"It's gone, Doctor. Destroyed," Ray said.

"Ah… Well, the good news was that I was a few calculations away from knowing how to re-synchronize your quantum signature with the space-time baseline."

"Okay, hold on. A bass line has something to do with music, so…" Lewis reasoned.

"He is going to fix us, Lewis," Ray said.

"That was the past tense, boy. *Was*. The only device in the world capable of administering the adjustment has apparently gone 'very away.'"

"So now what?" asked Lewis.

"Now I'll have to build a new one. Without the military industrial complex funding it, it isn't going to be easy."

"Great. That's just great," said Ray.

"Whatever you did here probably registered on the Richter scale. That sort of thing coming from a military base will attract some three letter acronyms," Dr. V said. "We should get moving."

"Okay, Dr. V. I just gotta say goodbye to Ricky, and then we can go." Lewis looked up to the creature. "Well… you proved something to me today, Ricky. Just because you're pointy doesn't mean you're bad. … Which I guess explains hedgehogs."

"You're not much for sentimental moments, are you, Lewis?" said Ray.

Ricky reached down and pulled up a piece of rubble. With little difficulty, he carved it into a medallion with an intricate design and an indecipherable inscription on the back. He handed it to Lewis. He selected another piece of rubble and created a similar one for Ray.

"Aw," Lewis said. "Thanks a lot big guy. Feel free to stop by anytime."

Ray looked to Ricky. "Uh… No offense, but please don't."

Ricky removed the hat and put it on Lewis's head.

"So long, Ricky," Lewis said with a sniffle.

Ricky faded away, and the boys followed the elderly scientist as he trudged back up the stairs.

"Well," Lewis said. "So long as we sneak back into our houses okay, it'll be like none of this ever happened. Some adventure, huh?"

Ray was silent.

"Oh, come on. Don't pretend you didn't have fun," Lewis said.

"… Okay. *Parts* of it were fun."

"So… once the grounding is over, you wanna come over and help me with my homework? I'm still confused about that 'carry the one' thing."

"Yeah, I guess so. After all, what are friends for, right?"

The group left. The battled had been harrowing, and Dr. V. was in a hurry. Had that not been the case, perhaps one of the three of them would have remembered to lock a few of the doors on their way out.

But they didn't.

A few minutes later, Nancy arrived with her bike helmet on and a flashlight in hand.

"Hello?" she called. "Wow, what happened in here?"

She stared at the wreckage through the hole in the wall, then kicked at some dust. A glimmer among the debris caught her eye. She picked it up.

"Cool… A necklace." She brushed it off on her shirt and stuffed it in her pocket. "I'm going to have to keep a closer eye on those two."

After a moment or two of additional investigating, she decided it was probably not a good idea to linger. She turned and headed for the surface. Behind her, just before she shut the door, a fairy hauling a ray gun fluttered by.

###

Afterword

Thanks for reading the second collection of Patreon stories. If you enjoyed them, you can get more of the same *as they are written* by supporting my Patreon. And if you'd like to keep tabs on future releases, consider signing up for my newsletter. The details of both can be found at bookofdeacon.com

I'd like to take a moment to give special thanks to some of the people who made this collection possible:

Chandra Free: Artist of the story covers for *Uncle Easy, Comfortable Dragon, Time Loop, Dragons in Space, The Front Way, The Pencil Hoarder, Soft Summoned,* and *The Tale of Amberbelly.*

Ashe: Artist of the cover illustration for *The Dwarfendam Run.*

SwagginMun: Artist of the cover illustration for *Soft Summoned.*

Adam J. Hall: Artist of the cover and co-creator of *Weird Nothing.*

Tammy Salyer and **Anna Genoese**: Editors who cleaned up the vast majority of these stories (as well as my novels).

From the Author

Thank you for reading! If you liked this story, or perhaps if you found it lacking, I'd love to hear from you. Leave a review, or contact me directly on social media or via email. You can find the relevant links (as well as my newsletter sign-up) at bookofdeacon.com/contact

Discover other titles by Joseph R. Lallo:

The Book of Deacon Series:
Book 1: *The Book of Deacon*
Book 2: *The Great Convergence*
Book 3: *The Battle of Verril*
Book 4: *The D'Karon Apprentice*
Book 5: *The Crescents*
Book 6: *The Coin of Kenvard*

The Big Sigma Series:
Book 1: *Bypass Gemini*
Book 2: *Unstable Prototypes*
Book 3: *Artificial Evolution*
Book 4: *Temporal Contingency*
Book 5: *Indra Station*
Book 6: *Nova Igniter*

The Free-Wrench Series:
Book 1: *Free-Wrench*
Book 2: *Skykeep*
Book 3: *Ichor Well*
Book 4: *The Calderan Problem*
Book 5: *Cipher Hill*
Book 6: *Contaminant Six*